WOLVES OF THE SEA

EDWARD J. MCFADDEN III

SEVEREDPRESS

WOLVES OF THE SEA

WWW.SEVEREDPRESS.COM

ISBN: 978-1-922861-45-0

"You could start now, and spend another forty years learning about the sea without running out of new things to know." -Peter Benchley, The Deep

1

Stag Harbor, Orcas Island, U.S., 10:19 PM PT, June 14th. Sixteen days until the start of Pink Salmon Season.

The yellow kayak slipped through the inky water, tiny ripples rolling over the still harbor like a miniature tsunami. Moonlight filtered through the scattered clouds, the bay's surface shimmering silver, the slap and tinkle of Kylie's paddle dipping into the water carrying softly through the night. A tall gray and black cliff face rose from the water to the west like a wall, the sparkle of lights and the dark shapes of trees running along its crest. To the east, boats of various sizes and economic prowess bobbed and listed in a gentle sea breeze that brought the scent of low tide and evergreens.

Kylie loved night paddles. It was her favorite part of the trip. While Dave sat on boats waiting on fish he didn't eat, she paddled the many estuaries, ponds, bays, and straits of the San Juan Islands, and she found particular solace in moonlight paddles. Fishing adventures weren't as relaxing as sitting poolside in the Caribbean or touring Europe, but they were close. Her husband was what real anglers called a "tripper", an amateur who fished for pleasure and mostly cared about the location, not what type of fish he went after. That's why they were staying at the Stag Harbor Inn for three hundred dollars a night. In two weeks, when the pinkies started running, the place cost eight hundred a night and had a five-night minimum.

She'd snuck from her room without waking her husband from his nap because he would have hassled her, arguing that paddling alone was dangerous, especially at night. He would have insisted on coming with her, and that was exactly what she didn't want. She knew these waters well, and she relished the solitude. It reset her brain and recharged her batteries.

The night air was crisp, but pleasant. A tiny school of mackerel surged around the kayak, their silver scales glinting in the pale light, dorsal fins knifing through the sea, forked tails jetting back and forth. Kylie rolled her shoulders and laid the paddle across the kayak's cockpit. She stretched her hands as the wind tugged at her, gently pushing the boat toward the dark maw of the harbor mouth and the black mound of Fawn Island beyond.

Kylie glanced down at the blinking red light on the front of her lifejacket to verify that her marine radio was on and functioning. The device had a beacon that could transmit her location in the event of an emergency, though given the calm seas it was just a precaution. She didn't even have a sprayskirt covering the open cockpit because it didn't fit right and was difficult to get on. She was a good paddler, but her skill at Eskimo rolling was suspect, so a skirt wouldn't help much. If Kylie flipped, she'd be forced to jettison from the kayak and tread water while she used the emergency hand pump to clear the boat. Not a big deal and the water was only a nipple-twisting sixty degrees.

She lifted her paddle and dug in, the kayak knifing between larger boats moored on the outskirts of the harbor. There were large pleasure crafts and sailboats mixed with beaten clippers, gillnetters, and transport vessels. The guidelines of mainsails tapped aluminum masts, windsocks flapped, and the squeak of boats straining against their mooring lines stirred the stillness. The gentle sound of music emanated from one of the boats, and blue and white light leaked around curtains and from dark pilothouses. It looked as though every mooring slot was filled, which wasn't surprising given the pinkies were coming. Pink Salmon only ran every other year in the San Juan Islands, and the rules and traditions surrounding their preservation and capture went back hundreds of years.

A single light shone in the blackness of Fawn Island. Kylie paddled hard, the kayak surging forward, the wind picking up as the yellow fifteen-foot sea kayak sliced through the growing chop. More lights appeared along the rocky shore of the mainland as she left the harbor, long docks, like metal fingers, reaching out into the undulating channel, boats, gazebos, and storage trunks at their ends.

The current was strong around Steep Point, and Kylie braced the kayak as a light chop rolling west to east rocked the boat. She shifted course, staying along the shoreline, constantly adjusting, and keeping the nose of the kayak into the wind. A cool breeze scattered her hair and brought the scent of grilled meat. One of the residents along the shoreline had their BBQ going, and her mouth watered, despite the fantastic meal of cod and local vegetables she'd had for dinner.

Pinpricks of red, green, and white navigation lights dotted the North Pass, pleasure crafts out for nightly excursions and casual fishing. Gulls cooed and cawed gently, as if even the air rats knew it was quiet time. Kylie took a deep breath and released it slowly, and whatever stress and worry she'd felt scattered like so many dead leaves on the wind.

There was a splash, a faint huff, and a glimmer of white appeared in the water as Kylie jerked her head toward the sounds. Moonlight splashed across the silvery sea, tiny streaks of white foam glowing in the darkness. She stopped paddling, spiders marching down her spine as the kayak was slowed by the wind and tugged south by the current.

Kylie stared at the moon-drenched spot where she'd seen the burst of white, but there was nothing except swirling black sea. She edited out the wind, the trickle and pop of the water, and the faint murmur of the trees along the shoreline.

An eerie cadence of sharp clicks, short whistles, and tapping echoed over the water.

In the darkness to her left, bathed in the moon's glare, three knife-like dorsal fins scythed through the sea, each at least five feet tall, their dark forms like solitary soldiers marching across a blackened windswept battlefield.

Excitement sprouted in her gut. Seeing orcas up close in their native habitat was an incredible opportunity. Tension hummed just beneath her skin, the practical portion of her brain reminding her it was dark, she was alone, and that killer whales are apex predators. To that, her primal voice argued that orcas rarely showed aggression toward humans, and she'd kayaked alongside larger creatures. Kylie had seen orcas in the wild, but never up close and personal. These beasts were in town for the same thing everyone else was; pinkies would be on the menu soon.

Her stomach danced with eagerness, and Kylie eased her paddle into the water, stroking slowly, being as silent as possible as she angled toward where she'd seen the dorsal fins.

Kylie couldn't shake the feeling that the beasts could be swimming beneath her in the blackness. If one of them breached, or inadvertently came up to breathe with her above them, she'd end up in the drink. This was highly unlikely because similar to sharks and dolphins, orcas utilize SONAR-like echolocation to detect and locate prey and other objects in the water, so she was confident the creatures were aware of her and would leave her be.

The eerie chorus of ticks, hoots, and drumming returned, and a loud sucking sound rose above the wind and a spray of seawater splashed the kayak.

Kylie jumped when she saw a red eye rimmed in yellow floating in the dark water before a patch of white. Orca eyes are normally dark and barely perceptible, but this one was engorged and red, as if irritated by toxic smoke. The sea wolf twisted slowly, the moon shadow of its dorsal fin falling over the kayak. Kylie was transfixed by the beast's smooth motion, its elegant form camouflaging muscled fury beneath.

Her breath caught and Kylie stopped paddling, terror gripping her.

Dorsal fins knifed from the water all around the kayak.

The icy fingers of panic and worry massaged Kylie's shoulders and a million guppies wriggled in her stomach as perspiration dripped down her back. Suddenly she felt very alone.

Moonlight painted the scene in harsh black and white, the white spots on the orcas glowing in the darkness. The massive sea wolves were all around her now, six tall dorsal fins sticking from the sea forming a horrific carousel.

Orcas are torpedoes of steely flesh with large powerful jaws filled with savage teeth, and yet Kylie believed them to be beautiful. Dolphin-like in shape, she had been told males can get as big as thirty feet long, regardless of the subspecies, and she'd been surprised to learn that though the coloration of white patches on black often appears random, each type of orca has a distinct pattern that identifies them as male or female and part of their particular subgroup.

She turned toward land, and the distant lights of the houses and docks suddenly seemed far away, though she was less than half a mile offshore. The current was strong, and it tugged the kayak south, away from land, and she adjusted her paddle strokes, angling the boat between two towering dorsal fins.

An orca blocked her way, rolling onto its side and revealing its white belly.

Kylie pulled up, bracing the kayak as the boat spun. All around her patches of white shined in the dark water, pale moonlight painting the sea in a garish glow. Bubbles erupted beneath the kayak, popping and snapping on the surface as the kayak spun faster. The beasts were creating a whirlpool, and she was trapped within it.

One of the massive creatures breached and crashed back into the sea twenty feet away, and a wave of whitewater crashed against the kayak.

A black tail fluke with a ribbon of red pustules like poison oak cutting across it rose from the water before the kayak like a leviathan. The huge wing hung in the air for an instant, dripping water, before crashing into the sea next to the kayak, missing Kylie by mere feet.

The orca rolled, spitting bubbles, its pectoral fins massaging the water.

Kylie's flight reflex took control and she paddled hard for a red light at the end of a dock, not heeding the loud slap and plunk of her paddle or the echo of her ragged breathing.

Another tail flute smacked the water and missed the kayak, and the ensuing swell of water roared over the boat. Kylie struggled with the paddle, fighting the whitewater as she tried to keep the kayak from capsizing. She'd paddled class five rapids on rivers several times, but the sea kayak was long and narrow and wasn't designed for quick adjustments in extreme whitewater. Despite these hindrances, she managed to keep the boat upright, though her victory was short-lived.

A white cloud of bubbles surged from the dark water, a knot pushing from the sea as a dorsal fin appeared beside her. Then Kylie was sailing through the night, paddle in hand, the red light from her emergency radio casting a cloud of red on the black water as she faceplanted into the sea.

Whitewater, streaking bubbles, then blackness. She held her breath as the current tore at her clothes and twisted her around, giant white patches sliding past in the darkness, the chuff, tap, and hoots of the beasts reverberating through the water.

Her lifejacket buoyed her to the surface, and Kylie sputtered and spit as she got her bearings. The yellow kayak floated upside-down several feet away, and she still gripped her paddle.

Huffing and sprays of water erupted all around her, dorsal fins climbing from the darkness, tail flutes slapping the surface. For a moment she considered trying to get back into the kayak. If it was upside-down, it couldn't be filled with water, but as she gazed at the red dock light in the distance, she reminded herself that the kayak could be replaced.

Kylie swam for shore, stroking easily, trying not to splash, though she knew the effort was useless. The orcas would sense her movements and there was nothing she could do about that.

A wave of pressure pushed her onward, a fist of roiling whitewater surging from the sea, but it died away, waves cresting on her back as she swam. The red dock light was getting further away, and Kylie realized with a sickening dread that she'd been pushed off course. She was swimming northwest, parallel to land.

She was growing tired, her lungs burning, her muscles protesting as she angled north, stroking hard.

The shadow of a tall dorsal fin fell across the oily sea beside her, the white glow of teeth rising through the water. Pectoral fins fluttered as a black and white conical head emerged, two elongated patches of white behind swollen fiery eyes. The beast chuffed and whined, jaws flexing wide, its stingray-like tongue lulling out as the sea wolf sank back into the depths.

Relief flooded through Kylie, and she stopped swimming, her head spinning, muscles aching from the exertion. The red dock light was closer now, and she saw the dark outline of the rocky shoreline and the illuminated windows of a house beyond. She was going to make it. Filled with hope she swam on, an unreal heat wrapping her in a warm cocoon.

Kylie's body jerked backward as her legs were tugged hard, bringing her to a stop and pulling her beneath the surface. Surprise and terror fought for control of her body as the warm sea bubbled around her, moonlight casting a spotlight on the surreal scene. A slick of hot oil covered her face as she fought back to the surface, and with sinking dismay, she understood the oily substance was her blood.

She broke the surface and tried to kick her legs and resume swimming, but realized she no longer had legs. Shards of broken bone, gristle, and frayed flesh protruded from the stumps where her legs had been, and hot blood pulsed into the cold sea. Kylie was overcome with pain and panic as she desperately floundered, her blood filling the water all around her.

Stars wheeled overhead as an orca knifed from the sea, a determined missile of muscle, rage, and hunger. Time slowed, and Kylie stared at the beast, her legs hanging from the orca's mouth as it tossed its head back, her legs disappearing down its gullet as the sea wolf crashed back into the churning water.

Blood bubbles popped and snapped as Kylie screamed, the cry stinging her throat, pain filling her mind as she struggled to understand. The irony that she would be the first human killed by an orca in the wild was too much to endure, and as darkness crept in around the edges of her vision, her muscles betrayed her, and Kylie sank back beneath the surface.

Another orca knifed through the water, gliding up from the depths, homing in on the hot stream of blood pouring from Kylie's severed appendages. The sea wolf breached, jaws open, its black and white head driving Kylie from the water. Its jaws snagged her like a frog snatching a fly, a stone-crushing vise that broke bone, mashed organs, and broke Kylie's torso in half.

The last thing Kylie saw as life left her was the yellow kayak tumbling on the undulating sea.

The orca crashed back into the sea, mounds of red-streaked foam glistening in the moonlight. Beneath the surface, the orca shook its head like a dog, pieces of flesh, bone, and clothing leaking from its mouth as it swallowed. Chunks of the corpse got stuck in the orca's five-inch teeth or floated to the surface, and the pod moved in, cutting through the cloud of blood and flesh, taking their fill.

Pieces of bone sank into the depths along with the radio, its blinking red light trailing into blackness like a strobing electric eel. Pieces of Kylie's life vest and paddle floated on the surface in the blood, shreds of fat, and muscle that bobbed in the red slick.

A gust of wind flattened the sea, and windchimes adorning a nearby house sang a mournful melody. The orcas dove, chuffing and tittering, and leaving behind swirling pinwheels in the water. The sea calmed and the whitewater dissipated, and the blood slick thinned as it was pulled away by the current. The yellow kayak rolled onto shore, slapping against rocks, the hollow thuds echoing through the darkness.

2

Lake Washington, Washington, U.S., 8:59 AM PT, June 16th.
Fourteen days until the start of Pink Salmon Season.

The floatplane shuddered and threw spray as it powered through the light chop that blanketed Lake Washington. The single prop DHC-2 Beaver's engine cycled up, and its landing pontoons shook on their supports, water splashing the plane as the pilot fidgeted with knobs and levers, adjusting the water and tail rudders.

John Starker stared at his blurred reflection in the plane's window, dark blue water racing away beyond. His graying black hair was tousled, dark bags hung beneath his brown bloodshot eyes, and his puffy white cheeks were windburned red, his salt and pepper goatee on the borderline of unruly. Two days ago, Starker had been packing his apartment and preparing for his new assignment in Seattle, and now he'd been diverted to Orcas Island for one last assignment out of the Marysville Office of the Washington State Conservation Department.

The pilot, whose name was Jesse, pulled back on the yoke and the plane stopped shaking as it lifted into the air, water bubbles streaming along the windows like marching ants. Jesse made a note on his log, which was affixed to a clipboard that hung next to the control panel. The radio crackled and Jesse reported their status, then looked over his shoulder at Starker, who was the only passenger.

"They're asking where you want to go?" the pilot said.

Starker said nothing. If the pilot didn't know where he was going, he sure as hell didn't. All his arrangements had been last minute. A civilian fishing vessel had gone down off Waldron Island following the disappearance of a kayaker, and he'd been ordered to investigate and report back before heading to his new position in the WSCD main office.

"Weather's good," Jesse said, as if the statement might spark an answer, but it only generated another question.

"What does the flight plan say?" Starker said.

"Says I'm to drop you at Stag Harbor."

Starker recalled he was staying at a place called the Stag Harbor Inn. He said, "So, there?"

"I just thought…" Jesse adjusted a control nob and made a note in his log.

"You thought what? Help me out here."

"I know why you're heading up this way," Jesse said.

Starker said nothing. It was to be expected that multiple deaths at sea would rankle a small sea community like the San Juan Islands. "Again, I say, so?"

"So…" The pilot shook his head. "The water is calm, so if you want. Pala said I could bring you out to the scene of the most recent… disappearances. Or we can go see the chief in Friday Harbor. Or we can follow the original flight plan. Your call. I just figured you might want to get started right away."

"What's a Pala?"

Jesse laughed and the plane's wings waggled slightly. "Pala is the local ECON officer. Also, there are the pinkies to consider."

Starker nodded. His WSCD contact, Officer Rankin, and the pink salmon. He sighed. Starker planned to be long gone before the season opened on July 1st.

As the plane climbed, the houses and rocky shoreline of Lake Washington faded, and the barren green fields of Fort Flagler appeared to the west, a thick line of puffy clouds blocking the distant view of Seattle. Forests of evergreens dotted with an occasional house and accompanying patches of grass filled the eastern horizon. The Beaver's engine coughed, then resumed its steady cadence, and Jesse made a control adjustment.

"Stag Harbor isn't far from Waldron Island, right?" Starker asked.

"A stone's throw."

"And you're sure Officer Rankin is on scene?"

"Pala's up there with a knot of boats."

Starker shifted his gaze from the green landscape fleeting by below to Jesse. "Who else is there?"

The pilot shrugged. "Don't know for sure, but there's at least two coastie vessels, the local fuzz, plus a gray boat or two that's got to be the Navy or the Department of the Interior."

"You can land there?"

Jesse nodded. "On a calm day like today I can."

"Then what? I swim to the inn?"

"I'm sure you can catch a lift with Pala, and you've only got that one bag."

"10-4," Starker said, slipping into military lingo. "Take me there." He pulled his phone and called up the email containing the preliminary report that had triggered his deployment.

An eighteen-foot civilian fishing vessel, The Braggard, capsized under clear skies on flat seas. Reports of floating debris began streaming in late the prior day, and a father and his two sons were missing. As of this morning, no bodies had been discovered, so the family was still holding out hope that the three missing anglers might be injured along the shoreline or had been pulled out to sea. Thorough searches of the area revealed nothing of note except additional debris suspected to have come from the capsized vessel.

Forty-five minutes after take-off Jesse arced the plane northeast, a tangle of islands, channels, straits, and ponds slipping by below them. To the left, the town of Friday Harbor sat on a hillside like an angelic settlement of another time, and to the right was the green lump of Shaw Island. Starker was familiar with the archipelago, having lived and served in the Pacific Northwest most of his adult life. "I guess you'll be busy the next few weeks, huh?" he said.

"Life Changing Tours is always busy. There are always rich folks looking to get to their vacation homes, so I get a steady stream of Seattle people. But yeah, pinkie season is a big one. We're here."

Waldron Island sat next to Orcas Island, a narrow strait separating them. The island was sparsely inhabited, the isle nothing more than a gray-black rock with a scant covering of evergreens. The dark waters of Cowlitz Bay lapped against a yellow mossy shoreline, and a knot of boats floated in a loose circle several hundred yards offshore at the center of the bay.

"Buckle up, please," Jesse said as he adjusted the Beaver's drag flaps, reducing the aircraft's speed as he worked the yoke, the floatplane gently descending.

Starker rolled his shoulders and cracked his neck. Now the games began. Local law enforcement looking to cement their power, out-of-towners looking to exert authority, and residents trying to save what little livelihood they had left. They would all want something different from him, and there was a lot at stake.

A gentle tremor ran through the Beaver as the plane alighted on the foam-streaked water, throwing spray as the engines cycled down. Jesse reported their landing as he taxied toward the gathering of boats, one of which had separated from the pack and was streaking across the water toward the plane.

The floatplane eased to a stop, rocking gently, its propeller spinning slowly, the aircraft's engine humming resiliently.

Starker touched the grip of his Glock 19 where it rested in his shoulder holster. He'd never fired the weapon in the line of duty, but the gun was a necessary evil. He checked his badge, making sure it was clipped securely to his belt. A gust of wind dosed the plane with sea spray as Starker grabbed his bag and inched open the plane's side door.

"Careful there," Jesse said. "It'll be slippery."

Starker eased out onto the aluminum landing pontoon, being careful to step on the rubber tread. A gray SAFE boat with an aluminum pilothouse sped toward his position, a woman with dark black hair at the helm. Starker figured the woman was Pala.

The SAFE boat slowed, its wake slapping into the plane. Starker gripped a pontoon support, his bag's strap falling from his shoulder, the weight of the satchel jerking his hand free. He danced for an instant, sure he was tumbling into the drink, but his bag swung back like a counterbalance, and he managed to grip the Beaver's open door and keep his feet under him.

"Ahoy," said Pala as she exited the pilothouse. She wore dark green pants and a sand-colored uniform shirt partially covered by a green life vest, her gold badge glinting in the sunlight that painted the water white. Her reflective sunglasses said cowboy cop, but her casual speech and easy posture made Starker relax.

"Good luck," yelled Jesse as he cycled up the Beaver's engine. "Maybe I'll see you down the road."

Starker waved to the pilot and closed the plane's door.

"Well, hello," Pala said. "That was quite the entrance." She held out a hand. "Step carefully."

Starker cinched up his bag's strap, grasped her hand, and deftly stepped onto the gray inflated gunnel of the SAFE boat. "CO Pala Rankin." She released his hand, and Starker thought he detected a slight red tinge on her light brown cheeks.

"John Starker."

"Well, Officer Starker, I assume based on your arrival you want to get right into it."

"Call me John. Any reason not to?"

She made fish lips and shook her head as she motioned for him to follow her into the pilothouse. The sound of arguing seagulls faded as Pala slid the pilothouse door closed. "There's not much to see, really, but maybe you'll see something the rest of us haven't."

"I do have experience with aquatic crime scenes."

Her eyebrows scrunched. "Crime scene?"

"Until we know what happened here, how can you rule out foul play?"

Pala puckered her lips again, then said, "We can't, I guess. But none of the cops are calling it a crime scene."

"There were no witnesses, correct?"

She nodded.

"Did yo… do you know the missing fisherman?"

"No, but from what I can gather Mr. Dingman has been on the water since he was a kid. Very experienced." She started the twin Yamaha 150s and eased down the control levers. The engines grumbled and popped as the SAFE boat picked up speed.

"Anything unusual not in the report?" Starker asked.

"Nothing specific. The whole thing is odd."

"How so?"

"We don't get many capsized boats around here," Pala said. "These inland seas can get rough, and sometimes the wind rips through the straits like a hurricane, but I've never seen a boat go down because of the weather, and this entire week has been beautiful."

"No preliminary cause has been identified?"

"No, a potential cause has definitely been identified," she said.

Starker waited and when Pala didn't elaborate, he hiked his shoulders, and said, "And?"

"I don't want to put ideas in your head. Take a look and then tell me what you think first."

Made sense. Preconceived notions could destroy an investigation before it got going, but something in the tone of Pala's voice told him what he was about to see wasn't of the ordinary variety.

Pala eased back on the throttle arms and the engines fell to a low hum as the SAFE boat knifed between larger vessels from various agencies. Pala's twenty-six-foot SAFE boat was the smallest of the group.

"The coastie cruiser has most of the collected debris laid out on their aft deck, but the wreck itself hasn't been moved. As you can see it's rolling a little in the current."

The eighteen-foot Grady White center console was upside-down, its bottom a peeling mess of blue paint. Pala moved the SAFE boat in close, and Starker leaned over the side and examined the sea-worn and faded hull as the SAFE boat circled the capsized vessel.

Most of the boat appeared undamaged, except for a section of the forward hull where the fiberglass was cracked and spidered as if from a collision. "What do the experts make of that?" Starker said, pointing at the damage.

"Not sure," Pala said. "There are no traces of stone or wood in the fiberglass, so the working theory is the vessel didn't hit a rock or piece of water debris."

"Have divers been underneath?"

"Yip," she said. "Nothing of note other than a nasty surface slick."

A rainbow-colored oil slick surrounded the vessel as fuel leaked into the sea, and pieces of what looked like shredded cloth clung to the boat's dirty new waterline ring.

"What's around the waterline there?"

"We think it may be shreds of clothing, and we've taken samples."

Starker headed back into the pilothouse with Pala in tow. "Anything else of note from the first responders? There was something in the report about a blood slick?"

She nodded and fished about on the top of the command console until she found a short stack of photos. Pala frowned as she handed them over.

The pictures showed the site at dawn, the sun just peeking above Waldron Island in the east. The boat was in basically the same position, but cushions, chunks of Styrofoam, shredded lifejackets, and other debris littered the water all around the capsized boat, but it wasn't the floating trash that drew the eye.

A red slick snaked between the bits of the garbage, pieces of what looked like fat and gristle floating within. There were several closeups. Starker cycled through the photos and whistled.

Pala said, "We're still waiting on testing, but the responding officer had no doubts that the slick was human blood mixed with..." She stared out the windshield at the undulating bay.

"Mixed with?"

"Some other type of blood. Maybe tuna. Again, we're waiting on samples."

Starker made a mental note to call one of his new colleagues at central and ask to have the tests prioritized. He said, "Still no sign of the bodies?" Though Starker knew things weren't always what they seemed, he was already ninety percent certain the three fishermen were dead.

"Well, not no sign," she said.

Starker lifted an eyebrow.

"There was a development this morning."

A tremor of excitement raced through Starker. "Do tell."

"It's best you see for yourself."

3

The captain of the Coast Guard endurance cutter met Starker at the top of the Jacob's ladder that climbed from Pala's SAFE boat to the deck of the coastie ship. Captain Raynard was a slight man who looked like he might disappear if he turned sideways, and his face twisted as he escorted Pala and Starker aft where the evidence was laid out on the rear deck like a plane crash investigation. Everything was tagged, and a folding fish filleting table sat open on the far end of the deck, a series of baggies atop it.

Uniformed men and women, some in blue and others in green, watched Starker like he was a shark swimming through a crowd of frolicking kids as he strolled through the evidence. He'd debated internally about if he should wear his uniform and had decided against it, even though he knew his jeans, white collared shirt, and outdoor tactical vest would separate him from his fellow law officers. They would see him not only as an outsider, but as an authority figure they couldn't fully trust, and he was counting on that.

Starker eyed the retrieved fishing gear, a cooler, beer and soda cans, a nautical chart of the area destroyed by water, snack bags, and trash, and a variety of marine items, none of which looked damaged. A gaff with dried blood on its sharpened tip caught his eye, but when he examined it closely, he saw fish scales. Captain Raynard didn't offer to answer any questions, and Starker didn't ask any.

Pala trailed behind, smiling at people she knew, making sure everyone knew she wasn't with the newcomer.

A loud pop reverberated over the water and everyone's gaze fell on the capsized fishing boat as it shifted in a windblown swell, pockets of air snapping, the bay water crackling and foaming.

Starker's breath caught in his throat when he reached the table of bagged evidence. Chief among the items was a severed forearm and hand packed in ice that looked to have belonged to a child. He opened his mouth to berate the captain and ask why the limb hadn't been sent out to pathology, but the skinny man beat him to the punch.

"In case you're wondering, we just found the arm this morning. Floated onto shore."

Starker closed his mouth, sucked his lips, and nodded.

The arm had been severed just below the elbow, and he could tell it was a right arm because of the position of the thumb on the hand. A stump of bone and gristle hung from the end of the appendage like boiled chop meat. It didn't take an expert to see that the ragged wound wasn't caused by a single sharp cut, but instead resembled a serrated and torn gash, like wounds caused by teeth. The arm hadn't been torn off, otherwise the break would have been at the joint.

Several of the other bagged items were splattered with blood; pieces of two different life preservers, and clothing, some of which matched the colors of the small shreds clinging to the capsized boat's greasy waterline. Starker didn't ask about the blood. There were no doubts left. The fishermen were dead, most likely killed when they'd somehow ended up in the water and were attacked by a shark. Whatever remained was most likely rolling along the bottom with the tide, and whatever wasn't eaten by the local sea life would find its way into the vastness of the Pacific Ocean.

Starker chuckled to himself. Sharks got blamed for everything, but not without cause. Unlike orcas and other sea predators, there were many shark attacks each year, and the apex killing machines were most likely in town for the feast of pinkies.

"So?" Pala said.

"How much does the family know?"

"It's just the wife… mother, and she only knows they're missing."

"I think missing is overly optimistic at this point," Starker said.

"Without bodies, what are we supposed to do?"

Starker shrugged.

"You got nothing? You're supposed to be a special investigator, right?" She said that last part loudly so the surrounding peanut gallery could hear her, and sure enough, one of the officers chuckled.

Starker licked his lips and said nothing. Less is more and leave them wondering were his mantras.

"Got it all figured out?" the captain asked.

"Where are you bringing the capsized boat? I'd like to take a look at it after you pull it from the water."

"Do I have your permission to do that?"

Now it was Starker's turn to laugh. "Permission? Since when does the Coast Guard bow to the econs?"

"Professional courtesy." The captain smiled.

"Has nothing to do with the mountain of paperwork and questions, does it? Or maybe being late for leave?"

The captain raised an eyebrow.

"Fine," Starker said. "Mark the spot with a buoy and haul it. Try not to break anything."

"10-4," the captain said. "It'll be in the yard at Friday Harbor by the end of the day."

"I assume I should inform Mrs. Dingman of the current situation?" Starker said.

"Which is what? We've found one of your kid's arms, some bloody garments, and torn life preservers, but no corpses? They're lost at sea until they're not unless there's something you're not telling me," Captain Raynard said.

"Still," Starker pushed. "She deserves to know the status of things. If you can't do it, I'll go and sp—"

"You'll do no such thing. I'll update her this evening in person."

Starker nodded, turned on a heel, and headed for the ladder.

"Meow. Meow."

A black cat with haunting gray eyes appeared before Starker and he stopped walking. The feline sat before him and curled its tail around its body.

"Oh, yeah, I forgot about the cat," Pala said.

The animal stared at Starker, appraising him before pushing to its feet and rubbing his legs as it purred.

Several of the officers laughed, and the captain said, "Looks like you've got at least one friend."

Starker turned to Pala and lifted an eyebrow.

"They found him wet as a drowned rat, balancing atop the capsized boat."

"Family pet?"

"Nope."

Starker's brow wrinkled. Cats had a long and storied history when it came to maritime legends.

Cats were said to bring good luck on ships and prevent bad weather. Starker didn't know if he believed that, but they did catch rodents, which helped make sea voyages safer, thus further fueling superstitions. He'd seen many stray shipyard cats. What better place to snag unwanted fish parts? Starker was a dog man himself, but as the black cat rubbed against his legs, tail in the air, he felt an urge to stroke the animal.

"Marina cat?" Starker asked.

"Maybe. Nobody seems to know," Pala said.

When the cat followed Starker and jumped down onto the SAFE boat, nobody protested. The captain was surely happy to get rid of the beast, and the least Starker could do was ensure that the cat made it to a shelter.

Back in the pilothouse, the cat resting atop the command console, Pala said, "What's next? Do you want to get settled in?"

The sun had rolled past noon, the thin cloud cover gone, the day a comfortable seventy degrees, a gentle sea breeze making it feel like sixty-five. Gulls screamed overhead, and Starker's stomach grumbled. "The kayaker's boat was found on Steep Point?" he asked.

Pala nodded. "And we know that was her last known location because of her emergency beacon."

"It was recovered?"

"Yes, along with a piece of her lifejacket."

"Blood on the jacket?"

Pala nodded as she powered up the boat, put it in gear, and slowly pulled away from the Coast Guard cutter.

"If I'm not mistaken, Steep Point is on the southernmost tip of Orcas Island, yes?"

Pala nodded as she pushed down the boat's throttle control and the SAFE boat leapt from the sea, knifing through the calm water, light spray splashing the windshield.

"Let's take a look on our way back," he said. "Where's the kayak and other items that were recovered?"

"The sheriff's office has an annex in town. We can head there before I drop you at the inn."

Judging by the tone of her voice, and the sharpness with which she said, "drop you," it was clear there wouldn't be a dinner invitation forthcoming, at least not tonight. He was wounded somewhat. They were on the same team and departmental power struggles and overbearing egos had no place in law enforcement, but that was like saying there was no business for performance-enhancing drugs in professional sports. There were the rules, and then there were the real rules, the ones everyone actually followed.

The twin Yamahas roared as the SAFE boat arced around the southern tip of Orcas Island, shooting a fifteen-foot rooster tail, Jones Island Marine Park a mound of hemlock and stone to the west.

The cat leaped onto Starker's lap, and the investigator jumped.

Pala coughed to contain a chuckle.

The feline stared up at Starker, gray eyes blinking as it meowed.

"Spooky looking thing," Pala said.

"That's what we'll call him until we find him a home. Spooky "

The beast purred and closed his eyes.

Pala slowed the boat and brought it to a stop, and Spooky jumped from Starker's lap, anticipating disembarking. The boat bobbed and listed, the cat steadying himself on the deck as he looked back at Starker. When the beast realized the trip wasn't over, he leaped up onto a chair and curled up with his back to Starker and Pala.

"Something I said?" Pala asked.

"You know cats," Starker said, though he'd never owned one himself.

Pala handed him binoculars. "The kayak was found on the shoreline by a resident." She pointed. "The debris was all over the bay and channel."

Starker pressed the binoculars to his eyes and adjusted the focus as he scanned the shoreline. Four red traffic cones with yellow hazard tape strung between them sat atop a scree of tumbled gray stones. He handed the field glasses back to Pala.

Stag Harbor was churning like an ant's nest, boats of all types coming and going, the smell of charred meat and evergreens floating on the gentle breeze. The Yamahas gurgled and popped as Pala piloted the SAFE boat to an open section of the dock at the end of a long pier.

Starker slid open the pilothouse door and Spooky leaped from his seat and darted through the opening, and that was the last Starker expected to see of the animal. He stepped out onto deck and went about tying off the bowline as Pala shut down the engines and joined him on deck. As Starker looped rope around the aft cleat, he said, "Any way we can grab something to eat on the way?"

She nodded, but said nothing.

With the boat secured, Starker grabbed his bag, checked his badge and Glock, and jumped from the boat to the dock. He found Spooky laying lazily atop a wood docking pole, and when Starker walked past the cat, he vaulted from his perch and followed.

The small hamlet of Stag Harbor was subdued. People moved quietly about the cobblestone streets as Starker and Pala made their way through town, stopping to grab sandwiches and water. Starker paid, and as the duo ate, he asked, "So, Pala. A different type name. Is it Lummi?"

She nodded. "Dad left the reservation when I was four."

"So you're not far from home."

Pala said nothing.

Spooky lounged on the ground between Starker's legs, having finished the water and dollop of tuna he'd been given.

"Anything ever happen out here that doesn't involve a drunk tourist or a misplaced pet?" he asked.

"I spend most of my time chasing poachers and measuring cod and salmon."

"Sounds thrilling."

"I have my moments."

The Sheriff's Annex was a single-room wooden structure that looked like it was visited once a year. Crab apple bushes and weeds surrounded the structure, and several deer bolted through the foliage when Pala opened the building's roll-up bay door.

Spooky meowed and planted himself in the open doorway, his gray eyes locked on Starker.

At first glance, the yellow kayak appeared undamaged, but closer inspection revealed four deep scratches along the boat's side as if it had been raked with a mighty claw. It looked nothing like a shark bite. The torn lifejacket was splattered with dried blood on one side, the opposite side cleaned by the sea. The radio was undamaged, as was the hand pump, safety whistle, and water bottle.

"So now you've seen it all," she said.

There was an unspoken question there and Starker decided to answer it. "I'm sure at first you thought the same thing I did. Had to be a shark. What else could it be? But now…"

"Yeah," she said.

Sharks rip and tear, and though it was possible the scratches on the kayak had been made by a great white or one of its relatives, it was unlikely. Sharks have powerful jaws that would have crushed the polyethylene boat, but he was unable to come up with another scenario. If it had only been the kayaker, or only the capsized fishing vessel, as single events they could've been written off as an odd event. But with both incidents occurring so close together, it was hard to believe there wasn't some type of connection.

Starker didn't believe in coincidence. Everything happened for a reason, though as Spooky meowed beside him, he wondered if that was still true.

4

The Stag Harbor Inn was like the rest of the San Juan islands; rustic yet clean, practical but dignified. The place had a homey feel, as did the married couple that had been running the place since the 70s. He made a mental note to question the innkeepers because the deceased kayaker had been a guest.

Starker had a cottage out back of the main inn, one of six small bungalows that were scattered amongst the forest of cedar and fir that wrapped the entire complex. He had no car, so he'd walked through town, gathering odd stares as he went, his new partner, Spooky, walking beside him like he owned the place. Cats. His cottage had a small porch, and was one room with a kitchenette, bathroom, and a double bed.

Starker undid the hasps on his valise and hung it from a hook on the back of the bathroom door. When he went to use the head, he found Spooky blocking his way. The feline's gray eyes stared up at him, tail wrapped around his body like a protective snake. The animal meowed as if asking for something. He'd given the cat water and tuna at lunch, but Starker figured it was time to pick up some cat food. He grabbed a bowl from the kitchenette, filled it with tap water, and placed it on the floor.

Spooky slinked across the room, sniffed the water, then looked up at Starker as if to say, "What's this?"

"I'll get you something better when I go out," Starker said, and the cat slurped gently at the water before jumping onto the bed and curling into a ball.

It was a little early for dinner, so Starker cleaned up and changed his shirt before plopping down onto the bed next to Spooky, who was sleeping and purring softly. He rifled through the local travel magazine hailing all the attractions, and the many companies and guides that would help you enjoy them. The lead story was about Orcas Island, and the text reminded him that the island hadn't been named after the sea predators. Orcas is a truncated form of Horcasitas, from Juan Vicente de Güemes Padilla Horcasitas y Aguayo, a Viceroy of New Spain who'd sent an exploratory expedition commanded by Francisco de Eliza to the Pacific Northwest in 1791. During the voyage, Eliza explored part of the San Juan Islands, but he didn't apply the name Orcas specifically to Orcas Island, but rather to a section of the archipelago.

Shaped like a pair of saddlebags separated by the village of Eastsound, and two bays, Westsound and Stag Harbor, Orcas Island had an area of fifty-seven square miles, and was slightly larger, but less populous, than neighboring San Juan Island, home of Friday Harbor. Eastsound is on the island's northern end and was the largest population center on Orcas Island and the second largest in San Juan County. The demographic information was accompanied by a picture of Eastsound from above, and the article was surrounded by ads for pink salmon charter boats.

Starker closed the magazine and pushed up from the bed.

Spooky opened his eyes but didn't move.

He switched out his tactical vest for a windbreaker, checked his Glock, and grabbed his mini binoculars. The room darkened, the sunlight fighting its way into the room around the edges of the window shades fading. Starker unplugged his phone from its white lifeline, pocketed the device, and stared in the mirror on the back of the room's door. His hair was combed, but stubble still fought through his skin making his face look dirty.

"Meow. Meow. Meow." With the stealth of a soldier creeping toward their enemy, Spooky had jumped from the bed and fallen in behind Starker.

He laughed. "You think you're coming with me?"

"Meow."

For a second Starker considered bringing the cat, but then thought better of it. He didn't know where he'd end up having dinner, and he didn't think the local restaurants would appreciate him bringing a stray cat into the dining room. "I'll be back soon," he said, as he slipped out and closed the door quickly behind him. The sound of mewing came through the door, and Starker felt like shit, though he wasn't sure why. The feline had gone to the bathroom, drank water, and eaten, and he'd pick up some cat food on his travels.

Starker strolled down the inn's main driveway to Stag Harbor Road, white smoke billowing through the windbreak of evergreens, the scent of BBQ carrying on the breeze from Toby's Smokehouse. His mouth watered, but he wanted to see more of the town, so he continued, winding down toward the marina through houses and small shops until he reached Channel Road, where he made a left and headed down toward the harbor.

The hamlet of Stag Harbor wasn't much. Channel Road ran through the center of town, which was comprised mostly of residential homes painted in pastel colors, some with terracotta roofs. Interspersed within the houses were shops supplying all manner of goods. There was a sandwich shop, and takeout fish place, and a convenience store called Orcas Island Market – South. In the market, he picked up three cans of cat food and got some advice from the lovely young cashier who smiled so wide at him that Starker thought she might be flirting, but then he remembered where he was. The people of the San Juan Islands were always sunny and polite.

"I'd like to have a sit-down dinner. Maybe grab a steak. I'm famished," he said.

"If it's meat you're after, try The Swimming Steer."

Starker raised an eyebrow.

The cashier chuckled. "It's a nice place. Really. Just follow the channel past the Cayou Marina and you'll see it perched up on the cliffside. They've got a nice outside veranda if you're into such things."

He thanked the woman and pushed back out into the fading light of early evening.

The land sloped down toward the bay as he walked. The marina was a hive of activity; supplies being loaded on boats, dinghies running back and forth from main dock to vessels moored out on the bay. Charter captains and their crews lined the docks, setting-up fishing poles, cleaning boats, everyone preparing for the arrival of pink salmon season.

Starker's phone vibrated and he pulled it free. His mother. Starker rolled his shoulders and cracked his neck. His father had died the prior year and his mom had been devastated—still was, and she called Starker every night. The calls were mostly a pity fest and an interrogation, but it was what it was. He tapped accept call. "Hi, Ma. What's happening?"

"I'm falling apart is what's happening. The doctor said that growth on my back might need to be removed. I don't want any more surgeries, John. I just can't take it."

Starker said nothing as he waited for her storm to blow itself out.

"Where are you?" she asked.

"Up on Orcas Island."

"Lucky you. It's beautiful up there."

"I'm working mom, not on vacation."

"Still, it's better than staring at these four walls."

"Why don't you take a walk? Call Harriet and go out to dinner?"

"Have you heard from Cindy?"

So there it was. Thirty seconds into the conversation. "No, mom, I told you we broke up."

"I'm still hoping it doesn't stick. She's such a nice girl. Are you ever going to tell me what you did to her? What you did to drive her away? You're a good-looking boy."

Starker was thirty-seven, hardly a boy, and he took a deep breath, going to his well of patience that had become deeper since his dad passed away. He had no siblings, and he was all his mother had.

His breakup with Cindy had been amicable. The main issue had been Starker moving to Seattle, and Cindy not wanting to move there. Their relationship wasn't that solid, and she disliked the city and certainly didn't want to live there. None of these practicalities showed up on his mother's RADAR.

"You there?"

"I'm here, Mom."

"Where are you going?"

"To get something to eat. I think—"

"Get down off there," his mother shrieked.

Starker sighed. His family dog, Henry, had been allowed on the furniture his entire life until the last six months, and the canine was having none of it.

"When's he going to learn?"

Starker almost uttered the interminable phrase that solved all the world's ills, "You can't teach an old dog new tricks," but he said nothing. He'd reached the end of Channel Road and he could see The Swimming Steer perched atop a slab of gray stone that jutted out over the harbor. "Listen, I've got to go."

"What? What's more important than me?"

"Nothing, Mom," he said. Starker told her about his day and about Spooky.

"A cat?" Her distaste for the creatures evident in the tone of her voice. "Don't bring it here."

Starker cracked his neck and said, "My table is ready. Talk tomorrow. Love you." Before his mother could respond, he tapped end call.

The Swimming Steer looked to be carved from the cliffside, its dark wood façade disappearing behind gray stone, its metal roof reaching out over a natural stone veranda just like his new friend at the market had described. Gas torches licked the growing dusk, the harbor below an oily dark expanse dotted with moored boats. The joint wasn't crowded, but more than half the tables in the dining room were full, as was the veranda. Three patrons sat at the bar; a couple, and an old man who looked like a permanent fixture. The guy sipped a beer, a shot of whiskey at his right elbow as he stared up at a TV showing SportsCenter, a picture of Russel Wilson, the Seahawks quarterback who'd been recently traded to the Broncos, filling the screen.

The maître d' offered Starker his choice of tables, and he said, "Can I eat at the bar, since it's just me?"

"Certainly, sir," said a dour man who looked more suited to working in a mortuary.

The bar ran along the back of the main dining room, and a series of sliding doors had been peeled back, opening the east side of the building to the veranda and the harbor beyond. The scent of charred meat knotted Starker's stomach, the tinkle of glasses and silverware, and the faint chatter of diners leaking through the restaurant.

Starker sat in a bar chair and smiled at the couple two seats down on his left, and he nodded to the old man one seat down on his right. The bartender brought a menu, and Starker ordered a Jonnie Walker Black and settled into his seat. The old guy hadn't even looked his way.

"The Hawks going to be any good this year?" Starker said, referring to the report on the bar's TV.

The old guy turned his head slowly toward Starker, like an ancient eagle appraising a varmint. The man shrugged and turned back to the TV.

"Don't mind Pinter. He's just grouchy," the bartender said. The guy wore a nametag that read Jerry. "What can I get you to eat?"

"Steak with fries, another scotch, and back Mr. Pinter up for me."

"Pinter is his last name, he's kind of the unofficial mayor around here." The barkeep chuckled.

The old guy looked over and shook his head in admonishment. "And don't mind Jerry, he just sticks his pecker of a nose where it don't belong."

Starker and Jerry glanced at the couple sitting at the bar, but they were engrossed in each other, and if they'd heard Pinter's comment, they showed no sign.

Jerry laughed. "When you're right, you're right." The bartender scuttled off to put in the food order and make the drinks.

"John Starker, WSCD, special investigations." Starker held out a hand, and the old guy eyed it like it was the head of a snake. Starker was preparing to pull back because Pinter was leaving him hanging, but after ten seconds the old guy smiled and gingerly took Starker's outstretched hand.

The bartender returned with the next round of drinks, and Starker drank in silence, waiting for his opportunity to engage Pinter, maybe get a feel for what was being said via the community's coconut telegraph of gossip. His dinner came, and he was halfway through his steak and the mountain of fries when his phone vibrated. It was Pala, so he answered. "Miss me already?"

"Apparently we hit it off because I've been officially assigned as your local liaison. I'm to shadow you and assist in any way possible."

"You don't sound so happy about it, Pala," he said, and Starker felt Pinter's eyes briefly flick in his direction.

"It is what it is, as the k_ds say."

"You've got kids?"

"And a husband. Surprised?"

"No, I—"

"Don't sweat it, Starker. I'm not a flower. What time do you want me to pick you up in the morning?"

"8 AM work?"

"Yup," she said. Starker heard an innocent young voice calling mommy. "Be at the end of main dock."

"O.K., I'll…" He trailed off when he heard the click of Pala cutting the connection.

Pinter inched into the vacant seat between himself and Starker "You here because of the missing people?"

Starker nodded. "What do you know about it?"

The old guy hiked his shoulders. "Just talk. Word is body parts, bloody clothes, and such have been found in both cases, so folks are worried."

"About what?"

Pinter laughed, which turned into a hacking cough. He took a pull off his beer and followed it up with a pull of whiskey. "About what? They're worried about a big fish, and what that might mean for the pinkies and those that covet them."

Starker said nothing as he sipped his scotch.

"You're working with Pala Rankin?"

"Eavesdropping?"

Pinter threw his head back like he'd been punched, and then made a show of looking around. "You can hear people's thoughts in here."

"I'm working with Pala. Do you know her?"

"Sure," the old guy said, and he followed up his statement with a long pull of beer. "She considers herself a Lhaq'temish, a person of the sea, and her ancestors were of the Native American Lummi Tribe, though her family hasn't lived on the reservation since her father left as a young man."

"Seems like a nice lady," Starker said. "From what I can see she cares about her work."

Pinter nodded.

"I've heard of the Lummi," Starker said.

"They have a long history and many traditions relating to the salmon hunt, and their ways are respected by the local governments. Pala's life is Orcas Island and protecting its habitat. She's been in the CS since she got out of the Navy."

Starker nodded again. A busboy came and took away the remnants of his food, and he switched from scotch to wine. "Set my man up here again before you cash me out, will you?"

"To what do I owe the honor?" Pinter said.

A gust of wind pushed through the restaurant, blowing out candles and jostling bills on their tiny clipboards.

Starker leaned in close. "I'm guessing you're in here every night?"

Pinter hiked his shoulders.

"I'm going to be around for a few days, and I'd appreciate it if you could keep your ear to the ground for me. Get the pulse of the island. I want to step on as few toes as possible."

The old guy finished his whiskey and held up his glass.

Starker nodded, pushed up from his seat, collected his wine and windbreaker, and went out onto the veranda to get some fresh air. It was almost dark, and the bay below glimmered with the last light of day, the sparkles on the water blinking out like tiny dying flames.

Long finger-like shadows arced across the harbor mouth, tall dorsal fins sticking from the water. Starker pulled his mini binoculars and focused on the fins.

Orcas surged and dove through the sea, their sleek bodies glistening in the fading light, their white eye patches glowing. The pod was moving fast, chasing what looked to be a school of mackerel. Starker couldn't see any real detail, but he counted eleven dorsal fins of various sizes.

Starker put the binoculars back in his windbreaker's pocket, puzzling over what he'd just seen. It wasn't uncommon for the sea wolves to be up this way, especially this time of year, but eleven orcas together was a little unusual. He knew pods were usually comprised of four to six beasts, but he also knew females can live ninety years, and as many as four generations can travel together.

He finished his wine and waved toward the bar as he left. Tomorrow was another day.

5

Stag Harbor, Orcas Island, U.S., 7:46 AM PT, June 17th. Thirteen days until the start of Pink Salmon Season.

Monday morning dawned bright and clear. Starker pulled back the curtains and cracked open the window, and a chill breeze pushed into the room. He put out a fresh can of cat food and water, but Spooky only sniffed at the offerings, tail up, before planting himself before the closed door. After being left behind the prior night, Spooky was having none of it, and the cat eyed Starker with suspicion.

Starker pulled on his shoulder holster, clipped on his badge, and grabbed his windbreaker. Spooky hissed and mewed as Starker lifted him and placed him on the bed, but before Starker could slip out, the cat jumped from the bed and blocked his way.

"Meow. Meow. Meow."

He had learned over their short partnership that when the beast meowed three times in a row he was agitated. Starker put his hands on his hips and stared down the cat, whose gray shining eyes met his. "You know you can't come with me, right?"

Spooky's tail whipped around him, curling and uncurling.

"Actually," Starker said. The Friday Harbor Animal Protection Society was the perfect place for the cat and odds were Starker would end up in San Juan Island's largest town at some point during the day. "Can you behave until I drop you off?"

Spooky stood as if asking "What are we waiting for?"

Starker walked into town, Spooky at his side. Stag Harbor was bustling; charters heading out, residents going to work, grabbing breakfast, and running errands. The air was thick with the scent of bacon and baking bread, and his stomach growled as locals nodded and waved as Starker made his way down main dock. Nobody appeared to give Spooky a second glance as if it was perfectly normal for a state investigator to have a cat as a partner.

Pala's SAFE boat was docked at the end of the pier, and the officer sat behind the command console sipping from a Styrofoam cup, the pilothouse windows slightly steamed. She greeted Starker out on deck. "Sleep well?"

He nodded. "Do you folks put something in the air up here?"

She chuckled, but her mirth fell away when she saw Spooky, tail up, gray eyes aglow. "What's Tonto doing here?" Pala asked. "We've got a meeting with the sheriff. He wants to meet you, but I think he's allergic to cats, at least symbolically."

"I let him come along so we can drop him at the shelter."

Pala shook her head. "Not today. APS is closed Monday and Tuesday."

Spooky did a purr-meow thing that sounded like laughter to Starker.

"Can't you make a call or something?" he said.

She hiked her shoulders. "The folks that work there are mostly volunteers."

"What if there's an emergency? Who feeds the residents?"

"Tippi, the full-time person is off, so students and volunteers fill in. If there's an emergency Tippi comes in, but given the situation," Pala tossed her head toward Spooky, who had taken a load off and was lounging on the dock cleaning himself.

"Should I bring him back to the inn?"

The cat stopped licking himself and stared up at Starker.

"Might make sense. If we…" Pala trailed off as Spooky pushed to his feet, jumped from the dock onto the inflated gunnel of the SAFE boat, then to the deck. He walked past Pala, tail up, through the open pilothouse door, and leaped onto the command console, where he resumed the methodic cleaning of his fur.

"Guess that settles that," Starker said.

As the SAFE boat taxied out of the harbor, Starker told Pala about the orca pod he'd seen the prior night.

"Eleven?" She whistled. "Unusual, but not unprecedented." Pala fiddled with knobs and levers on the control console, waved at the open pilothouse door, and said, "Close that, will you?"

Starker nodded and complied, the incessant arguing of the gulls falling to a dull roar.

When they'd passed the moored boats, Pala inched the throttle levers down, and the twin Yamahas purred.

Thin lines of whitecaps broke across Steep Point as Pala dropped the hammer and the SAFE boat jumped from the sea, coming on plane as it zipped through the chop. A steady wind out of the west was blowing the sea spray onto the windshield, so Pala changed course, heading southeast as she piloted the vessel down Upright Channel, the greenery of Shaw Island slipping away to the east, the San Juan Marine Preserve fleeting by to the west.

"So, the boss says I should treat you right. He said you're off to the main office."

Starker nodded, but said nothing.

"Is that really a promotion? I mean, I'm sure you're getting more money—which is why we work—but you're cool riding a desk? Writing summonses to the ferry and fishing companies?"

"I can affect policy at that level. Out here—you're just trying to take the salt out of the sea."

"Maybe, but the air sure is cleaner."

"You got me there." What he didn't tell her was he was never big into fieldwork. He was best suited to the big picture, looking at the entire chess board, and that meant moving up whether he wanted to or not.

Pala nudged the ship's wheel, arcing the SAFE boat around the point into Friday Harbor. She eased back on the throttle and the boat slowed, a large white brick-like ferry pushing across the harbor before them.

Spooky was stretched out in the gap between the windshield and command console, eyes closed, chest rising and falling as the feline slept. Starker pointed at him and said, "You ever see a cat that could sleep while getting bounced around?"

Pala hiked her shoulders and slowed the vessel further.

Not unlike Stag Harbor, Friday Harbor was postcard-like, yet much larger. As the heart of the San Juan Islands, the harbor accommodated multiple ferries from all around the Pacific Northwest, fishing charters, whale-watching boats, as well as floatplanes, and pleasure craft from all around the world. At the center of the harbor, off the eastern tip of Brown Island, the US Coast Guard endurance cutter sat watching the harbor's entrance. Starker thought he saw Captain Raynard standing on the forward deck, but he couldn't be certain.

"We can stop and see the coasties anytime you want. They're patrolling the area with response boats and drones, and the captain promised to alert us if there are any new developments."

He nodded.

The village of Friday Harbor climbed a gentle south-facing slope; houses, restaurants, and public service buildings all intermingled, the quaint architecture reminding Starker of the tiny towns that dotted the northern portion of the U.S. west coast.

Starker went out on deck to deal with the mooring lines, and he had the SAFE boat secured before Pala exited the pilothouse with Spooky in tow.

"You have to wait here." Starker lifted the cat, despite Spooky's frenzied protest. He dropped the feline in the pilothouse and quickly closed the door. "We'll be back soon." Starker inched open one of the windows to let fresh air enter the cabin, though it wasn't hot. The morning mist had burned off, humidity had settled in, and the cat would be fine.

Starker blocked out Spooky's ceaseless mewing as he and Pala wound through the maze of boats and docks to the mainland.

"Hungry? We're early," Pala said.

He nodded vigorously.

The pair grabbed egg sandwiches and coffee at a local bakery, and wandered through town, slowly heading west toward the sheriff's office.

Pala pointed at the open door of the orca museum, and Starker's eyebrows inched up.

The sand-colored building was decorated with murals of orcas, large and small, and the old man at the reception counter waved Pala through without looking up from his computer screen. The joint had a historic feel, and it was comprised of a little science, some theater, and a fascinating collection of orca bones and activities for children. A giant orca skeleton hung from the rafters in the main hall, surrounded by Native American totem poles, orca skulls, and an illustrated history of orcas in the region.

"Here," Pala pointed at a large display board labeled Basics. "I'm sure you know most of that, but…"

Starker read the description. "Orca or killer whale (Orcinus orca) is a toothed whale belonging to the oceanic dolphin family, and it is that group's largest member. It can be identified by its black-and-white patterned body. Orcas live in all the world's oceans in a variety of marine environments, from Arctic and Antarctic regions to tropical seas; they are absent only from the Baltic and Black Seas, and some areas of the Arctic Ocean. Orcas have a diverse diet, although individual populations often specialize in specific types of prey. The San Juan Islands host two types of orca: Southern residents, which feed exclusively on fish, and transients, or Biggs, that hunt marine mammals such as seals and dolphins. Transients have been known to attack baleen whale calves and even adult blue whales. Orcas are apex predators, and they have no natural predators, but they are highly social, and some populations are composed of matrilineal family groups, or pods, which are the most stable of any animal species. Their hunting techniques and vocal behaviors are often specific to a particular group and are passed down through the generations. Wild orcas are not considered a threat to humans, and no fatal attack on humans has ever been documented in the wild."

That last part stuck in Starker's brain like a fishhook as he and Pala strolled the rest of the way to the sheriff's office, the pod of eleven from the prior night coming back like the tide.

The sheriff's office looked slightly out-of-place, its red brick façade institutional and drab. The building housed the local court and other county offices, and Pala led Starker through a series of hallways, waving and nodding at people she knew.

Sheriff Klep was short, fat, and bald, and his hawkish gray eyes constantly shifted in his head. If Starker hadn't known better, he would've thought the guy was nervous. Klep's uniform shirt was creased from multiple ironings, and his badge shined under the harsh LED light.

Pala introduced Starker and the three officers took seats around a small conference table in the corner of the sheriff's office. Sheriff Klep asked, "Can I get you anything? Water? Coffee?"

Pala and Starker shook their heads no.

"How's Joel, Pala? I haven't spoken to him for a bit, but I see his boat is usually full."

"You know how it is. It never rains but it pours." Pala looked over at Starker and added, "My husband runs a local orca-watching business." Then back to Klep, "We've had some cancelations because of the... incidents, but it'll blow over."

Sheriff Klep nodded. "So, Mr. Starker, how can we help the WSCD?"

The "Mr." burned Starker's stomach, but he pressed on. "Exactly what you are doing. Keep in touch with me while I investigate. I intend to share anything I find, and I'd hope you'll do the same." He ran through everything he knew, including the pod of orcas he'd seen the prior night. "I put a call into the main office and asked to have all the forensic tests prioritized."

Sheriff Klep waved a hand. "We'll need that stuff for the reports and probably court, but I don't think it's any mystery what happened out there."

Starker lifted an eyebrow and said, "Do tell."

"We've got a hungry great white, maybe more than one. The fish scares the kayaker, she ends up in the drink, hence the minimal damage to the kayak, and you can figure the rest. Dingman's boat is a bit more of a mystery, but knowing his boys they probably tried to gaff the monster, got pulled into the water, and..." He trailed off and threw up his hands.

"I'm not sure," Starker said.

"Really? What do you think?"

"Nothing I've seen so far says shark."

"I guess that's why you're here."

A clock ticked, and the sheriff's small refrigerator buzzed.

"Anything new on your end?" Pala asked.

The sheriff sucked on his teeth. "I'm staying on the coasties, and they're giving me regular updates, but there's been nothing new to report."

"How long are they going to hang around?" Pala asked.

Klep hiked his shoulders. "Until they get bored. Once the pinkies start running, there'll be plenty of food for everyone."

"And you think the attacks will stop?"

"I do. This type of thing isn't that unusual. The timing sucks, but a few years ago—"

"Sheriff!" A woman in civvies with a knot of blonde hair atop her head like a beehive burst into the office.

"What is it, Sheila?"

"Captain Raynard called. He's sending a patrol boat out to Obstruction Pass."

Sheriff Klep opened his eyes as wide as he could.

"Oh, right, they're responding to a report of an orca pod fighting with a shark. I've dispatched Cooter."

The sheriff threw up his hands. "See? Shark."

"And orca," Starker said.

6

A Coast Guard patrol boat streaked away from its parent cutter as Starker and Pala jogged through the maze of piers and vessels to the SAFE boat. People stepped out of their way, and Starker almost laughed to himself. They were running around like kids. Even if they managed to get on scene before the dustup was over, what were they going to do? The coasties had better photography equipment, and the sheriff's office was surely already on scene. Still, he picked up his pace. "Come on," he said. "We can't let Raynard beat us there."

"What do you think? He's Captain Kirk? I'm pretty sure he's not heading out on a routine call."

"This one he will."

She skidded to a stop before the SAFE boat and thrust out a pinky. "Dinner?"

Starker gripped her pinky with his, then went to work on the mooring lines.

The Yamahas thundered to life, and Spooky didn't even glance in Starker's direction when he entered the pilothouse. The harbor was clogged with boats because a seaplane was coming in for a landing, and the Coast Guard boat got held up and Pala and Starker caught up with them.

"Looks like you owe me chow," Starker said.

Captain Raynard stood at the helm of the coastie response boat, his baby blue uniform standing out against the two sailors in dark blue that stood behind him.

The seaplane came in smooth, and the Coast Guard boat chirped its siren and cut the line of vessels waiting to exit the harbor.

"Screw that," Pala said as she jammed down the throttle control. The SAFE boat leaped from the sea, propellers clawing at the water as the boat came up on plane. She spun the ship's wheel, putting the SAFE boat fifty yards back of the coastie vessel, riding inside its wake in the flat white churning water of the motor wash.

The procession of two arced around Brown Island, and when they reached Shaw Island, Pala pointed the vessel north, away from the southern fork that led to the Pacific. Muddy brown hardpan beaches covered with patches of green seaweed gave way to evergreen forests on both sides of the channel, and Pala deftly piloted the boat around rocks and sand bars, slipping past Canoe Island and across South Sound. The water was choppy, and sea spray lashed the pilothouse windows, the wind stirring the spray like the flow interrupter on a lawn sprinkler.

The radio crackled to life as Pala eased back on the throttle. Obstruction Channel opened before them, Obstruction Island to the south, Orcas Island to the north. "This is Captain Raynard. WSCD and SJ Sheriff's Department are to stand down. Do you copy? Stand down and we'll pipe in our drone feed. Over."

Pala opened a channel and said, "We copy, Coast Guard."

The gray aluminum sheriff's boat sat at the center of the channel, the current pulling the vessel in a circle. The coastie boat came to an abrupt stop, bobbing and listing as its wake crashed into its transom.

Starker put his binoculars to his eyes.

A knot of whitewater churned a hundred yards off the coastie boat's port bow. Tall black dorsal fins moved in a large circle, the smaller gray fin of a shark knifing through the turbulent sea. A drone hovered thirty feet above the chaos.

The glare of the two control console monitors lit Pala's face as she tapped at a keyboard and supplied the coasties with an email address. As she waited for a reply, she said, "What's happening out there?"

"Nothing yet," Starker said. "It looks like the orca pod is trying to create a whirlpool around the shark, but toothy is having none of it. The beast keeps breaking their containment and striking at the orcas. There's blood in the water and from the looks of things it's orca blood."

Spooky stretched, pushed to his feet, and jumped from the seat onto the command console. He sat, peering out at the sea, his tail whipping back and forth, ears twitching.

The shark and orcas danced for five minutes before a chime echoed through the cabin and Pala deftly brought up her email account and accessed a link sent from the command center on the Coast Guard cutter. She clicked on it, and a window opened on her NAV screen. She resized it to fit the entire monitor.

Starker pocketed his binoculars and fell in behind Pala, eyes locked on the display screen.

The image showed the scene of the fight from above. Orcas surged and dove through the water, blowing spray, their tall dorsal fins encircling a smaller gray fin that slithered and shifted through the churning water. The white foam was tinted red.

"That's odd," Pala said.

"I think you need to be more specific."

"I think these orcas are residents. See how some of the dorsal fins are tipped and have the sharp corner?" She put her finger on the monitor. "This is typical of female residents."

"Why is it odd?"

"This entire situation is odd. I can count on one hand the accounts I've heard about orcas fighting sharks, but Biggs eat larger prey, and are normally more aggressive than residents."

"Could it be the pod I saw last night? Not all members of the family hunt, right?"

"True," she said. "It's one of the only times that pods separate for a short time."

The drone moved in closer, and the screen blurred, then sharpened.

Eight orcas, dorsal fins swaying, circled the shark, but the great white was undaunted. Its caudal fin swept back and forth, its dorsal fin appearing and disappearing as the beast made strafing runs on the orcas. The shark's jaws flexed, rows of razor-sharp teeth taking a chunk from an orca as it darted through the circle of tall dark fins.

Blood filled the channel, but the orcas didn't back down. The sea swirled, sucking at the shark, the killer whales thick black missiles of fury as they closed in.

"Look at the size of that one," Pala said as one of the orcas breached, the beast's entire body coming out of the water in a dramatic surge of black and white. The whale crashed back into the sea, blood boiling in the whitewater and foam.

"Did it look hurt to you?" Starker asked. It was hard to tell, but it looked like the orca had a large bubbling gash on its side, but it didn't appear to be bleeding.

"Looks like it has a massive case of poison oak," Pala said.

The great white was tiring, and it thrashed and fought, the fish taking a pounding. The orcas rammed and bit the shark from all directions, the massive black and white beasts taking turns attacking. With one last surge, the shark breached, jaws flexed open, teeth glinting in the sunlight as the orcas mounded on the fish like ants on a fallen lollipop. A fist of whitewater filled with a knot of gray and black fury rose from the sea as if hell itself was bubbling to the surface.

One of the larger orcas surged from the water, huge mouth agape, a row of five-inch chisel-like teeth visible all around the open maw like a bloody fence. A hollow *womp* echoed over the channel, and the orca bit the shark, blood spraying the water.

Orcas circled the two alphas like kids in the schoolyard, but the shark didn't have much left, and it soon fell still. The eleven orcas took turns knifing the dead fish, taking out chunks of flesh as blood filled the water. The drone moved in closer as the shark's corpse got pulled apart like a roasted chicken. The largest of the pod took a large chunk of the dead fish and moved away, its tall dorsal fin disappearing as it dove.

"Taking food to the rest of the pod," Pala said as she took note of the retreating whale.

The sea calmed, the orca dove, and a gentle breeze pushed the slick of blood, fat, and gristle across the undulating sea.

"Damn," Pala said. "I've never seen anything like that."

"Really?" he said. "Orca have been known to attack sharks, right?"

"Yes, but it's rare, but the way these orcas took that shark down... it's just..."

"What?"

Pala sighed. "I've never seen that level of aggression from an orca. Not even from a mother protecting her calf."

The radio crackled to life.

"Show's over, folks." It was Raynard. "I'll have my people go through the video and see if there's anything we missed. Coast Guard out."

The roar of an outboard cycling up echoed over the channel and the coastie boat jumped from the water, its orange inflatable sides disappearing within the sun's harsh glare as it darted east.

"Well, O.K.," Starker said.

Pala moved the SAFE boat toward the blood slick, but Starker decided against taking a sample. What was the point?

The drone image disappeared from the display, and it was once again filled with a color SONAR image of the depths. Starker adjusted the screen resolution, the depth and strength of the SONAR, but the pod of orcas was gone.

"What now?" Pala said.

"Let's patrol. Show me the sights and we'll see what's to be seen."

Pala nodded as she put the Yamahas in gear and headed east through Obstruction Channel.

When they were cruising along at a comfortable thirty-five knots, the SAFE boat spitting a fifteen-foot tail, Pala said, "So are you going to say it, or should I?"

Starker smiled and lifted his eyebrows. He wasn't certain what she was going to say, but he had a good guess.

"Is it just me, or do you think this rogue orca pod might have had something to do with the death of the kayaker and the capsized fishing boat?" she said.

Starker pursed his lips and hiked his shoulders. "It appears plausible at this point."

"The damage on the underside of the capsized boat, the way it looked like something had rammed it. That's exactly how orcas attack."

He'd had the same thought when he'd examined the upside-down vessel.

"And after what we just saw." Pala shook her head. "Those things looked sick. It would certainly explain most of their odd behavior."

To that Starker had no response.

The day wore on, the sun arcing across the sky and settling like a fat purple eye on the western horizon, and Starker was about to call it a day when the sheriff's office dispatched a boat to Sylvan Cove to investigate a civilian report of a whale washed up on the beach.

"We should check it out," Starker said, and without a word Pala changed course and pressed the throttle control arms down, the engines singing as the boat jerked forward.

The coastie drone buzzed overhead and Pala tried to follow it, but the device was too fast, and it soon disappeared within the glare of the dropping sun.

Sylvan Cove was carved into a notch on the northwest corner of Decatur Island, and to get there it was a fast five-minute shot through Lopez Bay. Pala brought the SAFE boat to a crawl as she entered the mouth of the narrow cove, a sandbar jutting from the western shore like a land bridge. There were a few boats moored in the cove, and inland at the southernmost corner a dock with boats lined up along its length extended out into the calm water.

The coastie drone was nowhere to be seen, but a sheriff's office vessel was beached on shore. A crowd of five people, including an officer dressed in tan, stood on the shoreline gazing down at a massive gray lump of flesh.

Starker brought up his binoculars. "Looks like a humpback."

"Not surprising," Pala said. "Humpback whales have been rare up this way, but recently they're straying closer to shore. Back in 2015, a pod of humpbacks entered the mouth of the Columbia River, drawn in by salmon."

Pala spun the ship's wheel and killed the motors as Starker dealt with the mooring lines.

The humpback was fresh. There were no signs of rot or decay, and at first glance, the whale looked like many others that found their way into coves and bays only to beach themselves and die struggling to get back into the water. However, closer inspection revealed puncture wounds all over the humpback's body. Huge round bite marks that hadn't been caused by a great white shark.

"The cause of death is those bite marks? There is no doubt, yes?" Starker asked when they were back on the SAFE boat.

"Whales do sometimes beach themselves when death is near," Pala said.

Spooky meowed twice. It was once for no, twice for yes. The feline looked directly at Pala, still giving Starker the cold shoulder.

A bruised sky smeared the western horizon, dusk leaking over the water as the silvery sheen faded to inky blackness.

7

**Friday Harbor, San Juan Island, U.S., 9:51 AM PT, June 18th.
Twelve days until the start of Pink Salmon Season.**

Starker heard the phantom mewing of Spooky in his head as he sipped his coffee. He'd tricked the cat, and he didn't feel great about it, but the feline had fresh food, water, and a bed that was more comfortable than the one in Starker's last apartment, so it was what it was. He actually missed having the cat around, but based on the prior day he figured the feline was better off at the inn than locked in the pilothouse of Pala's SAFE boat. The shelter was open tomorrow and Spooky would continue his journey to a new home, but the thought of it burned his chest.

Pala coughed gently. "You in there?"

The partners sat at an outdoor cafe, having breakfast, and mentally preparing for the day. Cars rolled lazily down Front Street, gulls cried, and a stiff sea breeze blew the remnants of the morning mist across the harbor.

"I was just thinking about Spooky."

She chuckled.

"What?"

"Here I am thinking you're puzzling over the complexities of a case that has three presumed fatalities and enough sea weirdness to keep researchers humming for a decade."

The lady had a point, and Starker sipped.

"I've got to ask..." She stared out at the line of charter boats trailing from the harbor. "The coasties pulled up anchor yesterday. How long are you going to play this out?"

Starker chuckled. "You want me gone?"

She licked her lips and rolled her eyes. "You've got to have a girlfriend waiting for you? Your new job?"

He shook his head. "She didn't want to move to Seattle, and it didn't matter. Things had played out, as you would say."

"Family then?"

"Dad died and mom is. . mom."

Pala stared at the table. "I've got two children, Starker." She looked up at him then, locking eyes in the unbreakable partner bond. She was telling Starker that she didn't intend for her kids to grow up without a mother.

"I understand. It's just. ."

"What? It's just what?"

"Something isn't right in all this. You have to see that?"

"What's the end game? Yesterday settled things, no? I mean, other than response aren't we out of this?"

"Rabid orca? Sounds like we're right in the thick of it, whatever it is." The more he thought on it, the more Starker's working theory that the orcas were diseased made sense.

"And? What the hell does that change? You're a marine biologist now? Isn't there a stack of papers in Seattle with your name on it?"

Starker smiled. The lady had another point, so he shifted gears. "So, I got word from the sheriff this morning. The analysis has come back on the blood samples taken at both scenes, and there was one notable surprise, though now it makes sense."

The deep hollow bleat of a horn boomed from a ferry as it pulled out, the sounds of a grumbling engine and bubbling water echoing over the harbor.

"All four victims' blood was identified, but it wasn't mixed with tuna blood as we thought."

"Orca?"

Starker nodded and took a bite of his buttered roll. "Sheriff said without corpses he's going to keep the investigation open, but he plans to lay things out for the husband and widow today."

"There may be legal entanglements. Life insurance and such."

He nodded. "If either party pushes for a confirmation of death, he's prepared to issue such."

"Requiescat in pace," muttered Pala as she made the sign of the cross.

"Excuse me?" He thought the words were Latin.

She sighed. "Sorry. Means rest in peace. Those poor families."

"You're Catholic?"

"As far as it goes. Most Lummi tribal members converted to Christianity in the late 1800s, including my ancestors."

"When missionaries were crawling all over the place."

She nodded.

"What do you think the Lummi have to say about what's happening with the orca?"

Pala shrugged. "The Lhaq'temish are known as people of the sea, and many Northwest coastal tribes live by collecting shellfish, hunting game, and most importantly, salmon fishing. Though they also gather plants, such as camas, a root vegetable, and different species of berries, but the fish is their bread and butter, so to speak."

"So it's safe to say they care a great deal."

Pala nodded. "The Lummi developed a fishing technique known as "reef netting," used for taking large quantities of fish in salt water."

He nodded understanding. "I know, and the Washington Department of Fish and Wildlife acknowledges the technique for selective fishing."

"Yup, and in twelve days, when pinkie season opens, the Lummi will set reef nets on Orcas, San Juan, Lummi, Fidalgo, and Portage islands, and near Point Roberts and Sandy Point."

"We should probably pay the elders at the reservation a visit then, no?"

She pursed her lips. "If they'll see us, and like I said, I think we're out of it."

"If it wasn't for the—"

The radio on Pala's hip squawked. She pulled it and responded, "Copy."

"Pala we've got a 1021 over on Deception Pass. Copy?"

"10-4. Starker and I are on our way."

Static. "Pala, please check with Officer Starker to confirm assignment. I forgot you were ferrying him around, over."

Pala looked at Starker, who was searching his mental code book for 1021.

"It's civilian vessels getting too close to wildlife," she said, reading his mind.

"Find out what type of animal. If it's just sea lions, then we'll pass."

"Central, Starker wants to know what animals are involved, over?"

"From what I can gather it's researchers and tour vessels, and they've surrounded a group of residents that are harassing transients."

Starker pushed up from his seat.

"Copy. On our way. Pala out."

The rumble of the engines filtered into the SAFE boat's pilothouse, which was oddly quiet without the purring and meowing of Spooky. He considered calling the inn and asking that he be checked on, but then Starker recalled he was dealing with a cat, not a dog. Felines usually weren't into drama, and he'd make it up to the animal by taking him for a walk and treat him to some fish when he got back to Orcas Island.

Pala cycled up the Yamahas as she cut around pleasure craft and fishing vessels that clogged the harbor mouth, her motions fluid and practiced.

Starker pulled his phone, but other than emails from his commanding officer requesting an update and a request for information from his new office, there was nothing of note.

Pala caught him scanning Knowpedia for information on orca and said, "You can just ask me, you know? My husband runs a whale-watching vessel. Remember?"

He'd forgotten that. "Sorry, yeah." He slipped his phone into a pocket of his windbreaker and the clank as it hit his mini binoculars echoed through the still cabin. "It's odd for transients and residents to socialize, right?"

"Odd?" She laughed. "Understatement of the century. They ignore each other like the jocks and burnouts at a high school dance."

She glanced in his direction and Starker lifted his eyebrows. "The researchers are always interested in the transients, for obvious reasons. They're not around much. Transients eat mammals and can be aggressive. They'll feed on anything from harbor seals to minke."

"Whereas the locals depend on the fish?"

She nodded.

Deception Pass was a narrow channel that cut through Deception State Park into Skagit Bay. Thin concrete-like sand beaches etched with black rock and seaweed ran on both sides of the waterway, and forests of evergreens climbed into the hills beyond. The current was swift, and small rapids curled and popped around the supports of Deception Pass Bridge as the SAFE boat passed beneath it.

The pass opened up, and a sheer cliff face rose from the water to the north, the pass dotted with islands and fishing boats. Nothing drew fishermen more than a spot where thousands of gallons of seawater constantly moved, pushing and pulling on fish as they fought with the current. The only other entrance to the bay was way down south around Whidbey Island.

A cluster of boats floated with the current off Yokeko Point, a series of tall black dorsal fins parading around as they dipped and dove from the water.

Pala didn't slow the SAFE boat as she tore across the channel, the bow jumping and throwing spray, the deck and pilothouse windows getting splashed. The SAFE boat zigzagged through the knot of vessels, still not slowing, Pala calmly working the ship's wheel, the boat's wake knocking around even the larger vessels.

Starker laughed as he watched tourists grab for gunnels and captains attempt to steady their crafts.

Before the barrage of incoming complaints could materialize, Pala lifted the communication handset and flipped a toggle switch, turning on the external annunciation system. "You are all in violation of the minimum distance requirements relating to these endangered animals.

Slowly move back or you will be ticketed, fined, and your license to operate in Washington State may be revoked."

That last part kicked everyone into motion and Starker noted several pleasure crafts slinking away along with a few charter boats and whale-watching vessels. Starker wondered if Pala's husband was among them.

Reading his mind yet again, Pala said, "Joel knows better."

Starker feigned confusion.

"In case you were wondering if my husband was here."

He nodded, but said nothing.

The research vessels eased back, except one, a little red center console bearing the markings of the University of Washington that stayed in tight, floating with the current and slowly getting closer to the knot of sea wolves.

Pala inched the SAFE boat forward, pulling alongside the red boat.

There was one person on the vessel, and she was perched in the boat's bow, peering into a camera with a lens the size of a rocket ship. She didn't appear to notice the SAFE boat's approach, so Pala blew her air horn.

The researcher jumped, hit her face on her camera, then steadied herself on the gunnel as she jerked her head back to locate the source of the intrusion. Her face softened when she saw Pala and Starker staring at her from the SAFE boat's pilothouse.

The woman waved a hand and made her way aft.

Starker slid open the SAFE boat's pilothouse door.

The woman said, "I'm so sorry. I've got my radio off."

Starker hopped onto the SAFE boat's inflated gunnel and jumped across the two-foot gap to the red research vessel. A fast check of her command console showed that the woman was telling the truth.

"You're supposed to have your radio on at all times," Starker said.

The woman nodded emphatically. "I know. It's just the noise was distracting, and it was…"

"Scaring the whales?"

She nodded.

"That's because you're too close."

The woman looked around, and finding no imaginary backup, she said, "Yes, of course, Officer, I'll move right away. I'm Dr. Travalon from WSU. My apologies." The researcher glanced at Pala as if she knew her, but Pala showed no signs of recognition.

Out in the middle of the channel, tall black dorsal fins knifed through the water, orcas of various sizes dipping and diving through the churning sea. Tail flutes surged through the water pushing forth conical heads filled with teeth, ribbons of pustule-filled gashes marring the beasts' slick skin.

Starker jumped back to the SAFE boat, but as he did so he asked, "Are they feeding on something?"

"They appear to be fighting over something, yes."

"And that's very odd, right?"

"More than odd. It's unheard of."

"Which group are the aggressors?"

"That's the funny thing. It's the residents, not the Biggs."

"Clear out of here," Starker said. "Now."

A hundred yards away the sea bubbled with whitewater, black and white polished flesh, and blood. Shockwaves slammed into the SAFE boat, showering the pilothouse, tail flukes slapping, wing-like pectoral fins stroking the water. Conical black and white heads with smiling mouths of spike-like teeth exploded from the channel, the beasts in a frenzy.

Starker stared through the binoculars, trying to count the creatures, but it was like trying to count a knot of cats, all of which were almost the same color. The creatures tousled and ten minutes slipped away. His rough count was seventeen orcas, and it appeared six transients were being corralled by eleven residents.

"Camera on," said Pala. "This type of behavior has never been seen before."

"Never?"

Pala killed the motors and let the SAFE boat slide in slow.

Water sprayed over the boat and two orca calves jumped from the sea, but they didn't look like any orca young Starker had ever seen. The beasts were great white shark-like in size and demeanor, their red engorged eyes standing out before white eye patches. Ribbons of pustule-filled gashes covered both beasts, and the pair swam in perfect symmetry as they moved in on a full-grown Biggs.

"Are they going after that big guy?"

"It would appear so."

Tail flutes flapped and pushed, pectoral fins flexed, and the two smaller orcas heaved and dove through the sea, cutting in on the Biggs like lions taking turns taking chunks out of prey. The sound of clashing muscle, tearing meat, and mumbled growls echoed over the water.

"This is unbelievable," Pala said.

"Believe it," said Starker.

8

The orca rumble at Deception Pass was still in full swing when the Coast Guard drone arrived. The thing sounded like a giant fly as it buzzed the SAFE boat, moving in close, its camera eye zooming in and out before moving away and settling over the melee, hovering twenty feet above the sea. All the boats that had been warned off, including the red research vessel, had cleared out. Pala managed to keep the SAFE boat on the edge of the chaos as she constantly adjusted the throttle and made corrections to their course as the current pushed them through the channel toward Rosario Strait.

The resident orca continued to attack the Biggs, roiling black and white patches of slick skin shining in the harsh sunlight that baked the sea. Whales breached and rolled, the residents ramming and biting the more aggressive Biggs, who looked to be searching for a way out of the tangle the larger pod had created.

A severed pectoral fin floated past the boat, blood and gristle leaking from its end. The fin looked like a surfboard floating in the water, its trail of blood and fat drawing in one of the smaller resident orcas. The creature's conical head shot from the water, a black and white bullet ringed with teeth, and it chomped on the severed pectoral fin like it was a corn chip.

Starker heard Pala squeak, and when he glanced over at her he saw her hand resting on the handle of her Glock.

"What do you plan to do with that?" he asked.

"Maybe a warning shot would break it up?"

Starker returned his gaze to the undulating knot of black and white flesh rising from the whitewater before the SAFE boat. Water tainted with blood sprayed the front of the boat and one of the beasts wailed, a great moan of pain that sent a tremor of fear running through Starker. He said, "We're not supposed to interfere with the natural actions of wildlife." He left the "but" go unspoken.

"I guess they're only hurting themselves." She let her hand drop from the gun.

Gulls circled above like buzzards, squawking and arguing, and Starker caught the scent of rust on the breeze that pushed through the open pilothouse window.

Minutes slipped away as orcas surged and breached all around the SAFE boat as they fought.

"Here," Pala said as she handed Starker a life vest, and he slipped it on over his windbreaker.

The eleven residents circled and managed to separate a medium-sized transient from its pod. The killer whale lacked the rounded tip on its dorsal fin, its saddle patches a solid and uniform gray. The transient pod left the separated creature for dead, and the five remaining transients fled, five black dorsal fins hissing through the sea.

Pala said, "Transients generally travel in small groups, usually of two to six animals, and have weaker family bonds—not like residents, so it's not unusual for transients to shun their own kind."

The remaining transient tried to break the residents' containment, surging and diving, breaching from the sea as it probed the residents' defense, but the larger pod spiraled in tighter. When the transient killer whale had no space left, the largest resident rammed the creature, jaws extended, teeth biting into black flesh, and blood stained the whitewater as the injured sea wolf slipped beneath the sea. The other residents took turns strafing the creature, and the transient finally fell still, the sea bubbling with red foam. Pieces of black and white flesh floated on the surface as the residents fed.

"This is more than habitat loss and hunger," Pala said.

"Come again?" Starker said.

"This behavior," she said. "As you know, orcas are considered threatened or endangered due to prey depletion, habitat loss, pollution, capture, and conflicts with fishermen, but this is different. Even different than what we saw yesterday."

"Because orca never attack their own?"

"Cannibalism has been noted in almost every species of mammal, including humans, but not orca. They typically take care of their own or ignore each other, but this. I have no doubts any longer that this is something else."

One of the resident orcas breached right next to the SAFE boat. The beast hung in the air for an instant, bloody water running down its length. Like some of the other orcas he'd seen, this sea wolf appeared to have gashes running its length, white pus-like boils spilling out of the wound like fat. The killer whale's large swollen red eyes stared up at the blue sky as it plunged back into the sea, its massive tail flute landing on the bow of the SAFE boat.

"Shit!" Pala yelled as the bow dipped sharply and seawater crashed over the bow, swamping the boat.

SAFE boats are hard to sink. Their inflatable gunnels have multiple chambers, and there's a self-bailing gap between the deck and the sides that allows the vessel to drain quickly. Starker heard the bilge pump snap on, but the deck was already clearing, the boat settling and the seawater draining away.

The feeding frenzy was breaking up, the transient orca nothing but a riddled corpse floating with the current, chunks of its body missing, the stark whiteness of its bloody bones standing out against the blue undulating water. The residents faded back into the sea, powering away, a slick of blood, fat, and gristle leaking down the channel with the current toward the Rosario Strait.

With the show over, the Coast Guard drone buzzed away, dipping its nose at the SAFE boat as it disappeared into the glare of the late morning sun.

Pala let the current pull the boat through the strait, the sea flattening, the blood slick thinning. "We don't need a sample of the slick, right?" she asked.

"I think we know what happened here, and the coasties got good footage I'd imagine. Still think we're out of this?"

She sighed. "I've never seen anything like that, and I've been on these waters my entire life."

"The question is, what do we do about it?"

Pala rolled her shoulders, the stress of the question tearing at her normally smooth features. "I feel useless. Helpless." She put the SAFE boat in gear, spun the ship's wheel, and brought the vessel about, pointing the bow west. Water gurgled and popped as the current pushed the boat along.

"I know the feeling well."

"Really? You'd never know it by the looks of you." She pressed down on the throttle control arm and the engines grumbled as the boat eased up on plane.

"I wasn't always this cool."

She laughed. "I never said you were cool."

"You implied it."

"Did I?"

"Anywayyyyyy, I remember my first real case. I threw up when I got on scene. Literally hurled my breakfast all over the deck. My lieutenant was pissed."

"What the hell did you see that made you puke? You might not be cool, but I can't see you tossing your cookies for no reason."

"Do you remember the Grason spill back ten years or so?"

"I was in high school, but I recall something about it."

"I was on the job like a month. I hadn't done anything except write some tickets. Measuring fish, as you would say. Then we get a call about a transport vessel, The St. Pete. The captain miscalculated and hit a submerged rock off Port Townend Bay by Fort Flagler."

Pala glanced in his direction as she piloted the boat south down Rosario Strait, the engines humming purposefully, the twin Yamahas singing at 3500RPMs.

"You're familiar with the area, right?" he asked.

"A little," she said. "I know from school that it was once an artillery fort, and with Fort Worden and Fort Casey they once guarded Admiralty Inlet, the nautical entrance to Puget Sound."

"Correct," Starker said. "The triangle of fire. Anyway, we get this call that a small transport vessel carrying oil, gasoline, and canisters of compressed gas has grounded on a stone. We rush to the site, and I tell you, I've never been so disgusted in my life.

"My lieutenant drops into the middle of the chaos, the transport ship listing to port, the crew in lifeboats paddling toward the rocky shore. The entire surface of the water was black with an oil slick, and I heaved on the deck of the boat. No warning. If my lieutenant hadn't also looked a little green around the edges, I think he might have dressed me down. As it was, he and I got to work helping the wildlife."

Pala glanced in his direction, worry and sorrow leaking over her face, but she said nothing.

"The bay was like black mud, and it coated everything it touched with oil. We beached our boat and waded into the water like blind men, pulling birds and ducks from the sludge. They were black like they'd been charred on a barbeque. We didn't know what to do."

Pala nodded solemnly.

"I mean we had a clue, but as you know when oil sticks to a bird's feathers it causes them to mat and separate, impairing their natural waterproofing and exposing the bird's sensitive skin to the extremes of temperature, and that's exactly what happened." Anger surged through Starker, a pain that would never abate. "I really didn't understand why I joined the WSCD until that day. The death toll was tragic; birds, fish, sea otters, anything that touched the water. All of them painted black."

Pala said nothing as she arced the SAFE boat northwest across the Strait of Juan de Fuca, heading for San Juan Island.

"The damaged boat was leaking oil and gasoline into the water, and there were canisters of all kinds of compressed gases floating in the flotsam, and we had to stop fishing out animals to deal with them. It was a nightmare.

"There was this pelican, a huge pterodactyl looking thing, covered in oil. The poor creature struggled against me as I tried to pull him from the water, and I managed to get him out of the sludge, but there wasn't much

I could do except hose the bird down with water. That's really all I was able to do for any of them until the Oiled Wildlife Care Network from UC Davis showed up."

"I've seen them at work. Amazing stuff."

Starker nodded. "When they arrived on scene things improved, but we lost eighty percent of the animals my partner and I pulled from the spill."

"Those types of accidents take a long time to fully clean up."

He nodded, gazing south as he pictured the blackened shoreline and dead sea.

With his story done, Starker hid within himself, the memory of that fateful day polluting his brain like a bad dream he knew wasn't a dream. He thought of Spooky and wondered what the cat was up to. Probably lounging on the bed. He'd be back at the inn soon enough.

Pala piloted the SAFE boat all around the San Juan Islands, patrolling. All appeared copasetic, and the partners stopped for a fast lunch at Estal's in Roche Harbor where fish and chips could be had for five dollars, and they sold ninety-nine-cent tap beers. Starker and Pala abstained, however, and that took all the willpower Starker had left.

When the sun started its descent to the horizon Pala announced she had plans for the evening and was knocking off. Still, there was no invitation to come meet the family, no offer of a home cooked meal, and she owed him for their bet, but he didn't push. Starker understood, nowadays folk's schedules were packed, and Pala had two children. He wasn't certain exactly what that entailed, but he knew it was much more involved than taking care of a cat. His partner most likely had a recital, sports event, or some other kid-centric obligation.

Pala pulled back on the throttle control and arced the boat around Steep Point.

Starker brought his binoculars to his eyes and verified that the traffic cones and yellow hazard tape still marked the area where the lost kayaker's boat had been found, not that it mattered.

The harbor was buzzing like a beehive stirred with a stick, and as the SAFE boat wound through the moored boats, Starker felt the energy of anticipation running through the place like electricity. Pala put the motors in neutral, spun the ship's wheel, and deftly brought the SAFE boat broadside against the end of main dock.

"Get a good night's rest. I've got a feeling tomorrow is going to be crazier than today, if that's possible."

Starker nodded and opened the pilothouse door.

"Oh, and we're dropping the cat off in the morning, right?"

He nodded again, but as Starker mounted the gunnel and jumped from the SAFE boat, he wasn't so sure. He wasn't sure of much anymore.

9

Spooky sat within a fold of the closed curtains, peering out the front window of Starker's bungalow. The sun was setting at Starker's back, and errant rays of purple-orange light fell across the cottage, painting it a garish yellow. The cat's eyes glowed, but when the feline saw Starker, he turned his back on him and jumped from the windowsill, disappearing behind tussled curtains.

Starker was exhausted, so he'd picked up a sandwich and a sixpack of Heineken on his way back to the inn, but before he dove in and showered, he took Spooky out for a walk.

Dusk spread over the island, a bruised sky with orange bleeding around the edges stretched across the western horizon, a purple glow filtering through the trees, the surface of the harbor dark glass.

Spooky didn't look at him, and after he took care of his business he headed right back to the cottage. The cat appeared unmoved when Starker presented a peace offering: a can of StarKist tuna packed in water. The feline sniffed the food, turned his back on Starker, and lifted his tail, giving Starker a good view of his poop hole.

"Come on, man." Starker put his hands on his hips and stared down at the cat, who jumped onto the bed, walked in a circle three times, and sat down facing the wall. "Whatever."

Starker popped a beer, showered, and shaved, and he felt much better having washed the day off him. When he came out of the bathroom, he grabbed another beer along with his food and plopped onto the bed next to Spooky.

The feline lay in the same spot, staring at the wall, his tail wrapped around him, but the can of tuna was empty.

Starker smiled and tore open his roast beef on rye. He took several bites and dropped the sandwich onto its wax paper wrapping and scanned his phone. Emails from the IT guy at his new office wanting to know what type of computer he wanted. Another from his commander wanting a detailed update on the situation. There were four missed calls from his mother, but he decided his patience was running a bit too thin to talk to her, so he sent off a text saying he was swamped and that he'd call tomorrow. He got no response.

The gray light leaking around the window shades slowly faded to black as Starker ate and moved on to his third beer. He was watching the SportsCenter app on his phone when Spooky lifted his head and glanced toward the cottage's door.

"What is it, buddy?"

For the first time since Starker had locked the cat in the cottage that morning, the feline turned his gray eyes on Starker, shook his head slightly, and returned his gaze to the door like a child dismissing a parent.

Starker shut down his phone and took a long pull of beer, then held the bottle out to the cat, who still had his eyes locked on the door.

Spooky pushed to his feet as if he'd been poked, his tail shooting out straight, glowing eyes focused on the closed door. The cat strode past Starker, jumped from the bed, and mounted the windowsill, staring out into the darkness beyond. "Meow. Meow. Meow." Three meows meant the beast was agitated.

The cat hissed viciously, the fur on his back lifting slightly as if stirred by a breeze.

Starker put down his beer, got up, and stood behind Spooky, staring through the gap in the curtains into the darkness beyond. Nothing moved. The vegetation swayed gently in the evening breeze, and porchlights and accent lighting around the complex pushed away the moonlight.

Spooky hissed, mewed three times, then hissed again before jumping from the window's edge and planting himself next to the closed door. He looked up at Starker, wet eyes glowing.

"Do you need to go out?"

"Meow. Meow."

"O.K., then." Starker opened the bungalow's door and don't you know the faint warble of sirens could be heard in the distance. He turned to Spooky, whose chin jutted up with satisfaction and arrogance.

Starker walked across the parking area barefoot in his underwear and peeked around a hedgerow so he could see the harbor. The flicker of red flashing lights cut through the trees on the opposite side of the harbor by The Swimming Steer, and a police boat was tearing through the harbor, blue lights falling over the listing and rocking moored vessels.

"Meow. Meow." Starker looked down and saw Spooky sitting next to him.

"Yeah, I think you're right. We need to see what's happening."

"Meow. Meow."

Starker jogged back to his room and pulled on some clothes and boots, clipped his badge to his belt, and grabbed his Glock and windbreaker. When he went to leave, Starker found Spooky blocking his way, and he remembered he didn't have a car.

"You need to stay here."

"Meow."

Starker sighed as he inched the door open.

Fool me once, shame on you, fool me twice—Spooky sprang for the gap between the door and its frame, and Starker shut the door.

"Meow."

"I can't have you… oh, forget it." Starker opened the door and the cat bolted out into the night.

The inn was stirring. It was only eight o'clock, and many of the hotel's windows glowed blue from TVs, and the main office light was on. He strode purposefully across the parking lot and when he pushed open the door to the main office he found Gladys sitting atop a stool behind the reception counter, glasses perched on the end of her nose as she stared at a computer monitor, lines of pain wrinkling her face.

"Everything O.K.?" Starker asked.

"These damn banks." Then like she'd dropped an F-bomb she said, "Oh, I'm sorry Mr. Starker. Is something wrong? Can I help you?"

"Meow. Meow."

"Oh, I didn't know you had a pet." The woman looked worried. "We don't allow—"

"He's not my pet. Listen, I need a favor." Gladys knew who Starker was and why he was on Orcas Island, and as he explained what he needed her face smoothed.

"My car? Of course." She fished in a purse that looked like it contained everything the woman owned and came out with a dolphin keychain with a bundle of metal hanging from it.

The sirens were fading and sweat rolled down Starker's back as he waited for Gladys to pick through her keyring like he had all the time in the world.

"Here it is," she said. Gladys struggled to get the key off the ring, so Starker helped her. "It's the white Ford F150 in the corner of the lot."

"Thank you. I should be back soon."

"No worries," Gladys said. "I'll be here for another hour or two. If the office is closed up when you get back just hold onto the key until morning."

Starker smiled and left with Spooky in tow.

The Ford was old and dirty, but it cranked over on the first turn of the key. As he drove down out of the hills to the harbor, Starker saw flashlight beams bobbing around within the maze of boats docked in the harbor, and a car with a flashing blue light on its roof waited on Channel Street.

Spooky planted himself on the dashboard, peering at the flashing lights below.

"You really shouldn't sit up there. If I get into an accident…"

Spooky didn't even look in his direction.

As if it had been planned, the flashlight beams reached the waiting police car just as Starker entered town. He dropped in behind the cruiser as it passed The Swimming Steer and entered the woods that covered the top of the sheer rock face that plunged into the harbor. The road veered right and changed to Potlatch Road, and soon the lights of town were gone, and he and Spooky trailed after the police car as it raced through the blackness of a dense evergreen forest.

Starker didn't attempt to hide his presence, and he stayed on the police cruiser's tail as it made a series of rights and lefts, steadily climbing into the hills as they worked their way west toward the coast. After ten minutes of driving the forest gave way, and the road plunged toward the sea. Lights sparkled along the shoreline, and beyond them the shimmering waters of President Channel slipped past, dark and foreboding, save for the occasional boat marked by navigation lights.

Mailboxes appeared on the side of the road, one every sixteenth of a mile or so, and when the police vehicle made a right onto Cormorant Bay Road, Starker saw his destination.

A police vehicle sat parked at the end of a long driveway that disappeared into a thick evergreen forest. The flashing blue light paused briefly before continuing, but the officer directing traffic and holding the fort stepped out into the driveway and blocked Starker's way.

Starker pulled his badge from his belt and held it up. "What's happening?"

The deputy sheriff studied the badge, and said, "ECON?"

Starker tamped down a surge of anger. The way regular law enforcement said "ECON" burned him every time. "Investigations division. I'm here investigating the disappearances. Let me through."

The officer straightened, a scowl inching over his face. "I've got to check with the sheriff." The guy lifted a radio and explained the situation.

Between squawks of static, the sheriff said, "Is that who was following me up here?"

"Affirmative."

"Let him through."

The cop stepped aside and waved Starker on.

A long driveway wound through the trees, daggers of red, white, and blue flashing lights knifing through the thick wall of green. A knot of law enforcement vehicles filled the crushed shell parking area in front of the house, and Spooky meowed as Starker parked and shut down the Ford's engine.

The estate house was set back several hundred yards from the water's edge, and a female officer that reminded Starker of Holly Berry met him as he and Spooky slipped through a gate into the house's backyard. A luxurious infinity pool reflected moonlight as Starker was led down to a manmade beach that looked like a rich kid's sandbox, and Starker chuckled at the thought because that's exactly what it was.

The shoreline of Orcas Island is mostly bog and stone, but several of the waterfront homes constructed their own private beaches. The notch in the shoreline was surrounded by trees, and two boats, one large and one small, sat moored offshore.

The Holly Berry look-a-like handed him off to Sheriff Klep, who didn't offer his hand. He was in plain clothes, and he looked put out. "What brings you here?" When he noticed Spooky, he added, "And you brought a friend."

"Meow. Meow."

"I heard all the commotion and…" Starker shook his head. He was an investigator for the state, and he didn't need to explain anything to this man. "What's happened here?"

"Come. I'll show you."

The two men and the cat made their way down a brick path, past the pool, a greenhouse, a tennis court, and finally came to the beach. The scene was garishly lit and officers wearing gloves and holding flashlights scoured the tiny beach. Two old people, a man, and a woman sat on a cobblestone retaining wall, weeping and coughing.

"The owners?" Starker asked, throwing a thumb toward the whimpering people.

The sheriff nodded. "They heard a scream and came outside to investigate."

Sheriff Klep worked his way down to the water's edge and Starker said, "What happened?"

"Their daughter was outside taking a swim in the pool, so when they heard the scream, they were understandably concerned. They came outside and Kim wasn't in the pool, but there were wet footprints leading down the path to their beach. So, they followed, and this is what they found."

Starker's breath caught in his throat like a chicken bone.

The scene was rendered in harsh black and white, floodlights on stands drenching the glowing white sand. A thick trail of blood led across the beach into the water. Officers snapped pictures, took measurements, the entire area cordoned off with yellow hazard tape.

Starker walked to the end of the blood slick and dropped into a crouch, and Spooky sat beside him. There was a depression in the sand, perhaps two butt-cheeks. The trail of blood cut across the imported white sand, terminating in the black water. There was a deep groove in the sand as if a boat had beached, and the sand on both sides of the narrow trench was disheveled as if by many feet… or the pounding of dorsal fins.

"We think maybe somebody snatched her," the sheriff said.

"Somebody, as in a person?"

He hiked his shoulders, his eyes finding Starker's, testing him.

The blood trail was fifteen feet long, which meant Kim had been sitting at least that far from the water's edge. "So you think someone beached their boat, grabbed her, and she was injured in the fray during the kidnapping?"

"I've got nothing better at the moment. Maybe tomorrow, under the light of day, new evidence will present itself."

Starker almost laughed. "Good thing you don't sell cars for a living," Starker said, his patience gone. "Who are these people? Are they important?"

The sheriff hiked his shoulders. "Computers or something, but they're both retired."

"So, no motivation, really, and how would the kidnappers have known Kim would be outside at that time?"

"Maybe they've been casing the place."

"Maybe you're not seeing what's right in front of you."

Sheriff Klep pursed his lips, not quite smiling.

"I think Kim was sitting on the beach, and she was snatched by an orca."

The sheriff laughed, but there was no mirth in it. "Last time I checked, orcas can't walk on land."

"No, but they pluck sea lions off the shoreline all the time. I've seen it."

Now the sheriff was nodding. "The thought crossed my mind, but I was afraid to say it out loud." He knelt next to Starker. "So, the kid is sitting here, minding her own Ps and Qs, when the whale breaches from the water and takes her?"

"Yup. The groove in the sand isn't from a hull, but a sea wolf's torso and the disturbance in the sand on the sides is from pectoral fins as it struggled to get back into the water."

"Maybe, but isn't this far from the water? Fifteen feet?"

"Granted, that is far, but as you know we're dealing with some unusual behaviors."

The sheriff rolled his shoulders. "What the hell am I going to tell the press? The pinkies are here and I can't have people getting eaten."

Starker said nothing.

"O.K.," Sheriff Klep said as he drew himself up. "Be in my office with Pala tomorrow at 9 AM sharp. I'll call the coasties and Chairman Spollomen."

"Meow. Meow."

10

Stag Harbor, Orcas Island, 8:21 AM PT, June 19th. Eleven days until the start of Pink Salmon Season.

Seagulls shrieked, boat horns sounded, and the buzz of fishermen and vacationers echoed over the harbor. Starker sat at the end of main dock waiting on Pala, Spooky sitting beside him. The cat had his tail wrapped around himself, his glowing gray eyes staring at a school of tiny shiners darting around the dock's support columns. In a normal situation, Spooky would have a bag with all his food, toys, and other belongings in it. Things Starker could give to the shelter to make the animal more comfortable, but Spooky had no possessions—no squeak toys or balls. All the feline had was Starker.

He stroked the cat and Spooky purred, leaning in and rubbing against Starker's leg. Spooky had forgotten—more likely forgiven—Starker for his abandonment, and as he thought about giving the cat up his stomach burned, though he wasn't sure why. He'd never been a cat person, and he was moving to the city where a cat would be confined to a seven-hundred-square foot apartment and a litterbox.

"Could you give this all up? You don't seem like an alley cat," Starker said.

"Meow. Meow."

Starker chuckled.

Spooky stood up, peering at the harbor mouth through the tangle of moored boats.

Starker heard it also. The roar of a boat engine.

Pala's SAFE boat rounded the point and entered the harbor, the grumble of the outboards lessening slightly as she powered down the motors. She was coming in hot, and the moored boats rocked and listed as Pala brought the SAFE boat in broadside.

"Hurry up," she chirped through the open pilothouse window.

Starker and Spooky jumped aboard and the SAFE boat was pulling away from the dock before Starker got the pilothouse door open.

Pala cycled up the motors, violating the no wake rule as she streaked from the marina, but nobody looked askance at her. Fishermen went about tending to their boats, charters loading, and getting ready for the day. Everyone knew Pala and her boat, and they understood if she was in a hurry there was probably a good reason.

"What's up?" Starker asked as he closed the pilothouse door. "Sheriff get a stale donut?"

"Meeting has been postponed until 10:30. We've been dispatched to Open Bay."

Spooky jumped on the copilot's seat and used it as a springboard to vault to the top of the command console. There he sat and stared out the windshield, shifting slightly with each bump and slap of the SAFE boat as it bounced through light chop.

Starker said, "I'm afraid to ask."

"I heard about last night," she said.

He sighed. "I was going to fill you in, and I didn't disturb you last night because there was nothing to be done. The only reason I was on scene was because of this guy." Starker pointed at Spooky.

Pala glanced over at Starker, then at the cat, who was licking his fur.

The sea was aglow, endless sparkling pinpricks of light, the water painted silver. Thin ribbons of foam cut across the channel, a heady wind out of the northwest pushing around the evergreens that packed the eastern shore of San Juan Island.

As Pala piloted the boat through the San Juan Channel toward the northern portion of San Juan Island, Starker filled Pala in on the prior night's events. How Spooky had heard the siren, the Ford, and the sheriff.

"Yup," Pala said. "Plucked her right off the beach was the way it was described to me."

Starker nodded. "Given the events of the last few days nothing else makes sense."

"The sheriff agrees, and he's taking every precaution."

Starker lifted an eyebrow.

"The Roche Yacht Club does their sailing lessons in the morning, and the sheriff didn't think that was the greatest idea. Boats are one thing, but blowing around without a motor on a twelve-foot sailboat doesn't seem smart at the moment."

"Meow. Meow."

"You agree, huh?" Pala said to Spooky. Then to Starker, "We'll stop at the shelter on the way to the sheriff's office. I spoke with Tippi and she's expecting us."

Starker's stomach knotted like he'd eaten bad chili.

Pala adjusted the resolution on her NAV screen and changed course slightly as the barren brown pasture of Spieden Island stretched out to the north, Roche Harbor to the south. A dark jagged line ran along the western portion of the chart delineating the border between the United States and Canada.

Starker pulled his binoculars.

Eleven orcas slithered and plunged through the sea, tail flutes driving through the water, black and white skin glinting in the sunlight.

Pala eased back on the throttle. "What've we got?"

Starker pressed the binoculars to his eyes, straining to see beyond the sun's glare, eleven black dorsal fins marching past the harbor mouth. "Looks like the eleven."

Pala lifted the radio handset and opened a channel to command and apprised them of the situation.

"Double-time it to those kids" was the order, and Pala pushed the throttle control to max, the twin outboards clawing at the sea, throwing spray, and spitting a fifteen-foot rooster tail.

The pod of eleven orcas was heading due west like a swarm of giant sharks, their boat-like wake a trail of frothing white foam, their white and black missile-shaped bodies surging from the water, dorsal fins scything the air. Gray rock shoreline covered in seaweed and moss fleeted by on both sides of the narrow channel, a smattering of houses tucked within the thick forests of evergreen and cedar.

A seaplane took off from Roche Harbor as Pala piloted the patrol boat past the harbor mouth, trailing after the eleven around the northern shore of Henry Island.

"Isn't it faster to cut through the harbor?"

Henry Island sat off San Juan Island's northern tip separated by the harbor and Mosquito Pass.

"I'd say it would take the same amount of time, and I want to stay on their tail," Pala said, tossing her head toward the windshield and the pod of orca beyond.

Henry Island was made up of three main landmasses loosely connected by a thick sandbar-like bog, with Open Bay at the island's southern tip.

"I lost them," Starker said. He adjusted the focus of the binoculars, but the sun glare was too intense.

Pala played with the SONAR, but the SAFE boat was too far away.

Starker said, "Should we reach out to the sailing instructor?" He knew the sailing instructor would be on a power boat at the center of the small sailboats, giving instructions and keeping the boats corralled like a mother bear keeping track of her cubs.

Pala sighed. "I don't want to cause a panic, but…"

"Better safe than sorry."

Pala nodded as she arced the SAFE boat around Kellet Bluff. Gray stone hills covered in brown grass and shore pines tumbled to gray rock beach covered with debris and driftwood that looked like piles of large bones. Yellow and blue sea kayaks were pulled up on the shore, but Starker saw no people and his mind raced back to the prior night.

Starker lifted the handset and went to the emergency channel. He put out a general hail to anyone in Open Bay but received no response, so he issued a warning to clear the water, though he didn't say why.

"There they are," Pala said. "Shit."

The pod of eleven orcas had rounded Kellet Bluff and was heading into Open Bay, their dorsal fins rising and falling as they glided through the sea.

Spooky got to his feet and pressed his nose to the windshield and hissed.

Open Bay was like black glass, a tangle of tiny white sails barely moving over the still water.

The eleven knifed into the bay, making straight for the sailboats.

Starker tried to hail the yellow center console at the center of the chaos, but again he got no response. "I'm going to rip this instructor a new one."

The SAFE boat screamed into the bay, and Pala lifted the handset and activated the external annunciation system. "Warning! Warning!" she screamed, but the SAFE boat was still too far away.

"Take the helm," Pala said.

"What are you—"

Pala drew her Glock 19 and opened the pilothouse door. Wind gusted into the cabin, the scent of salt and low tide carrying on the breeze.

Starker took the wheel, keeping the nose of the vessel on the cluster of white sails. The orcas were a half mile out front, jumping and diving through the water, their wake a thick white line on black rippled glass.

Spooky jumped from his spot atop the command console and slipped out through the pilothouse door before Pala could close it.

The orcas reached the sailboats, tall black dorsal fins cutting through the water, dark forms rising from the sea, a knot of roiling tail flutes and whitewater lifting from the bay behind them.

Pala chambered a round, pointed her Glock at the blue cloudless sky, depressed the safety trigger, and squeezed off three shots.

This had the desired effect, and every head on every sailboat jerked toward the sound. The rumble of screaming and panic carried on the breeze and rose above the sound of the outboards as Starker eased back on the throttle and slowed the boat.

The orcas appeared unaffected by the gunshots, and they formed a circle around the knot of sailboats, churning the bay into a massive whirlpool.

"No, no, no," Starker said.

Pala fired four more times, but to no avail. Most of the children had stopped working their boats and were staring at the tall dorsal fins that cut in and out of the sailboats like sharks sizing up prey.

Starker pulled back the throttle arm as he arced the ship's wheel, cutting into the center of the sailboats.

One of the eleven breached, the papa, and the massive sea wolf hung in the air for an instant before crashing back into the water. The tiny sailboats rocked and heaved, and the resulting shockwave knocked three children from their boats into the bay.

"Starker!" yelled Pala. She had the Glock trained on the chaos, shifting it from dorsal fin to dorsal fin, but not firing.

The kids in the water splashed and panicked, and Starker moved the SAFE boat in close.

Pala holstered her gun and pulled kids from the bay, the weeping, wet children staring at the orcas as they surged from the water, cutting between the sailboats.

Spooky stood on his hind legs in the bow, front paws pressed to the inflated gunnel, head jerking back and forth as he surveyed the scene.

Chaos reigned as the sailing instructor tried to get control of the situation, but the kids were panicking, and tiny sailboats darted in every direction.

Starker dropped the SAFE boat into neutral and gunned the engines, the ejection ports spitting water, the churning of flywheels rising above the yelping and crying of the children.

With all the kids out of the water, Pala drew her gun and fired into the sky, adding to the engine noise.

The cacophony caused several of the orcas to peel away, filtering around the SAFE boat and heading for the mouth of the bay. Starker eased the boat into gear, slowly turning the ship's wheel and piloting the boat through the center of the fleeing sailboats.

The remaining dorsal fins sank into the bay as the orcas dove. The surface of the bay smoothed, and the children stopped shrieking.

Starker felt his constricted chest loosen as he spun the wheel, putting the bow of the SAFE boat on the sailing instructor's yellow center console. He spared a glance at the SONAR, then looked west toward the bay mouth. Eleven tall dorsal fins of various lengths tore through the water.

The SAFE boat bumped the center console and Starker dropped the engines into neutral as he tossed his head side-to-side and cracked his neck.

As Starker stepped out onto deck Pala said, "Calm down, Starker. No harm no foul."

"Bullshit." Starker mounted the inflated gunnel and stepped over the gap onto the sailing instructor's boat.

"Wow," said a young woman with blonde hair that Starker pegged as no more than twenty. "What did I—"

"Shush," Starker said, and he held up a finger as he checked the UHF radio mounted beneath the ship's wheel. The unit was on, but the red indicator light was dark. Some of the anger drained from Starker. "Did you test this radio when you left port this morning?"

The girl stared at the deck. "I turned it on and heard static, so I figured…"

"Wrong," snapped Starker, his adrenaline draining. "You figured wrong."

The kid said nothing. Smart girl.

Like a dying storm, Starker huffed and puffed one last time, but his heart wasn't really in it, and it showed. "Please be more careful. You're responsible for these children."

The kid nodded, and Starker heard Spooky meow twice.

11

Nerves still jangling, lower back aching, Starker sat in the bow of the SAFE boat, Spooky sitting between his legs. With the close call at Open Bay in the rearview, Starker and Pala were taking a fast break to answer texts and respond to emails before heading to the sheriff's office. There was nothing new happening for Starker, and he wouldn't have been able to concentrate even if there had been. Big decisions needed to be made, dangerous and important factors considered, and all he could think about was the black hairball.

Spooky purred, rubbing up against Starker. The morning chill was long gone, and humidity blanketed Friday Harbor, the day's heat settling in. The faint *womp womp* of helicopter rotors leaked over the harbor.

"That must be the coasties. We better get going if we're going to stop at the shelter," Pala said as she checked the SAFE boat's mooring lines and locked the pilothouse door.

Starker pushed to his feet and Spooky jumped onto the gunnel and continued onto the dock, where he sat, staring at Starker.

Pala watched Starker, the edges of her lips curling up as she attempted to contain a smile.

"I don't want to rush this," Starker blurted. "I'd like to spend a little time, make sure he's comfortable before I leave him alone."

Pala's eyebrows rose, and she nodded.

The Coast Guard copter came in low, flying over Brown's Island toward town.

Starker opened the pilothouse door and whistled.

Spooky licked his paw and watched.

"You can't come with us. Understand?"

"Meow."

"Let's go or I'll drop you off now. Want to go in a cage for the day?" Starker pointed at the open pilothouse door.

Spooky looked at Pala, whose gaze was focused on something far away. Then to Starker's surprise, Spooky appeared to understand his options. The feline got up, jumped onto the boat, and sauntered into the pilothouse like he was captain. He jumped onto the pilot's seat, spun three times, and sat, curling his tail around himself as he watched Starker through the pilothouse window.

The coastie helicopter thundered overhead, its white fuselage gleaming in the sun, an orange stripe slashing across its nosecone.

As Starker and Pala made their way through the marina she asked, "What's with you? Are you thinking about keeping Spooky?"

Starker harrumphed like that was the stupidest question he'd ever heard, but the burn in his throat kept him from speaking.

"Might be good for you," she said. "Companionship and all that. He seems to like you."

"You sound surprised."

"I am. Cats are usually pretty perceptive."

"What are you trying to say?"

"You said it yourself. You aren't a cat person."

So he had.

The Coast Guard Jayhawk jostled treetops and stirred up dust as it settled on the concrete pad behind the brick building that housed most of the county offices. Pala and Starker waited for Captain Raynard, and the trio was ushered into a conference room where Sheriff Klep waited.

"Good morning," Pala said.

"It is thanks to you two," Sheriff Klep said. "I heard what happened out there. Close call."

"What?" Captain Raynard said.

"While you were en route these two scared the eleven away from a crowd of children," the sheriff said, and quickly recounted the morning's events.

"I guess that brings us right to it," Captain Raynard said. "Do we impose restrictions?"

"Hang on," Sheriff Klep said. "Let me get Chairman Spollomen on the horn... the screen, and we're waiting for Mayor Hendricks."

The sheriff fumbled with the audio-visual system and managed to place a video call to Chairman Spollomen, leader of the Lummi Nation. When the chairman's wizened face appeared on screen introductions were made and the mayor made her appearance.

Dorothy Hendricks had been mayor of Friday Harbor for twelve years, having run unopposed in her last two election cycles. She was a sixty-two-year-old retired teacher who looked like she belonged in midtown Manhattan, not in the backwoods of Washington. She'd grown up on San Juan Island and was universally respected.

"Greetings, Detective Starker," the mayor said as she nodded to the rest of the participants, who she knew well.

"Just an investigator, but thanks for the promotion," Starker said, and he forced a smile.

When everyone was seated around a faux oak conference table, the sheriff said, "Captain Raynard, I believe you're the ranking authority here. Do you want to run this shindig?"

Raynard laughed, but Starker could tell it was forced. "It's your show, sheriff. The Coast Guard is here in a support capacity until… we're not." He pressed his lips together and looked around at the assembled group, meeting each of their eyes in turn.

"Right," the sheriff said. "So, I assume you've all read or seen the news?"

Starker and Pala exchanged glances.

"The press caught wind of last night, and they've tied it to the other disappearances. They're calling the orcas the Ocean's Eleven."

The mayor chuckled and Captain Raynard sighed.

"Any George Clooney sightings?" Starker asked, but nobody laughed.

"With news choppers buzzing around things will get more complicated," the captain said.

"That's what we're here to avoid," the sheriff said. "So far, the reports have been pretty tame, and all the interviewed experts agreed that the whales' behavior is extremely odd, almost impossible, and that something is wrong with the animals. Is that the position of conservation?"

Starker coughed gently. "I would say so, but who am I? There are ramifications for such a claim, yes?"

Nobody answered.

Captain Raynard said, "We could eliminate the threat. We've got the means."

Chairman Spollomen spoke for the first time, his brown jowls jiggling. He said, "The Lummi Nation can support no such action."

"Nor I," said the mayor.

Chairman Spollomen continued, "The Lummi term for killer whales is qwe 'lhol mechen, meaning 'our relations below the waves', and the tribe feeds the ailing orca salmon via a yearly ceremony, and my people don't want the creatures harmed in any way."

"That is also the position of the many environmentalists and social justice warriors that have already contacted me," the mayor said. "I have to say I agree. The last thing we need is footage of us killing the beasts showing up on the nightly news."

"There also appears to be some conflicting facts with respect to the fishing boat attack," Chairman Spollomen said. "The fishing boat was on the edge of restricted waters and killing the beasts to advance pink salmon season would be a grave injustice and damage a population that's already under a real threat of extinction."

"But there's a danger to the populous. Doesn't anyone care about that?" Pala said.

Silence.

"We do have to remember these creatures are endangered," Starker said.

"And dangerous, as you've seen firsthand," Captain Raynard said.

To that Starker had no response.

"If we can't terminate the creatures, then what?" Sheriff Klep asked

"Before you answer that, take a look at these." Captain Raynard handed a flash drive to the sheriff, who looked at it like it was dog droppings.

"Here," Pala said. She snagged the drive, mounted it in the AV computer, and with a few swipes and taps of the mouse she had the main screen split, half showing the chairman, the other a closeup underwater picture of an orca.

The mayor gasped.

Sweat dripped down Starker's back, a block of ice forming in his stomach.

The photo was of a young orca, maybe a year or two old. The shot was from the front, the beast's swollen, red-rimmed yellow eyes staring out from the image. The beast's mouth was open, its spike-like teeth bloody, but none of that was what drew the eye. A large gash, bubbling open with pustules, ran down the center of the orca's conical head between its eyes. As the group watched, Pala cycled through the photos.

"Are you seeing this, Chairman Spollomen?" the captain asked.

"Yes, but I can't say I understand it."

"We've seen similar wounds," Starker said. "Is this a picture of one of the eleven?"

The captain nodded. "We got it yesterday with one of our underwater drones."

Air moved through vents and outside a crow cawed.

After several minutes dripped away, Starker said, "Have you sent those pictures upstairs?"

The captain nodded. "We're waiting to hear back from the bigheads."

"So where does that leave us?" the mayor said.

"Ideally, trapping the creatures would be best, but I don't think that's realistic at this time," Starker said.

"Trap them? Where?" The mayor smiled as she looked around the table for support.

"We could dart them," Starker said. "At least then maybe we'd be able to track the pod."

The sheriff, mayor, and captain all nodded their heads vigorously.

"I like that," the sheriff said.

"And conservation can take care of that, yes?" Captain Raynard asked.

Starker and Pala exchanged glances. He hadn't tagged an animal in forever, and the last time he did had been a near disaster. Heat spread through him, that uncomfortable feeling of being put on the spot. He said, "I think we can handle that. We only need to get one or two of the big ones."

Nodding and murmurs of approval.

"In the meantime, Sheriff Klep, draft me a guidance letter to send out to the public and press," the mayor said. "Just a gentle warning to pay close attention when on the water, and until the situation resolves, citizens should avoid the shoreline."

"And my office will issue situation specific restrictions for any unnecessary water activities, such as occurred this morning," the sheriff said.

"And don't forget the pinkies. We need to be careful how we spin this, or cancelations will flow in like the red tide," said the mayor.

"Agreed. We need to keep a close eye on things," Captain Raynard said. "Let's make this a standing morning meeting until... we agree it's not needed. I can't promise I'll be here in person, but since you've figured out how to work your AV I can video conference in."

"I will send an official request to you and the sheriff today requesting increased patrols, Captain," the mayor said.

"Already underway, but do cover your ass," the captain said.

The mayor took the rub in the spirit it was intended, and she smiled her best politician's smile.

"Press conference?" Sheriff Klep asked.

Captain Raynard licked his lips, but said nothing.

The mayor looked at Starker and Pala, then shifted her hawkish gaze to Sheriff Klep. "Thoughts?"

"Until we have something to say..." The sheriff hiked his shoulders.

"With four people missing and no corpses, having a press conference and answering questions could do more harm than good," Starker said.

"I agree," Pala said.

The sheriff and mayor, both elected officials and thus hankering to show their constituents they were on the case, said nothing.

Interpreting silence as acceptance, Captain Raynard pushed to his feet. "If there's nothing else, let's get to it."

"Captain Raynard, your crew is available to help us out?" Starker asked.

"Doing?"

"Dropping acoustic telemetry receivers."

The captain heaved a heavy sigh. "They'll be on boats doing Coast Guard type things?"

"10-4," Starker said.

The meeting broke up, and Pala and Starker grabbed an early lunch before heading back to the SAFE boat. The harbor was a hive of activity, two seaplanes waiting to take off, a line of boats stacked up at the harbor mouth. The air was thick with the scents of charred meat and salt, and as the pair threaded through the docked boats, Pala asked, "You're O.K. with all that?" She hiked a thumb in the direction of the sheriff's office.

"I don't see how I can justify more," Starker said. "It's not like there's people swimming in our frosty sea."

Pala chuckled. "It's not Amity Island."

That got a chuckle from Starker.

"Still, I feel like it's not enough, not after everything that's happened," Pala said.

"I hear that, but unless you've got other ideas, we've got our marching orders."

"The trackers," Pala said. "Yeah, it might surprise you to know I've never darted an animal."

Starker threw his head back in surprise. "Really? Not even during training?"

"Nope," she said. "So I hope you know what you're doing."

"I do."

Spooky waited atop the command console, his gray eyes glowing as he watched Pala and Starker

It was time to say goodbye and Starker's chest tightened, his stomach knotting.

Pala slid open the pilothouse door.

Spooky jumped to the deck, but didn't leave the pilothouse. He stood by the open door, tail beating back and forth.

"I'll call Tippi and let her know we're on our way," Pala said as she pulled her cell.

"Meow."

"Wait," Starker said.

Pala paused with the cell halfway to her mouth.

"Do you mind having him around? On the boat, I mean?"

She lifted an eyebrow, smiled, but said nothing.

"I'm not sure what I want, but giving him away right now doesn't feel right. At all."

Spooky exited the pilothouse and sat on the boat's deck.

Starker had spent most of his life following his gut, and never ignoring the internal voice that provided what his mother called "tough love." He could bullshit just about anyone, except himself. "I think I need a little more time to figure this out. Can we postpone the drop off a couple of days?"

"Not my call, boss."

"You never answered my question. Do you mind having Spooky around? Is he impeding our work in any way?"

"Double no."

"O.K., then." Starker dropped to a knee and tickled the top of the cat's head and scratched his neck. "Do you want to hang with us for a little longer?"

Spooky purred so hard a vibrating chill ran up Starker's fingers.

12

Racoon Point, Orcas Island, 10:11 AM PT, June 22nd. Eight days until the start of Pink Salmon Season.

The buzz of hydraulics as the outboards angled up from the water echoed off the cliff face as the SAFE boat crunched onto a gray pebble beach. The notch in the shoreline was surrounded by black and gray rock covered in juniper and pine, a thick green underbrush of grass and weeds spilling over the edge of the rockface. The beach gave way to a tumbled deadfall of driftwood and garbage, and the place smelled like a fish store's dumpster.

Starker jumped from the bow and secured a claw anchor behind a large stone.

"It's perfect," Pala said as she stepped from the pilothouse. It was warm, and she wore a dark green t-shirt and jeans, a WSCD baseball cap tilted back on her head. She had her cop shades on, her dark hair pulled back, and the way the sunlight fell across her back made her look like a goddess stepping from the heavens.

Spooky sat atop the command console, supervising from the spot he'd claimed over the last two days as Starker and Pala searched for the Ocean's Eleven, who appeared to have gotten bored and were hiding out. There had been no sightings since the near tragedy at the sailing camp, and the level of urgency had dropped considerably.

"Grab this," Pala said. She fetched two black plastic carrying cases and handed them off to Starker.

He said, "What are we going to use for a target?"

"O ye of little faith."

"You are Catholic."

The breeze was gentle, and tiny waves rolled onto the rocky gray shore. Gulls circled overhead, Starker and Pala having disturbed their foraging amidst the exposed seaweed that clung to the shoreline like a green beard.

Pala balanced herself on the SAFE boat's gunnel, a paper cup with an adult sippy lid on it containing the remains of her coffee in one hand, the other out for balance.

"Are you sure we've got enough room?" asked Starker as he placed the two black cases on the ground above the waterline.

"Yup," she said as she jumped from the SAFE boat onto shore, landing in two inches of water and splashing her boots and pant legs. "What did you say the range on that thing is?"

"Accurate to seventy-five yards, but we've got big targets. Could be a hundred or more."

She nodded.

Starker said, "Target?"

Pala took a long sip of coffee, placed her paper cup on a stone, and hiked across the beach to the deadfall. The Pick Up Sticks-like stack of driftwood and debris was packed against the cliff face, and she put her hands on her hips as she surveyed the pile.

"Can I help?" Starker said as he joined her.

"See that piece of blue marine Styrofoam under there?"

Wedged beneath a nest of driftwood held together by a tangle of fishing line and dried seaweed there was a rectangular chunk of blue compressed foam. "I do," he said. "Probably from inside a hull."

"Yup. Sure looks like bilge foam to me," she said. "Do you see a way to get it out of that mess without bringing the whole thing down?"

Like a game of Pick Up Sticks, if the wrong piece of debris was removed it could cause a cascading effect that could bury the particular bit of garbage they sought. Starker pulled his utility knife and flicked it open, revealing a five-inch stainless steel blade with notched back. He cut like a surgeon, removing fishing line, pieces of netting and plastic, and tossing the items aside like a bird building a nest. After ten minutes of careful work, he was able to wiggle the foam free, the squeak as it rubbed on driftwood filling the cove like the call of a pterodactyl.

Starker handed the prize to Pala, and she held it up for inspection. The blue hard block of sea tempered foam was dulled white from baking in the sun, and large pockmarks dotted the surface. The chunk was roughly two feet wide, a foot deep, and three feet high. She marched across the pebble beach until she was about thirty yards away. Then she stopped and placed the foam target several feet above the waterline. "We'll start easy."

"You're going to try at least, right?" Starker said. "In case I get hit by a bus or eaten by a fish?"

"If you're not a better shot than me we're in trouble."

Spooky jumped onto the SAFE boat's inflated gunnel and sat, his eyes glowing gray as he watched Starker and Pala.

The steel buckles on the black storage cases glinted like diamonds as Pala opened the larger case, revealing a Pneu-Dart G2 X-Caliber dart gun packed in black protective foam. The thing looked like a space trooper rifle, with its sleek black stock, scope, and hammer-forged thirty-nine-inch stainless steel barrel. Pala hefted the weapon and held it out to Starker, who accepted it.

The gun had been delivered to Starker via Captain Raynard at their daily briefing meeting. He'd never fired this particular model, and it was a considerable upgrade from the basic air-fired crack-barrel dart guns he'd trained with. Those dinosaur models only had a range of thirty yards, and they weren't very accurate. With a little practice, Starker was certain he could get the job done with the G2.

"We've got weighted practice darts here," Pala said as she opened the smaller black case.

There were two rows of darts, ten in all. One row was blue metal with stainless steel tips and yellow flight stabilizer tails. These were the practice remote delivery devices. The second row of five RDDs also had shiny steel tips, but these were backed by a red GPS locator the size of three dimes stacked atop one another. The tracker gave way to a yellow dart housing that ended in a blue and red stabilizer tail. Pala plucked out a practice dart and handed it to Starker.

"Only five tries?"

She shook her head. "We've got another case of ten GPS RDDs on the boat."

He nodded as he aimed the gun at the ground and twisted open the butt of the weapon's shoulder stock. Starker inserted the dart into the firing chamber and rotated the gun's butt until it locked back in place.

"I've never seen a gun load that way," Pala said.

Starker took the cap off the scope, and flipped the gun's safety toggle from SS, super safe, to F, fire. He sighted the blue chunk of foam, took a deep breath, and let it out slowly as he rotated the power control that adjusted the muzzle velocity. Out on the sea, even on a calm day, the SAFE boat would be listing and shifting, which would make the shot harder.

He squeezed the trigger and the gun farted. The dart missed, and the sound of it pinging off a stone rang across the cove.

"Jeez," Starker said. He reloaded and fired again, this time with better luck. He caught the upper right edge. After he'd placed the remaining three practice RDDs center mags on the blue Styrofoam, Starker handed the gun to Pala and retrieved the RDDs.

Pala was a natural, and soon the target was out seventy paces, and both Starker and Pala were hitting the foam consistently.

"Now to kick things up a notch," Starker said.

As Pala retrieved the practice darts from the target, Starker fetched a large piece of driftwood and a stone the size of a basketball. He laid the wood over the stone, creating a makeshift seesaw like those dangerous playground toys found in children's parks all around the world.

Starker loaded the G2 and balanced himself atop the moving driftwood, shifting his weight as he steadied himself and aimed the dart rifle. He missed on his first three tries, and the tips of the practice RDDs were bent and dulled when Starker and Pala achieved proficiency firing the G2 with their feet shifting beneath them.

In the end, Starker was the better shot by a baby's hair, and it was decided he would be the shooter. Pala handled the SAFE boat better than Starker anyway, so the arrangement made sense on multiple levels.

Pala pulled a GPS RDD from the case and held it up to the light. "How does this thing work?"

"Like a multistage rocket," he said. "The dart impales the animal, and the pressure of the hit forces out barbs on the RDD's tip that hold it in place. Then the dart housing and flight stabilizer falls off, leaving only the dime-sized tracker on the beast."

"What's the range? Global, I assume."

"Yup," Starker said.

"What about underwater?"

"That's why I'm going to have Captain Raynard's crew strategically place acoustic telemetry receivers at critical points we want to monitor, like harbor entrances."

Pala nodded. "We can mark up a map, but harbor entrances make the most sense. I'll put together a prioritized list to run by Raynard."

"Good," Starker said as he packed away the G2 in its case.

Back on the boat, Starker found Spooky purring softly as he slept. He stowed the gun as Pala lowered the motors until just the propellers were submerged in the clear water.

"Now all we need to do is find the eleven," Pala said as she cranked the engines, eased down the throttle arm, and put the SAFE boat in reverse. The snap of the gears engaging cracked over the cove like a gunshot—a real gunshot. The hard hull shrieked as it slid over stones and the boat eased back into the sea.

"Or they'll find us," Starker said. "I've only had to tag one animal in the line of duty and she sure as hell found me."

Pala arced the boat around the northern tip of Orcas Island, setting a course across the channel toward Sucia Island Marine Park. "Why do I sense there's a story in there?" she said.

Starker shook his head. "I was on the job a year or two, and me and my partner were investigating poaching in the Wenatchee National Forest. Wolves, grizzly bears, lynx, mostly, and I almost got myself mauled."

She pressed the throttle control levers down and the Yamahas sang as the SAFE boat bounced through the light chop, throwing spray. Pala tuned the SONAR to maximum, but there was nothing to be seen except fish and seals, and they were moving too fast for any real level of detail.

"It was a day much like today. Warm, the trees full, the forest buzzing with life. I was taking a leak, and a chill seized me. You know, that feeling you get when you're being watched?"

Pala nodded.

"There was a stand of trees before me, its canopy so thick it was almost dark underneath. I couldn't see anything in the blackness, but I knew someone, or something, was watching from within the cover of the shadowed tree line. I sensed a dangerous presence appraising, sizing me up. I zipped up, ants crawling beneath my skin as I stared at my dart gun which leaned against a stone twenty feet away.

"Then a gigantic grizzly bear bounded toward me. The alpha was old, gray streaks running through its dark brown fur. Patches of nasty mange covered the beast's neck and shoulders, and its massive jaws were open, dark drool leaking through broken teeth," Starker said. "I almost shit my pants."

"Almost?" Pala said.

He made fish lips. "Anywayyyy, I finally ran, not daring to look back. The thunderous thump of footfalls behind me was terrifying. When I felt the beast was right behind me, I threw myself to the side and tumbled to the ground. The bear slid past me, rocks and gravel carrying the animal on, its rear claws digging in and raking the ground. A massive claw swiped at me as the bear slid by, and the air between us shimmered. That's how close I came to dying."

"What happened to your sidearm?"

"I never even thought of it because I got up and ran for the dart gun, but the grizzly didn't give up. The thing was larger than any bear I'd ever seen, and I knew if it caught me, there'd be no escape. If it hadn't been for my partner darting the beast… I heard the puff of the gunshot, and the giant froze, as if in shock, eyes twirling in its head like pinwheels. It jerked and spasmed, huffing and grunting as it tried to right itself, but only one side of the creature's body was complying with its brain's instructions, and it slumped to the ground, let out one final exhalation, and fell still. My heart had been beating so fast I saw red."

Pala whistled.

"Meow. Meow. Meow."

Starker chuckled. "No worries, brother. It was a long time ago."

Pala arced the boat west and set a course for the Strait of Juan de Fuca, the midday sun painting the water in a glittering silver glow.

13

Haro Strait, San Juan Islands, 3:21 PM PT, June 26th. Four days until the start of Pink Salmon Season.

Three days slipped away as Starker and Pala searched for the Ocean's Eleven, but the legends telling of cats providing luck to sea-going vessels proved false. With no new sightings, footage, or missing persons, the news agencies had moved on, the coasties had backed off, and the sheriff had canceled the daily morning briefing. With the start of Pink Salmon Season less than a week away, tensions had eased as more and more pink gold was sighted in the San Juan Island's waters.

Spooky cleaned himself as Starker piloted the SAFE boat through thick chop. A stiff westerly wind pushed sea spray everywhere, soaking the pilothouse windshield.

Pala worked the command console keyboard, scanning SONAR images and correlating data from the coastie patrols. Plenty of orcas had been seen, plenty of pinkies, but no signs of the eleven. She'd synced all the RDDs to the monitoring software, and sent the links to the sheriff, the coasties, and Lummi police. "Looks like I got the issue with the app worked out," she said. "Once we deploy the RDDs we can get one-minute snapshots on our phones twenty-four seven. Theoretically. They dive and we lose them until they come up or pass an acoustic telemetry receiver. We're using the Coast Guard cutter's computing power and advanced aerial receiver array to pull and analyze the data."

"Captain Hook doesn't mind?"

"They're on a boat doing Coast Guard stuff."

Starker laughed as his thoughts strayed to Seattle and what awaited him there. Nothing, really. Was that why he was considering keeping Spooky? An idea that would have seemed insane just two short weeks ago? Being out on the water in the field with Pala had sparked feelings long buried, a love for the sea and the outdoors that had brought him to the WSCD. He leaned forward and stroked Spooky, who purred and closed his eyes. Starker felt Pala watching him and he said, "What?"

"Nothing." The condescension in her tone was so thick a stab of anger knifed through Starker's stomach, but he tamped it down. Pala was just busting his peanuts.

The sun had slid long past noon, and the SAFE boat was pushing thirty-five knots when the call came in about a sighting of the Ocean's Eleven at Deception Pass.

"Tourists hiking along the channel in the park called it in. A pod of eleven orcas plucking harbor seals off a rock. Copy?"

"We copy and we're en route," Pala said as she maxed the throttle control, and the SAFE boat surged forward.

Spooky sat up, tail lashing as he searched the strait.

"Go time," Starker said, and he retrieved the black storage case containing the Pneu-Dart G2 rifle.

The SAFE boat churned around the tip of San Juan Island and with the westerly winds at their back the partners zipped past Cattle Point Lighthouse under a gunmetal sky, the stone shoreline peppered with walkers and fishermen. The Strait of Juan de Fuca was windswept, thin ribbons of white foam stretching north to south like lines in a children's notebook.

The trip to Deception Pass took twenty minutes, and as the SAFE boat bounced along, Starker prepared the dart gun for firing. He activated a GPS RDD and inserted it into the gun before screwing on a new CO2 canister. The pressure gauge forward of the trigger read ninety-eight percent, and Starker made sure the safety toggle was on SS, super safety, before laying the weapon across his lap.

Lopez Island streamed by to the north, and ahead in the distance, Whidbey Island, a thin stretch of land that ran along the mainland separated by Skagit Bay, was a green line on the eastern horizon. Gulls shrieked, and whitecaps replaced the ribbons of foam, small breaking waves that dotted the sea like pimples.

The current was moving swiftly as the SAFE boat powered into the pass, the channel draining west as the water was sucked toward the Pacific Ocean with the outgoing tide. A small crowd of onlookers packed the shoreline just inside the channel, everyone gazing at the spectacle playing out in Deception Pass.

"I'm going to get ready," Starker said. "Bring us in slow and quiet." He hefted the dart gun and grabbed the case of extra darts.

"Starker."

He turned to look at her and Pala tapped her life vest.

"Got it." Starker put on his life preserver.

Pala locked her eyes on the tall dorsal fins shredding the water.

Starker slid open the pilothouse door and Spooky leaped from the command console and slipped out the door before Starker could admonish him, so Starker let the cat be.

The whine of the outboards diminished as Pala slowed the boat, and Starker made his way to the bow.

Eleven dorsal fins cut through the dark water, conical heads breaking the surface as the orcas tossed around a dead seal like it was a chew toy.

Blood splattered the water, creating a nasty slick that leaked through the sea like an oil spill. The slap and crack as the seal hit the water echoed through the channel along with the huffing and splashing of the orca. The seal's back bent a ninety-degree angle, the animal nothing more than a bag of bones. An orca snout surged from the sea and lifted the seal's corpse, tossing it across the churned-up water.

Pala piloted the SAFE boat around the pod of orcas until they were up current of the beasts. She spun the ship's wheel, bringing the vessel about as she killed the engines. Wind blew, and water popped and snapped against the hull, but an eerie silence fell over the SAFE boat without the engines chanting. The boat was still moving at about five knots, the current and momentum driving it toward the fray.

One of the larger orcas knifed from the channel, jaws flexed open, and the bloody corpse of the seal disappeared into the beast's gullet as the orca dove.

A great shouting, barking, and braying sounded over the water from a nearby boulder that jutted from the channel like a rotten tooth, several harbor seals yelling at the eleven.

"That's not very smart," Starker mumbled.

"Meow."

The orca pod shifted course like a swarm of bees, all eleven dorsal fins marching over the channel as if controlled by one mind, a team of muscular missiles all homing in on the bellowing seals.

Pala lit the engines and followed the orcas, positioning the SAFE boat fifty yards from the action. She shut down the motors again, letting the vessel's momentum and the current bring the SAFE boat in closer.

The Ocean's Eleven encircled the boulder, whitewater rippling around the stone as the seals, realizing their predicament, struggled to stay atop the giant rock. Slick black and brown bodies slithered from the sea, barking and yelping at each other as the seals fought for position atop the stone as if playing king of the mountain.

Starker dropped to his knees, placed the case holding the extra RDDs on the deck, and braced himself in the bow, using the inflated gunnel for support. He took the cover off the eye scope, brought the stock of the G2 to his shoulder, and pressed his eye to the scope. At first, all he saw was tumbling white and black in the crosshairs, but as he adjusted the scope's magnification, the churning water came into focus.

White foam tinged with blood surrounded the stone covered with seals, and one of the younger orcas breached, throwing itself onto the boulder and knocking off several seals like they were bowling pins. Chaos ensued as seals hit the water and orcas knifed through the tumult, tossing seals in the air with their white and black snouts.

Starker flipped the safety to the fire position and turned the control nob that adjusted the muzzle velocity, tuning the pressure to maximum as he tried to get one of the larger orcas in his sights.

The sounds of muscle tearing and bones snapping echoed over the channel as the Ocean's Eleven strafed the seals. Yelps and cries, like puppies being tortured, echoed over the water, and the shrieks and wails of pain ran through Starker like a knife, his mind spinning back to birds covered in oil.

It wasn't the responsibility of the WSCD to police animals in their natural habitats or interfere with the normal food chain, but Starker couldn't help but feel for the seals. Transient orcas ate seals all the time, but residents? It was unheard of, and therefore what was playing out before Starker wasn't normal, yet what could he do against creatures that weighed six tons with jaws that could crush a car?

The SAFE boat had stopped moving forward and was being pulled east by the current, directly toward the knot of orcas as they tossed around their lunch.

One of the big female orcas surged from the water, her conical head covered in gashes erupting with red boils, the beast's eyes bigger and redder than any of the other diseased sea wolves Starker had seen. The orca plucked one of the seals as it struggled to get out of the water, the orca tossing the creature over its head as if throwing food to its young.

A fist of seawater exploded from the channel, several black and white heads filled with teeth piling on the dead seal, ramming it and ripping it apart as blood bubbles popped and snapped atop the roiling whitewater.

Starker breathed slow, his eye hurting as the scope dug into his eye socket, the SAFE boat listing and bobbing as it floated closer to the chaos. He'd been trained to tag animals on areas of their body where there would be limited shifting of skin and muscles. With a sea creature that has a dorsal fin, behind the fin where it meets the creature's back was considered optimal.

A chunk of white passed before the scope, then black, and Starker fired, the puff barely audible above the howling wind, the shrieks of the seals, and the huffing and spraying of the orcas.

"Meow. Meow," bellowed Spooky, who had his front paws up on the gunnel, his gray eyes focused on the orcas.

Starker didn't look to see if the dart hit home, and instead loaded another into the gun. The process took a minute, and when he had his eye pressed to the scope again, he found another target and fired. He repeated the process five more times, Starker getting more confident with each shot. He was getting used to the shifting and heaving of the boat and was timing his shots with the lifting and falling of the bow.

If the orcas noticed what Starker was doing, they didn't show it. The sea wolves continued to attack the seals, pulling them apart and feasting as the water turned blood red, chunks of fat and gristle floating in the flotsam as the current dragged the slick through the channel toward the Strait of Juan de Fuca.

When the SAFE boat was thirty yards from the fray, Pala started the engines and backed the boat away from the eleven. Things were winding down, and Starker only had three darts left, so he was picking his targets carefully.

He squeezed off the last shot, and Starker saw the dart hit home, impaling an orca on the back of its head. Not optimal, but it would do. He pushed to his feet and let Spooky crawl up his arm to his shoulders, where the feline wrapped himself around Starker's neck.

The seals were braying and crying louder than ever, and whether it was the SAFE boat or the fact that the orcas had eaten their fill, the channel smoothed, and the tall dorsal fins of the orcas disappeared beneath the sea.

Back in the pilothouse, Spooky jumped into the copilot's chair.

As Starker stowed the G2, he asked, "Were you able to see how many hits I got?"

She shook her head no. "But take the helm and we'll see."

Starker took the wheel as Pala worked the main control screen.

"Looks like we've got significant movement on four of the ten darts," Pala said. "I've got four trackers heading north toward San Juan Island. The other six are out there somewhere." She pointed at the blood slick that undulated on the windswept sea.

Starker smiled. Four out of ten wasn't that bad.

Pala reported their success to the sheriff's office and the coasties, and both were able to access the trackers.

The sun started its descent to the horizon, and as if on cue, Starker's stomach rumbled. Then like she'd managed to do several times before, Pala read his mind.

"Hungry?"

Starker's eyes went wide, and he smiled. "You've got good ears if you heard my stomach grumbling over the roar of the engines."

"I owe you one, remember?"

He did.

"It's taco night at the Rankin house. That work for you?"

Before Starker could answer, two loud "meows" reverberated through the cabin.

14

A raspberry sherbet sky painted the western horizon, the sea sparkling as Pala piloted the SAFE boat into Friday Harbor. The day was winding down, boats were being secured, and lights along the dock cast their dim glow, faint circles of light on the dock every ten feet. Paula and Starker tied up the SAFE boat in its permanent slip along the inner marina, and Spooky sat on the dock watching, his tail flicking back and forth.

The duo checked on Joel's tour boat as they headed for Pala's car. Starker was impressed with the thirty-two-foot red Zodiac. It had stadium-like seating packed on the forward deck before the pilothouse, and Sea Adventure Tours was stenciled over the red in block letters.

"Water jet propulsion?" Starker asked.

Pala checked the mooring lines of her husband's boat, the vessel that helped put food on the Rankin table, not unlike the SAFE boat. She nodded as she stepped up onto the pier. "The law requires all tourist vessels to be electric by 2025, but Joel upgraded early."

"Easier on him?"

"The new boat sure is," she said. "He spent half his life working on his old rig's engine. Getting stuck out on the ocean with twenty-four tourists is no day at the beach."

"Wouldn't think so." As they continued down the dock he said, "Has that ever happened? Him breaking down on a tour, I mean."

Pala shook her head no. "Thank God."

"Joel at least," Starker joked, but Pala didn't laugh.

Pala's beat-up Ford pickup reminded him of the one he'd borrowed from Gladys at the inn, except it was black and newer. Children's toys—a bicycle, a bag of sporting equipment, and a small kayak, littered the back bed, and Pala stripped off her lifejacket and tossed it in a plastic bin held to the pickup bed's side via a bungee cord.

Starker opened the passenger door and Spooky leapt into the cab without hesitation. "Where exactly do you live?" Starker asked as he dropped in next to Spooky.

Pala fitted her old school key into the ignition and the truck's engine rumbled to life. "Over in Cheapside at the center of the island."

"Is anything cheap on this island?"

"Everything is relative."

Spooky curled into a ball and closed his eyes. Pala looked down at him and said, "The kids are going to love having a visitor."

"Cool. I'm great with kids," Starker said.

Pala chuckled. "I meant the cat."

"I know."

The light of the fading day cut through the trees casting long shadows across the road. Pala drove on in silence, making a series of rights and lefts as the town of Friday Harbor evaporated and the evergreen forests that filled the middle of San Juan Island materialized from the underbrush on both sides of the road. Fancy mailboxes at the ends of long driveways lined the streets, but as the pair wound deeper into the pine, juniper, and cedar, the driveways appeared closer together, and soon Pala was cutting through a neighborhood where the houses were stacked like sardines.

Pala's house wasn't what Starker expected. There were no toys strewn about the front lawn. No bicycles lying in the driveway. The house itself was a two-story cape with a faded cedar shake façade and white trim. The pickup came to a stop and Pala killed the engine and took a deep breath. A red Honda Civic with the Sea Adventures Tours logo on its doors sat next to the pickup, filling the driveway.

The house's front door was open, and the screen door fell back on its hinges, slapping the house as a young girl bolted through the door and vaulted off the stoop.

"Mom!" The child flew across the yard and threw her arms around Pala as she got out of the pickup.

"Watch my gun," Pala said, but her smile was so wide Starker thought her head might split open.

Spooky jumped from the truck and sat beside Pala. "Meow. Meow."

The child froze, staring at the cat like she might explode. "You got us a cat!" The kid jumped up and down, clapping her hands as she knelt before Spooky, who stared at the girl with his shining gray eyes, a quizzical amused look on his whiskered face.

"Oh no," Pala said. "No pets. Spooky is Officer Starker's pe... charge. Say hello."

The child made pouty lips and wrapped her arms across her chest. "Hi."

Starker got out of the truck and shook the girl's hand. "Very nice to meet you..." Starker looked at Pala when he realized he didn't know the child's name. He and Pala had been zipping around the island for almost two weeks, and yet they hadn't wadded very deep into each other's personal ponds.

"I'm Aurora," the girl said.

"Very pleased to meet you, Aurora."

Pala said, "Where's your brother?"

"Helping dad."

The interior of the house was immaculate—again somewhat of a surprise given the kids—but Joel was pretty much what Starker had expected.

"Pleasure to meet you finally," Joel said, sticking out his bear claw. The guy was huge, though not fat. He wore construction-like overalls and a t-shirt, his long black hair pulled back in a ponytail, his brown skin covered in perspiration from the steam rising off a skillet of chop meat that cooked on the range top.

Joel Jr. didn't look up from cutting tomatoes. The kid looked to be ten or so.

"Say hello to our guest, Joel," his father said, and the boy waved. "He's shy."

Starker freshened up as Pala got changed as dinner was put on the table. He rinsed his face, taking note of the picture of an orca breaching above the commode.

Once everyone was around the table, Joel Sr. said, "Aurora, would you like to say grace?"

The girl nodded and cranked out a standard blessing before everyone dug in, including Spooky who had been given milk and some boiled chicken. The feline sat beside Starker's chair, eating greedily. Starker made a mental note: chicken.

"So Pala tells me you're heading to the big city." Joel Sr. crunched on a taco.

"That's the plan."

"Those never work out, am I right?" Joel Sr. said.

"Sure seems that way," Starker said.

"Where do you see this going?" Joel Sr. asked with a sidelong glance at his wife.

Starker hiked his shoulders. "These things are unpredictable, but I feel we've got control of the situation now."

"Control?" Joel Sr. said.

Pala cleared her throat. "What Starker means is at least we can track the creatures."

Joel Sr. chuckled. "What did Chairman Spollomen think of that?"

Starker didn't answer. Instead, he said, "Are you also of Lummi descent?"

He nodded. "My family left the reservation two generations ago, but I still consider myself Lummi."

Starker glanced at Pala who had her eyes locked on her plate. So, a bone of marital contention and strain.

"We're done, dad, can we go?" asked Aurora. The girl's brown eyes sparkled like Pala's.

Spooky stood up, ears twitching.

"All your schoolwork done?" Pala asked.

Both children wagged their heads.

"Then you're excused," Pala said.

"Meow. Meow. Meow."

Starker looked down at Spooky, who was staring at the retreating children. "Well, it's OK with me if..." He looked at Pala and Joel and raised an eyebrow.

Pala nodded.

"Go ahead," Starker said, and Spooky bolted after the children. "Will do him good."

"Not for us," Joel said. "They've both been on our asses to get a pet. I've got enough on my plate and I'm not looking for more."

Pala sighed, but she was smiling.

"So you were saying," Starker said. "What do you make of all this? The chairman was adamant that we don't mess with the orca."

"Not surprising," Joel said.

"He did support the tracking efforts, though," Pala said. "So he's not totally in the 'leave the orca be' camp when it benefits him."

Joel sighed. "I love this woman."

"Where do you stand?" Starker said.

"None of this is good for business, for the islands," Joel said, then he took a bite of taco, and half of it disappeared.

"You haven't had to cancel any tours, right?" Starker asked.

Joel laughed, then wiped taco sauce from his chin. "If anything, reservations are up. Nothing like the potential for danger to bring out the weekenders. They want to see the orcas act up."

"Understandable, I guess," Starker said.

"I suppose if it wasn't my backyard and my livelihood," Joel said.

Pala paused with a taco halfway to her mouth.

"I didn't mean to discount the situation," Starker said. "All I'm saying is people are drawn to shiny new things. Getting a better story than their friends to tell at parties or getting a picture they can post all over social media to prove they have a life."

Joel laughed. "You get it."

The trio finished eating and moved out onto the patio to have coffee, the shriek of machine gun fire and explosions leaking from the house as the kids played video games. There'd been no sign of Spooky. The night symphony hummed and buzzed, but there were no mosquitoes as far as Starker could tell. The temperature was a comfortable seventy degrees and dropping as darkness leaked across the island like a creeping tide.

"The reason I asked about the chairman was because…" Joel looked at his wife who was eyeing him like he was a fox entering a henhouse, "…I was wondering if the chairman mentioned reef netting as a way to corral the diseased orcas, assuming that's what everyone wants."

"He didn't mention it, but Pala did." Starker looked at Pala who lifted her eyebrows.

"Our people are part of the Point Elliott Treaty of 1855, and the Lummi were paid $150,000 for their lands by the US. They were given an additional $15,000 in relocation costs and expenses and told to leave their ancestral homes." Joel shook his head. "The Lummi are the original inhabitants of the Puget Sound lowlands, and many Lummi still remember, and see the local governments as thieves. As to the chairman…" Joel waved a hand. "He's a politician and won't do anything to hurt his position, even if it's what's best for the Lummi and the citizens of Washington."

"That's the negative," said Pala. "Most Lummi today believe in cooperation with the local governments, and now it's a two-way street."

"With one lane much wider than the other," Joel said.

Starker leaned back and sipped his coffee, happy and upset that he'd sparked a family dispute, but judging by Joel and Pala's smirks they'd had this discussion many times.

"Come on," Pala said. "A few years back the Lummi Nation declared a state of emergency when the Cypress Island Atlantic salmon pen was breached. They recaptured most of the recovered non-native Atlantic salmon, with much local help."

"Because the local bigwigs were worried that the Atlantic salmon would interfere with their precious waters and rivers."

"Our precious water," Pala corrected.

Joel harrumphed.

"Tell me about reef netting," Starker said.

Joel nodded. "The Lummi developed the technique for taking large quantities of fish in salt water. As you know well, the WSCD acknowledges this method. Lummi usually set reef nets on Orcas, San Juan… a bunch of spots. They still plan to do this when the pinkie season opens."

"If it opens," Pala said.

"It'll open," Joel said.

"Why so sure?" Starker asked.

Joel rubbed his thumb and forefinger together in the universal sign of money.

"Do you think this method could be used to snag the eleven?" Starker asked.

Joel hiked his shoulders. "Maybe. You'd need pretty strong nets. But maybe."

With that, the conversation petered out and Pala said, "Let's get you back to the inn."

Starker nodded and pushed up from his seat.

"Have you checked where the illustrious eleven are?" Pala asked.

Starker pulled his phone and tapped the app that connected to the coastie vessel, which showed the position of the trackers. An hourglass spun and spun, but the position of the orcas didn't come up. "Looks like we're still buggy," he said.

Pala frowned. "I'll get it fixed in the morning."

"It was very nice to meet you, Starker," Joel said.

"And you." The two men shook hands and Starker thought the man held his hand a little longer than normal, squeezed his hand a little extra hard.

Starker was looking around for Spooky when his phone vibrated. He answered it, Pala watching him like he'd stolen some of her silverware.

"Got it," Starker said, and he tapped end call. He shook his head and sucked on his lips.

"What is it?"

"The pink salmon season is opening on schedule. No restrictions."

15

Neah Bay Inlet, Pacific Ocean, 11:21 AM PT, July 2nd. Second day of Pink Salmon Season.

Pink salmon season opened without a hitch. All the fishing charters were booked, and the inns and B&Bs were full of tourist fishermen and their families from all around the world. The shops and restaurants in Friday Harbor, Eastsound, and Point Roberts were booming, along with the tour operators like Joel who catered to the non-fishing crowd. The money was flowing, pinkies were being snagged, and all was right in the San Juan Islands.

That's why Starker's stomach was tied in a permanent knot. He and Pala had spent six days patrolling and trailing after the eleven as they cycled through the San Juan islands, spending most of their time out in the open Pacific Ocean. The western horizon was a dark smudge of clouds as a storm marched east across the sea. Tomorrow would be a washout, and the forecast for the next week was nothing but storms. He didn't mind. He was getting bored spending his days on the water, nothing new, no action. He thought of the desk that was waiting for him and his stomach soured.

The SAFE boat's engines were silent, and the vessel was floating at a gentle five knots as the current pulled it out through the inlet into the Pacific. Ahead, Seal Rock, a small uncharted island, loomed above the churning surf, a huge crowd of screaming harbor seals eating, fighting, and jostling for position atop it. The eleven periodically made a stop at Seal Rock, picking off any beasts that strayed from the pack. The constant cacophony of braying seals and shrieking seagulls was giving Starker a headache, but it didn't appear to bother Spooky or Pala.

"Looks like a bad one on the way," Pala said.

Starker nodded. "What does the weather report say?"

"Heavy rain tomorrow. Supposed to be like that all week. They've already moved the 4th of July fireworks show."

Starker licked his lips. "What does that mean for the pinkie seekers?"

Pala chuckled. "Are you kidding me? Most of the nuts think the fishing is better in the rain."

"Isn't it?"

"I suppose," she said. "Depends on who you talk to, but there is science behind it."

"Really? I just thought it was an old wives' tale."

Pala shook her head. "Come on. You hang with scientists, don't you?"

Starker said nothing.

"One of the bigheads in the agency once told me when the rain comes fish become more surface oriented. When it's raining that's the time when the birds tend to sit in the trees and stop feeding, so the fish are safer on the surface and don't have to worry about kingfishers and mergansers as much. Some insects go crazy too." Pala shook her head. "I think it's because the fish feel safe. It's like the cloud cover is providing them a respite from being hunted and they have an opportunity to eat."

"Makes sense, I guess," Starker said. "I've never heard it explained that way."

"Not a fisherman?"

"No," he said. "I enjoy a good fillet as much as the next person, but sitting on a boat holding a pole and doing nothing all day isn't my idea of enjoyment."

"I feel you," she said. "Either way, we've got a few days of crappy weather coming."

"What does Joel do if he can't run?"

She hiked her shoulders. "Office work, usually, but he doesn't like taking work away from his employees so usually he just sits around bored off his ass. At least he gets to pick the kids up from school and spend time with them."

Spooky rose from his spot atop the command console and stared out the window, his gray eyes reflected in the dirty glass. Suddenly he hissed, his tail going straight as the hair on his back stood on end.

"What do we have?" Starker asked. The cat had awesome natural RADAR and sensed other boats and fish approaching.

"Looks like the eleven are on their way in," she said. "Ten o'clock off the port bow."

Starker lifted his binoculars and looked beyond Seal Rock at the dull black expanse of the undulating Pacific Ocean. Three-foot waves rolled across the inky water, and at first, Starker didn't see the eleven. Without the sun's glare highlighting the black dorsal fins, there was no contrast, no shadows, and the orcas' black skin blended into the dark sea.

"Trackers are showing all four targets heading for lunch at the seal diner," Pala said. She lit the engines, and the purr of the twin Yamahas rumbled over the water.

The Ocean's Eleven were coming on fast, jumping and diving through the sea, tail flutes leaving a wake of foam, their black and white heads rising and disappearing with the roll of the ocean.

"Move us in closer," Starker said.

Pala inched down the throttle control and positioned the SAFE boat on the east side of Seal Rock.

The eleven broke around Seal Rock, tail flutes driving through the water as the beasts blew spray, but didn't engage the seals. Instead, the orcas moved around the SAFE boat, and headed inland across the Strait of Juan de Fuca.

"Time to go," Pala said, and she spun the ship's wheel and tailed the Ocean's Eleven. The channel was rough, two-foot rollers leaving thick ribbons of foam. The SAFE boat bounced as it knifed through the waves, doing thirty knots, the boat falling into the orcas' wake.

Starker's phone buzzed and he pulled it free. Commander Richie. He sighed.

"Who is it?" Pala asked.

"Command."

"Better take it. They might have info for us."

"Or it might be the end of the road for me." Starker held the phone out like it was nuclear waste, the reality of what answering the call could mean sending tremors of regret flowing through him like bad wine. Things had been quiet, and there was work waiting for him in Seattle.

"Meow."

Then there was Spooky. Starker tapped accept call. "Starker here."

"Starker? Richie. How's your little vacation going?"

Starker said nothing as he rolled his eyes and glanced at Pala, who was doing her best to act like she wasn't listening, but doing a poor job of it.

"You there, Starker?"

"I'm here."

"What's the status? Anything new to report other than a record salmon?"

"Haven't had one of those yet that I've heard about," Starker said. "We're actually two hundred yards behind the eleven as we speak. They're heading inland after spending most of the day and last night out at sea."

"I see," Commander Richie said. "Anything else?"

It was time to gild the lily. "Sir, these animals have shown aggression beyond anything anyone has seen from killer whales. Yes, things have slowed, but it's like a fire simmering just below the surface. Things can ignite at any moment. That's the general opinion here, including the coasties." Shit! He shouldn't have mentioned the Coast Guard. And what was he doing arguing and trying to delay his departure?

"Speaking of the CC, what are they up to?"

"They're around."

"When was the last time you saw Captain Raynard?"

It had been days, but Starker said, "I don't recall. I don't keep a bell on him."

"Meow. Meow."

"What was that?" Commander Richie asked.

"Nothing. Wave popping on the boat." He glanced at Pala who was no longer containing her smile.

"Look, your new boss calls me daily. Something about some new policy that needs to be vetted and reviewed. I asked him if he'd ever heard of email, but I don't think he appreciated the suggestion."

Starker laughed. Richie was a nut buster, but he was honest and easy to work for. Starker was going to miss him. "I'll reach out to him, and he can forward the materials. There's nothing to do around here at night anyway."

"Really? For a single eligible bachelor like you?"

Starker said nothing. Richie had tried to set him up with his wife's sister, and Starker had put the kibosh on it. The last thing he needed was to see Richie on Christmas and Thanksgiving.

"It sounds to me like everything is under control there, Starker," Commander Richie said.

Starker covered the phone and whispered, "Here it comes."

"It sounds like the trackers are working as expected," Richie said.

"They are," Starker said.

"And there have been no recent attacks?"

"No, sir."

"Then I'm having trouble understanding why you're still there."

"A watched pot never boils, sir. You know the second I pull out all hell will break loose." He knew the overused cliché was one of Richie's favorites.

"Yup," the commander said. "That seems to be our lot in life. What's the sheriff got to say? He pissed off we're looking over his shoulder?"

"No more than usual," Starker said. "I think that's another reason I should stay, at least for a few more days. I've developed a good working relationship with everyone here, and we need a strong presence."

"That's the part I'm struggling with," Commander Richie said.

"Let me paint you a picture," Starker said, and he threw Pala a wide smile. "The Ocean's Eleven, who we believe to be diseased, kill again, and I'm not here. I can see you on TV. 'Commander Richie, is it true you pulled out WSCD support days before the attack?' I can see your face and it's whiter than when you got back from your trip to Alaska."

A chuckle-squeak escaped Pala's lips and Starker put his hand over the phone to muffle his laughter.

"Yeah, you've read too many Clive Cussler novels," Richie said, then he sighed long and hard like he was making the biggest decision of his life. "But I see your point."

Starker saw his opening and he pushed. "Orders?"

"Let's get a week into pinkie season," Commander Richie said. "Let's talk again in a couple of days. If everything is still quiet, I'll push the decision upstairs."

"That's why they get the big bucks," Starker said.

"You got that right," Richie said. "Call me if there are any new developments. In the meantime, I'll update the bigwigs."

"10-4," Starker said, and Commander Richie closed the connection.

"Got a few more days?" Pala asked.

He nodded.

"Sounds like you don't want to leave."

Starker said nothing.

The Ocean's Eleven dipped and lunged through the Strait of Juan de Fuca, powering inland toward Victoria British Columbia. Pala opened a channel to a Canadian Coast Guard vessel that sat anchored off Oak Bay. The U.S. agencies had been sharing all their information with the Canadians, who had been doing the same. Technically, Pala and Starker had no jurisdiction once they crossed the dark black line on the NAV screen that separated the two countries, but that was just a formality. Pala knew the Canuck coasties better than the U.S. forces because they were around more, and there were no territorial disputes between the various law enforcement agencies. It was rare international detente.

"Hi, Pala, we've got them," rumbled a voice over the comm from the Canadian vessel. "Stay on them and consider us on standby."

"10-4," Pala said.

As if the Ocean's Eleven had heard the communique, the pod turned sharply east, cutting back over the international border into U.S. waters, their white wake like a magic marker line over the dull water.

Pala tracked the orcas under a slate gray sky, the dark clouds in the west a constant reminder of what was to come. The SAFE boat bounced gently through the surf, which was growing steadily less turbulent the farther inland they got. "Lookie what we've got here," Pala said.

A red tour boat with the Sea Adventure Tours logo on its side was jetting out of Friday Harbor.

Starker lifted the handset and opened a channel as he smiled at Pala. "Tourist vessel N0078, radio check, please."

"What do you want me to pick up from the store?" Joel asked.

"This is a restricted channel, necessary communications only."

"Yeah," Joel said. He waved out his pilothouse window as the SAFE boat and the red Zodiac raced past each other.

"Look at this," Pala said. She had one hand on the ship's wheel, the other on the SONAR screen.

The Ocean's Eleven had slowed and were circling in the open water. Dorsal fins knifed through the Strait of Juan de Fuca, but Starker only counted nine fins. He brought binoculars to his eyes.

Something orange tossed and heaved within the whirlpool created by the eleven. Starker adjusted the binocular's magnification, focusing on the churning sea, but all he saw was a roiling fist of whitewater.

"Bring us in closer," Starker said.

Pala eased back on the throttle control and the SAFE boat slowed to a crawl as the current tugged the vessel back toward the Pacific.

The Ocean's Eleven were in perfect form, circling the orange object, slowly spiraling inward as they closed their trap.

When the SAFE boat was a hundred yards west of the pod, Pala said, "Tell me that's not a lifejacket."

"It's not a lifejacket."

"Is it?"

"I think so. Bring us in, fast, break up the party," Starker said.

Pala cycled up the motors and dropped the throttle handles, the motors shrieking as the SAFE boat surged from the water.

The orcas broke formation, four heading south, the rest north.

Pala spun the ship's wheel and dropped the boat into neutral, whitewater slapping the SAFE boat's transom.

Starker bolted from the pilothouse with Spooky on his heels.

The wind had let up some, but two-foot waves still rolled over the Strait of Juan de Fuca, and the boat bounced and heaved as Starker leaned over the gunnel, reaching for the orange object. His hands gripped the item, and it was slippery, but Starker threw himself backward, using his momentum to tug the item from the water as he fell onto his ass.

Starker laughed, he couldn't help himself.

The eleven dove and disappeared beneath the surface.

"What is it?" yelled Pala.

Starker held up a deflated beach ball.

16

Kangaroo Point, Orcas Islands, 10:50 AM PT, July 6th. Sixth day of Pink Salmon Season.

There's an old saying among seamen that says, "With the weather comes great fortune and peril, but when it arrives angry everyone pays, one way or another."

Sheets of drizzle blanketed the cove in a thick mist, visibility down to fifty yards. The calm before another storm settled over the San Juan Islands, the western horizon an explosion of black clouds, the storm front leaking over the islands like Voldemort's snake head might come surging through it. The sea was dark, the wind a steady ten-mile-an-hour push from the west. The air smelled of salt and low tide, though Starker hardly noticed it anymore. He didn't know if that was good or bad.

Spooky was curled up in a ball atop an old lifejacket, eyes closed. The feline had stopped sitting up on the command console. Poor thing was probably just as bored as Starker. They'd gotten a few calls, and measured a few fish, but otherwise, the last four days had consisted of trailing the Ocean's Eleven, who were currently out in the Pacific. All vessels were staying clear of the beasts, and there'd been no provocations or incidents involving humans.

Pala had the SAFE boat churning at a steady twenty knots, the boat slicing through the water, hardly bouncing, the sea spray hitting the surface of the water the only sound. The gulls were sleeping in, and the low murmur of the Yamahas was like a soothing lullaby.

A beep resounded through the cabin and the NAV screen shifted to Kangaroo Point. Pala eased back on the throttle, the SAFE boat slowing to a crawl, water slamming the transom. Waves crashed on a rocky shore hidden by the thick mists, the Peapod Islands rising from the inky sea to the east. A large fishing vessel materialized out of the fog like a ghost ship, and Pala dropped the SAFE boat into neutral.

Starker lifted the comm handset intent on hailing the fishing vessel, but before he could, a gray boat glided from the mists, RADAR array spinning next to a red police light, Lummi Nation Police stenciled on its side in white.

Pala turned the ship's wheel, using the wind to turn the boat south so the Lummi police boat could pull alongside the SAFE boat. The gray vessel had an open pilothouse with no rear wall, and a tall slender man wearing a dark blue uniform and a gold badge with the Lummi Nation logo on it, a fiery eagle, eased out onto deck. He had long black hair pulled back in a ponytail, and his skin tone was darker than Pala's, his eyebrows thick.

The officer lassoed a rope around one of the SAFE boat's bow cleats and said, "Hi, Pala, nobody told me you were coming."

Pala and Starker went out on deck, and Spooky, stirred by all the activity, followed.

"Just patrolling," she said. "You haven't met my... partner, Starker, yet, right? He's in town for a few days to help with our little situation. Starker, this here is Officer Stanly Imirchio. Everyone calls him Mirch."

"Nice to meet you, Mirch." Starker held out a hand.

Mirch left Starker hanging and said, "Help out? Isn't that bigwig speak for watch and supervise?"

"Depends."

"On?"

"If said helper is a cowboy concerned with career advancement and being in charge and getting all the credit, or really wants to help."

"Which kind are you?"

"The latter."

"The what?"

"The second one."

An uncomfortable silence ensued, and Starker left his hand out there like a teenager leaning in for his first kiss.

Mirch eyed the hand like it was a piranha, then glanced at Pala like a child looking for his mother's approval. Starker was a little surprised when she said, "He's not that bad."

"Well, if Pala says you're O.K., then you're alright by me, Mr. Starker."

"Starker is fine. My dad was a Mr."

The two men shook hands and the uncomfortable hot cloud pushing away the mists dissipated.

"You want me to show you the nets?" Mirch said.

Starker nodded. "I'm interested in knowing the process."

"Everything the Lummi do here has been reviewed, documented, and approved by the WSCD, so if—"

"Not to worry," Starker said. He was a fish measurer after all. "I'm not here to police the Lummi, or anyone else. I... we... the royal we... were talking about maybe using the netting process to contain the Ocean's Eleven."

Mirch blew out a long stream of air. "I guess, maybe if you had Kevlar reinforced nets and enough power and weight to hold everything in place..." He rubbed his chin. "Let's go take a look. There's a dive platform on the back of this baby." He pointed at the large fishing vessel that sat anchored twenty yards off, a yellow net float hanging from it cutting across the dark water like a mechanical eel.

Pala put the SAFE boat in gear and slowly piloted it around the old fishing vessel and tied off on the rear platform. Mirch bumped into them and tied his boat off on the SAFE boat. Mirch mounted his gunnel and jumped on the SAFE boat, but pulled up short when he saw Spooky appraising him, eyes aglow in the drab light. The drizzle had coated the cat's fur, and he didn't look happy.

"What do we have here?" Mirch said.

"That there is Spooky," Starker said as he climbed up the Jacob's ladder to the deck of the fishing boat. "You wait down there, Spooky," he added.

"Meow," Spooky shrieked. The cat eyed the ladder like it was Mount Everest.

"Don't 'no' me," Starker said.

"Meow."

"I said—"

Pala lifted the struggling cat and locked him in the pilothouse as Mirch stood watching, a smile spreading across his face like a sunrise on a rainy day.

Up on the deck of the fishing vessel, they were greeted by the boat's captain, who gave Mirch free reign of the TipTop.

The ship had a small conning tower, its forward gunnels rising eight feet above the deck, the side walls tapering away as they ran aft, blending into the deck, the back half of the boat a platform. The work area was a smattering of fishing nets, floats and buoys, and piles of what appeared to be a tangled rope, but was carefully spooled in a loosely organized bunch. Deckhands and fishermen moved about, but nobody appeared to be in a hurry. The net was out, and there was nothing to do at the moment except wait.

Mirch led Pala and Starker to a huge empty spool mounted on the aft deck that reminded Starker of a giant fishing reel with no line wound around it. The yellow float line attached to the net trailed off the spool and over the inky sea.

"You're familiar with the basics of how this works?"

Pala nodded.

Starker looked at the deck, searching his memory. He knew nets were used, two boats... but that was about it. Pala patrolled the area and dealt with the net fishing every two years, but other than a briefing or two he was somewhat ignorant. He said, "Refresh my memory."

Mirch nodded. "Excuse me if I go on too long. My kids say I need an editor. You know what that is?"

Starker chuckled. "Do your kids get to do the editing?"

That made Mirch laugh. "So, this tradition goes back hundreds of years when one fishing crew could catch thousands of salmon in a single day. Those days are over, of course—much fewer pinkies, plus all the new rules, and ECON…" He trailed off and looked at Starker, his brown eyes searching for insult. When he found none, he said, "Reef netting involves the setting of a net suspended between two boats, which back in the day were canoes. The nets are placed at strategic locations where the natural flow of salmon was constrained." Mirch waved his arms expansively, indicating the Rosario Strait and surrounding seas. "The nets work like a sort of on-ramp that leads the fish up the net by creating an optical illusion of a rising bottom. When the salmon are in the horizontal net, still free, the boats move in and close the net, trapping the salmon."

"That still works?" Starker said. "I mean, with less pinkies in the water don't they get spooked?" Starker glanced aft toward where Spooky and the SAFE boat were moored, but the fishing vessel sat too high in the water and all he saw was the black sea and the rising mists.

Mirch chuckled. "My ancestors were smart. Smarter than pinkies."

"I didn't mean—"

Mirch held up a hand. "Just breaking your stones. Those are valid questions. What happens is the fish swim along the bottom through a path created in the kelp. Add to that…" He pointed at the islands, "The fish are constrained by reefs and islands. Before the net is set, the fishermen string the webbing with sea grass to create a false bottom, and as the fish swim above the net they are gently nudged forward by the lifting of the far end of the net."

Starker was shaking his head.

"I know what you're thinking, but it works, obviously," Mirch said. "The entire rig requires great stability and precision of placement. Look here."

The trio strolled aft, threading through piles of rope and netting, and the crew parted before them.

"See that line there?" Mirch said.

"The anchor line?" Pala asked.

"Yes, there's another in the front, and the second boat…" He pointed east, "…which you can't see because of the mist also has two anchors out. That keeps the two main boats extremely stable and in position."

"That's enough to keep the boats from shifting?" Starker said.

"That and the net anchors that run all along the net and hold its end to the seafloor. Many times the weights are nothing more than large stones that the Lummi reuse. They're covered in organic webbing to hide them."

"Tricky," Starker said.

"Smart," Pala said.

"They work too well," Mirch said. "That's why initially reef nets and other forms of fish traps were banned in both Washington State and British Columbia in an attempt to take control of salmon fisheries from Indigenous peoples." The Lummi officer looked at Starker with defiance.

"Well, it was also to manage the flow of salmon and other wildlife," Starker said.

"And let's not forget an exception was made for the Lummi," Pala said.

"All too true."

A horn sounded, men yelled, and Starker heard the forward anchor chain rattling over the deck. The net was being adjusted and pulled in.

Mirch led his companions to a spot away from the action, with a good view of the dumping bin where the nets would drop their catch. The captain stood out front of the conning tower, smoking a cigarette and staring into the mist.

The rear anchor was pulled as the boat's diesel engine thundered to life, and the deck vibrated as the screws notched into place and the boat slid slowly east, the net winding around the giant spool.

"Our boats aren't in the way?" Pala asked.

Mirch shook his head no.

A horn echoed over the water and another fishing boat materialized out of the mists to the east. It was a smaller vessel, but it had a similar spool on its aft deck, and it was also reeling in the net. Men on both sides pulled lead lines, drawing the far end of the net up as it scooped up whatever was within it.

The rain came in a sudden downpour like it all needed to fall at the same time, and the roar of water hitting metal and plunking into the sea filled the air like static.

Pink salmon dumped into the holding container as men in yellow rain suits guided the nets, the fish wriggling and fighting. Their white mouths had black gums, and they opened and closed as they sucked for air, their gills pumping as the bright silver fish thrashed, their dorsal fins bending, beady black eyes bulging, tail fins sweeping madly.

"Wow," Mirch said. "See that humpie?"

Pala nodded. "He's huge." During their spawning migration, males develop a pronounced humped back.

"The ones that spawn and make it back this way will be green and yellow," Starker said. He had to show Mirch he knew something.

Yelling and screaming echoed over the boat and the winch stopped coiling the net.

"What is it?" yelled the captain.

"Tiger shark!"

17

Rain lashed Kangaroo Point, large drops of liquid ice falling in a deluge, pounding the fishing vessel, and churning up the cove. The boat listed under the pressure of the nets and half-full holding bin. Silver scales glistened as the fish sloshed around and fought to free themselves. Black clouds reached for the sea, fingerlike streaks knifing toward the blue water. Muffled yells fought through the static of the rain, and Starker and company went to the back of the boat to see what all the commotion was about.

"Restart the winch!" the captain screeched, and a yellow-clad fisherman turned the machine back on, the tap of the chain rolling over metal ringing over the boat as the last portion of the net was hauled in.

Pink salmon tumbled into the holding bin along with a few crabs and seaweed. The fish wriggled and fought, but there would be no escape. Some would go to market, others to the Lummi people, and still others would be sacrificed to the orcas.

When Starker reached the back of the boat, he found two fishermen wielding extended gaffs and trying to untangle a tiger shark from the net. The second Lummi vessel was in close, and the beast was caught in the center of the net.

One of the largest surviving sharks, the tiger shark ranks in size behind the whale shark, the basking shark, and the great white. The shark's gray missile body writhed, its sharp-tipped dorsal fin caught in the net, its caudal fin thwapping back and forth. The shark's jaws flexed open, revealing razor-sharp teeth, which had pronounced serrations and an unmistakable sideways-pointing tip. The tiger shark bit a pinkie with teeth that could cut through flesh, bone, and other tough materials like turtle shells.

The net winches screeched to a halt, the shark still caught in the netting that hung between the two vessels.

"What the hell is that thing doing here?" Mirch screamed.

Pala shook her head in confusion. "They're mostly nocturnal hunters, and with the rain..."

"These guys also have the widest food spectrum of all sharks," Starker said. "They'll eat just about anything; crustaceans, fish–they love pinkies, seals, birds, squid, turtles, sea snakes, dolphins, and even other sharks."

"That's why they're called 'garbage eaters'", Mirch said.

The fishermen poked and prodded the shark with the round end of the gaff, forcing the creature out of the netting as it feasted on their pinkies.

"I don't have to tell ECON why they're not just gaffing the shark, right?" Mirch said.

Starker and Pala both shook their heads no. Though not yet endangered, the tiger shark is considered a near threatened species due to finning and overfishing.

The massive fish clamped its jaws on one of the few remaining pinkies in the net and doubled its efforts to shake free. The tiger's caudal fin thrashed as the fishermen pushed and prodded the creature with the gaffs.

The downpour faded to steady rain, but it was like drizzle after the downpour.

Starker wiped the water from his face, his raincoat slick, his jeans soaked through. His stomach rumbled, and he thought of Spooky, who was still locked in the pilothouse on the SAFE boat on the opposite side of the fishing vessel. The feline had missed all the excitement.

The tiger shark breached from the netting, flying through the air for an instant before crashing into the sea, leaving a bubbling swirl of whitewater tinged with blood and fish guts. The shark's sharp dorsal fin slid below the surface, caudal fin lashing back and forth as the giant fish disappeared into the rain-soaked murkiness.

"As I said," Mirch said, "The Lummi do things the right way."

"Nobody ever said otherwise," Starker said.

The captain of the fishing vessel yelled orders, and the fishermen set about separating the nets and getting them ready to be set again.

"I wonder how Joel made out with his tour in that rain?" Pala said as she, Starker, and Mirch headed back to their boats.

The invisible thread that binds couples of all persuasions, races, and sexes, is as odd as it is accurate. The handheld radio Pala had clipped inside her slicker squawked, and she opened a channel. "Pala here. What's up?"

"The Ocean's Eleven. Copy."

"I copy. Where they at?"

"The trackers have them moving north fast along the coast off La Push."

Pala and Starker exchanged worried glances, and Pala said, "I copy. Anyone within range?"

"That's why I'm calling. There are several tour boats out there observing a large resident pod. Two, actually. They're playing."

"Has the sheriff dispatched a boat? The Coasties?"

"This information is going out to all agencies."

"Copy. We're on our way," Pala said.

"Thank you for the tour, Mirch, and be sure to thank the captain," Starker said.

"You got a bit of a show," Mirch said. "Sharks don't get caught in the nets often."

The trio jumped onto the SAFE boat and Mirch continued onto his vessel. "See you out there."

"Race you," Pala said.

"You're on."

Starker untied the bowline before following Pala into the pilothouse. Rain thrummed on the roof and Spooky didn't even look in Starker's direction. The cat was back in his original position atop the command console, and Starker saw the reflection of the cat's eager eyes as he stared out the window.

Pala backed away from the fishing boat, slowly turning the ship's wheel, but not rushing. Mirch's boat was bigger, and she had him pinned between the men working on the nets and the two large vessels. He couldn't go anywhere until Pala moved.

The twin Yamahas sang as the SAFE boat surged from the sea, spitting a white tail as it drove through the chop. The boat came up on plane, throwing spray, the strong easterly wind pushing the storm across the San Juan Islands.

Mirch's engines cycled up, but they didn't sing. The diesel growled, a steady moan that rose above the tapping rain as the large gray boat fell into the SAFE boat's motor wash.

The SAFE boat bounced over the windswept Rosario Strait as Pala arced the boat into Obstruction Pass. Gray curtains of rain hung over everything, and the shoreline was shrouded by thick fog bellowing over the surface like smoke.

"It's like driving through a cloud," Starker said.

"Should I call Joel?" Pala's face was twisted in a way Starker had never seen before.

"I can't see how it could hurt, but command said the locator information went out to all agencies, that means a general warning has been issued."

She nodded, her face still sliced with worry.

"But let me take the wheel and you can call."

Pala glanced at him, then at the thick fog obscuring their path. "You sure you can handle this? You'll have to use the NAV screen to pilot, and we're going forty knots."

Starker harrumphed and playfully nudged her away from the ship's wheel.

The NAV screen showed the narrow East Sound, with Lopez Island to the South and Orcas Island to the north. The ship's wheel vibrated slightly, the engines churning at 5500 RPMs. Starker took a deep breath.

Pala tapped on her phone and Joel answered. "Hi," Pala said. She looked at Starker as she listened. "O.K., just making sure you got it." More waiting. "O.K. You've seen enough though, move away." She sighed. "I know. I know. Love you." She closed the connection.

"Being married is awesome, right?"

"That it is," Pala said. "He heard the warning, and he's preparing to leave the area. He said the two pods are playing and it's the best whale watching he's had in months. The tourists are elated. He's monitoring the situation and he'll be leaving shortly."

"La Push isn't that far from Joel's location, right?" Starker asked.

She nodded.

"How long would it take for the eleven to get there? Assuming they went straight there?"

Pala slipped away her phone and retook the controls as she hiked her shoulders. "It's what, about thirty miles? And they can travel at about thirty-five miles per hour? So, we've got about fifty minutes."

When the SAFE boat dropped into the San Juan Channel, Pala spun the ship's wheel, putting the boat on a southern heading. The strong wind pushed the fog west, and green patches of San Juan Island bled through the endless gray.

The Strait of Juan de Fuca was a wind-torn mess, whitecaps covering the entire surface as the sea between Canada and the United States was beaten by the storm.

Pala opened the comm and informed command that she was almost on scene.

The eleven were south of Seal Rock, but they appeared to be tracking out to sea toward the residents.

Starker looked over his shoulder, and he couldn't see Mirch's boat. So much for the race.

Fog funneled into the inlet, leaking around Seal Rock. Spooky meowed once and Pala pulled back on the throttle control, bringing the SAFE boat down to thirty knots. The rain eased a little more, and the barking and braying of harbor seals could be heard as the rock island appeared out of the gloom, the island covered with seals and sea lions like ants on a fallen lollipop.

The SAFE boat churned past the island, the seals and sea lions yelling and screaming at them. The wind gusted and pushed away the fog, and for a brief instant, Starker saw several tourist boats racing toward the inlet, a red Zodiac out front.

Pala breathed a sigh of relief, Spooky meowed twice, and the knot in Starker's chest eased.

The barking of the seals and the braying of the sea lions faded as the SAFE boat approached the cluster of orcas. The tangle of dorsal fins swayed and glided through the water as the killer whales breached and rubbed one another, blowing spray, their conical heads lulling from the dark water, mouths open like smiles. The beasts tossed around a knot of seaweed like a beachball, the younger wolves jumping from the ocean, twisting and biting like puppies.

Pala moved the SAFE boat in closer, knocking back the throttle and angling the vessel to the south of the frolicking pods, putting the boat between the residents and the oncoming Ocean's Eleven.

To the south, eleven dorsal fins leaped and dove through the sea, rain blurring the windshield, but the scene was clear as the brightest day. The Ocean's Eleven were heading straight for the playing orcas.

"Meow," Spooky shrieked. He hissed and pushed to his feet, tail out straight, face an inch from the windshield.

"Yeah," Starker said.

The wind gusted and sea spray lashed the SAFE boat, but Pala pressed on, increasing speed as the boat powered through the three-foot whitecaps. The vessel bounced and heaved, but it didn't appear to affect Pala or Spooky, both of which had their eyes locked on the eleven as they scythed through the Pacific.

One of the frolicking orcas, perhaps sensing the oncoming squad of muscle and teeth, peeled away from the group, and breached, presumedly to alert the others, and it worked. The knot of orcas scattered, dorsal fins disappearing beneath the rain-dappled ocean, leaving only churning whitewater.

Mirch arrived on scene and pulled up short behind the SAFE boat, and behind him was a sheriff's boat. All three vessels floated with the current as eleven dorsal fins arced north toward the fleeing orca.

"Do you think we should stay with them?" Pala asked.

Starker brought the binoculars to his eyes, but they didn't help much with the blurred windshield. The eleven hadn't shifted course and had picked up speed and were gaining on the two resident pods as they fled. The tourist vessels were safe, the other authorities were present, so they had backup, and nobody was in danger. He said, "Stay on them, but give them space."

18

Sensing the approaching pursuit, four of the larger fleeing orcas peeled away from their pods and circled back toward the Ocean's Eleven. From the looks of their dorsal fins, Starker thought there were two males and two females. They were big, thirty feet if they were an inch, their sleek powerful bodies knifing through the Pacific Ocean, dipping and jumping through the sea at a furious pace as they headed straight for the Ocean's Eleven.

Pala pulled back the throttle handle and brought the SAFE boat down to a cool fifteen knots. The Ocean's Eleven were five hundred yards off the port bow, their thick white wake still visible despite the rain.

Spooky stood on the command console, staring out the rain-blurred windshield.

Starker watched the harrowing game of high stakes chicken, that old-school childhood game that never failed to deliver chills and thrills. An odd sense of wonder filled him, delight, and excitement at seeing four apex predators bearing down on eleven diseased wolves of the sea that were performing well above their natural design parameters. It wasn't a fair fight. Starker reached into his jacket and felt the handle of his Glock, the cold steel reassuring.

Out on the storm-ravaged Pacific, the game of chicken continued, the eleven cutting through the sea like they owned it, the four residents churning toward what Starker believed to be certain doom. Didn't he have an obligation here? To protect the wildlife? Yes, there was the WSCD prime directive of "do not interfere," but Starker was tired of waiting for things to happen and then reacting. It was time to take the bull by the horns and at least attempt to gently step in-between these endangered bullies.

The comm crackled. It was Mirch. "Woo-hoo. I ain't never seen anything like this."

Pala asked, "Coasties coming?"

The sheriff's boat broke in. "Pala, it's Renne. The Coast Guard is inbound via helicopter. Over."

"Copy, Renne."

"You were here first, Pala, and it's animals, so..." Mirch's communication trailed off.

"So it's up to us," Starker said as Pala closed the channel.

The two charging pods of orcas were a quarter mile apart, neither side showing any signs of slowing or peeling off. The eleven had passed the SAFE boat, and Pala spun the ship's wheel and set a course to keep pace.

The gods chose that moment to turn up the rain spigot, and the skies opened, a deluge of rain that blinded Starker and his companions, the SAFE boat's windows so blurred that visibility fell to zero.

"Dang," Pala said as she adjusted the SONAR and called up the tracking software. Four red dots appeared on the NAV screen as they moved swiftly northeast to meet the defenders of the fleeing residents.

"Are they arcing back this way?" Starker asked.

The four red dots separated.

"I don't think so. They're preparing to surround the four."

Then as if the Earth had run out of water the rain stopped. It happened so suddenly, that Starker and Pala stood in stunned silence, staring at one another, the stillness in the cabin deafening despite the snap and crack of waves breaking on the SAFE boat's bow.

The SONAR showed six large masses approaching the SAFE boat.

"Meow." Spooky sat, his tail between his legs. The feline hissed with a viciousness Starker had never heard from the animal, but as the rain drained away from the windshield, he felt the cat's anger and fear.

Six tall dorsal fins surged through the sea alongside the boat, their conical black and white heads rising and dipping into the black churned-up water.

Starker reared back, his gaze falling on the NAV screen. The four red dots were still moving northeast fast.

The six dorsal fins next to the SAFE boat separated, three to each side as they surrounded the vessel.

"Are they..." Starker said. He couldn't find the words. He was too amazed by what he was seeing.

"It does look like they're trying to protect us," Pala said.

"Do you think the healthy orcas sense there's something wrong with the eleven? Maybe because of their behavior?"

"Definitely possible," Pala said. "We skipped the section in the killer whale museum, but orcas have the second-heaviest brains among marine mammals. They're second only to sperm whales, which have the largest brain of any animal on Earth. As you know, orcas can be trained in captivity and are often described as intelligent."

Starker nodded. "Sure, I was up in Alaska once, and I saw orcas playing with a ball of ice soon after a researcher threw a snowball at the whale. It was using it as a toy."

"Orcas will imitate and teach skills to their pod. Off the Crozet Islands, mothers push their calves onto the beach, waiting to pull the youngster back if needed."

The game of chicken was almost at its end, and the SAFE boat was just to the east of the action, the sheriff's boat and Mirch still trailing after, their six black and white honor guards flanking them.

"This is amazing," Pala said.

"Not really, I guess. I remember talking to a WSCD researcher who said Alaskan orcas have not only learned how to steal fish from longlines, but have also overcome a variety of techniques designed to stop them, such as the use of decoy lines."

"I've heard about that," Pala said.

"They tried to stop the thefts, but it became increasingly difficult," Starker said. "Fishermen tried placing their boats several miles apart, taking turns retrieving small amounts of their catch, in the hope that the whales wouldn't have enough time to move between boats and steal the catch. It worked well for a while. Then the whales split into two groups. Like these guys."

The SONAR showed the Ocean's Eleven and the four defenders were almost on top of each other, the blue-gray bottom of the Pacific streaking across the SONAR screen.

The orcas met in a momentous clash off the port bow. The sea erupted, the beats slamming into each other, breaching and rolling, black and white skin in a massive tangle. Tail flutes whipped and beat like bird's wings, the sea a churning mess of fury and teeth. The four were outnumbered and were quickly hemmed in by the eleven, five of which swam in a wide circle, containing the action as the rest of the pod attacked the four.

"Bring us in closer," Starker said.

"Do you think that's a good idea?"

"Not really," he said. "But maybe it'll break things up."

"And maybe it will put us in the drink."

Starker frowned. "We can't just sit here."

Pala's gaze strayed to Starker. It was the look that said her children aren't growing up without their mother. But she inched down the throttle levers and the SAFE boat picked up speed, and as it did, the six orcas flanking the boat tried to cut in front of the bow to stop their advance, but the SAFE boat was moving too fast and the six were forced to trail after.

Mirch and the sheriff's boat stayed back.

The orca brawl thinned out, the creatures giving each other some space. Killer whales breached from the Pacific, others joined up with partners and rammed their attackers, and still others bit and snapped at anything that came within their reach, spike-like teeth filling huge jaws.

Starker pressed the binoculars to his eyes and was surprised to find bloody gashes running along several of the Ocean's Eleven. "It looks like those strange pus-filled wounds on the eleven are breaking open," he said.

"We've got bigger problems," Pala said.

Starker jerked away the binoculars and focused on the NAV screen, which showed four red dots surging toward the SAFE boat. The SONAR showed the rest of the original frolicking pods were circling and working their way back toward the fray to help their family.

"Switching targets?" Starker said.

"It appears the residents weren't as done for as I thought." She eased the throttle into neutral and the SAFE rocked to a stop, the following sea slapping the transom and bubbling up to the outboard covers.

The six orcas guarding the SAFE boat stopped as well, falling in around the vessel like they were protecting a calf.

"Wow!" Pala said. "Look at these two spyhopping."

Two of the honor guard held their conical heads above the water as they surveyed their surroundings.

"Resident orcas have been known to swim alongside porpoises and dolphins, as well as boats," Starker said.

With the SAFE boat at a full stop, Pala's attention shifted to the SONAR and NAV screens.

The sheriff's boat and Mirch were back a half mile distant, a black cloud of gulls hanging below the dark clouds above Seal Rock behind them.

Spooky hissed, the feline's eyes aglow.

"They're almost on us," Pala said. "I'm going to—"

Suddenly, as if Starker had lost a tiny block of time, he and Pala went from observers to the center of the battle. The sea turned white as the Ocean's Eleven rammed the six protecting the SAFE boat. A feverous frenzy erupted around the boat, the sea a jumbled mass of black and white flesh and teeth.

It was like watching a soccer game with all the players wearing the same color jerseys with no numbers. Orcas bit and fought, a nasty slick leaking across the water, blood, fat, and gristle floating around the SAFE boat's waterline.

"O.K.," Pala said. "I'm backing us out of here."

Orcas fought and swelled from the ocean all around the SAFE boat, blocking their path, patches of white and black tumbling and streaking through the blood-tainted water. The sound of servos filled the pilothouse as Pala angled the motors up, leaving only the twin props in the water. The engines gurgled and spat as they fought to suck in seawater as a coolant, and with the SAFE boat in neutral, Pala raced the motors.

A thunderous roar echoed off the water, the rumble of a massive engine struggling to move a large object. A rooster tail of water shot fifteen feet into the air behind the boat, and the growl of the engines was enough to wake Poseidon.

For a heartbeat it looked like Pala's scare tactic might work, and the water around the boat flattened, tall dorsal fins circling the boat.

But the eleven weren't normal orcas, and unlike the rest of the sea wolves, they weren't frightened by the loud noise. It had the opposite effect, and the disease-ravaged eleven refocused their attack on the sound.

Pala dropped the engines, hydraulics singing, but it was too late.

One of the adult eleven breached, its massive blood-streaked form hanging in the air, its tail flute driving the creature out of the water. The beast came down on the SAFE boat's bow, and Starker and Pala were tossed forward into the command console.

Spooky slammed into the windshield as seawater flowed over the inflated gunnel into the boat. The engines screamed as the back of the SAFE boat lifted from the water.

The orca rolled off the boat, and the bow surged upward, the water flooding the deck and pouring across the windshield like a waterfall. The water drained away, and the bilge pump snapped on.

Spooky got to his feet and shook his head as Starker and Pala regained their positions behind the command console. The whining of the servos stopped, and Pala dropped the hammer, the SAFE boat leaping from the Pacific. The engines faltered as the propellors dug into flesh, and blood and gristle spit from both motor's ejector ports, spraying the undulating ocean.

The radio crackled to life, Mirch asking if they needed assistance, but Pala and Starker didn't have time to respond. One of the eleven nudged the SAFE boat with its tooth-filled snout, driving the boat to starboard as it struggled to come up on plane, but as the propellers clawed at the sea, the SAFE boat listed sharply.

Pala clung to the ship's wheel to stop herself from being tossed across the cabin.

Starker and Spooky weren't as adept. Spooky flew from the command console, but somehow managed to land on his feet as he hit the deck. Starker was thrown across the pilothouse, arms out in a useless attempt at balance. He slammed into the bulkhead wall, stars dancing across his vision before he lost his footing and hit the deck, his face landing in the two inches of water that had somehow leaked into the sealed cabin.

Pala made a sound like a pig taking a dump, and Starker braced himself against the bulkhead and pushed to his feet, using the cabin wall for support as he made his way back to the command console, the deck rolling and shifting beneath his feet.

Spooky hissed. The feline was soaking wet and trembling, his eyes down, tail between his legs.

Starker stood next to Pala and when he saw what had made her squeal, his stomach burned as if on fire.

The bow of the SAFE boat where the orca had landed looked to be losing air, and seawater lapped over the deflating gunnel.

19

The inflated gunnel of Pala's SAFE boat had eighteen separate and distinct chambers, and the entire inflated assembly sat atop a hard hull with a quarter-inch bottom plate and a reinforced keel beaching plate. The rig had a self-bailing drain gap between the deck and sides, and all this made the boat very hard to sink. Still, Starker felt little spiders crawling all over his body as he watched a section of the bow deflate, a growing stream of water lapping into the boat with each wave.

The ship's radio squawked as Mirch and the sheriff's vessel hailed, asking if Pala needed assistance. She told them to move in as she struggled to turn the SAFE boat's wheel as more seawater poured into the boat, the bilge pump spitting water from the side of the vessel.

"She's handling like a brick," Pala said as she worked the helm.

Starker shifted on his feet, and when he noticed Spooky sitting in the water at his feet, he picked the feline up and got no resistance. He stroked the cat's wet fur. The poor thing looked miserable.

Patches of white rolled beneath the dark water, an occasional engorged eye appearing before a patch of white. The sea wolves were all around now, and Starker couldn't tell friend from foe. Orcas breached, ramming and biting at each other, using their size to push the smaller orcas around. Blood filled the water, and Starker figured the sharks would be on scene soon.

As if reading his mind, as she'd done on several occasions, Pala said, "I think it's time we make like a tree."

Starker looked at her and she smiled. He didn't laugh.

"And leave."

Still nothing.

"Leave... like a leaf," she said, frustrated. When again he didn't laugh, she frowned. That was one of the many reasons Starker liked Pala. They were in the shit with a leaky boat surrounded by apex predators who were intent on eating each other—and maybe them, and she was making jokes. Bad jokes, but Starker gave credit for the effort.

Pala spun the ship's wheel as she cycled up the outboards, slowly moving through the field of orcas. The westerly wind helped spin the SAFE boat around. With the bow pointed east, the sea was attacking the rear of the boat, and less water lapped through the growing gap in the bow's gunnel. She pressed down the throttle just enough to lift the bow, and the boat pushed east in that awkward plow-like position, and the flow of water into the boat decreased. The Yamahas whined as the SAFE boat fought through the chop, the vessel rolling and jumping, orcas surging from the water around the boat.

The sheriff's boat and Mirch had come in close and was two hundred yards off the SAFE boat's starboard bow, mimicking its progress. Ahead, Seal Rock jutted from the undulating sea, waves breaking on the black stone as seals fought and barked and squirmed, waving their flippers, mouths open, revealing thick tusks.

Starker checked his life vest and gun out of habit, thoughts of ending up in the drink with three pods of fighting orcas not on the top of his bucket list. The rain came again, and the tapping on the pilothouse roof resumed, the endless static that filled the cabin with a cacophonous echo.

The Yamahas were struggling to keep the bow up so Pala inched the throttle down a hair.

The sound of metal-on-metal tore over the water and white smoke streamed from the port outboard.

No matter, Starker thought, that's why we have two. The engine ground to a stop with an earsplitting screech and the SAFE boat surged to port.

At the same time, two orcas breached, one on each side of the boat. Starker couldn't help but be impressed with the precision as the massive beasts crashed down onto the SAFE boat at the same time.

Pala, adjusting for the down motor, jerked the ship's wheel, trying to bring the SAFE boat back on course, and that may have saved their lives. The orca on the starboard side overshot the boat and the one on the port side undershot. The result was one orca mostly missing the SAFE boat, with the other crashing across the deck, pressing the bow beneath the waves.

A deluge of seawater washed over the windshield as the back of the SAFE boat lifted from the ocean, the remaining engine screaming as it sucked for water. Pala and Starker were tossed across the pilothouse, both slamming into the shatterproof glass window at the rear of the cabin.

This time Spooky managed to stay perched atop his seat. The wet cat looked small, but his eyes glowed with defiance as his head jerked around and he hissed at the world.

The orca rolled back into the Pacific, and the back of the SAFE boat came down in a shuddering crash, water pouring over the gunnels and filling the boat.

Starker and Pala struggled to their feet, and now six inches of water sloshed around the pilothouse floor. "This cabin is supposed to be sealed!" Pala screamed.

The seawater drained through the SAFE boat's bailing gaps, but seaweed and debris were clogging the drains. The bilge pump was going full tilt, but it was like trying to take the sugar out of a candy bar. Pala struggled with the ship's wheel, but with all the extra weight and one motor down, maneuverability was minimal.

Seeing the SAFE boat's vulnerable condition, Mirch radioed and asked if they wanted to be picked up.

Starker held the radio handset and stared at Pala, who looked out the windshield at the storm-swept sea, not meeting his eye.

Orcas circled the boat, still fighting, white patches knifing through the dark water. The eleven didn't seem to care who they attacked, the original residents or the SAFE boat. Killer whales rammed the vessel on all sides, and Starker's mind spun the scenario forward. He didn't want to abandon ship. Never thought he'd even consider such a thing. But he wasn't making Pala's children motherless, and the orcas were becoming increasingly hostile. It was in fact time to make like a tree, but on another boat. Seal Rock was a quarter mile distant, but the shoreline of Canada's Pacific Rim National Park was still several miles away.

"Are we done here?" Starker asked.

Pala's eyes flicked from the sea to Starker. "What are you saying? Leave my rig?"

Starker said nothing as he watched the nose of an orca push from the sea, its jaws open in a toothy grin.

"No way. I'm not—"

The SAFE boat was pushed to the side as if punched by a massive invisible hand. The vessel rose on a giant wave, then settled.

"They're coming up beneath us," Starker said, and he was surprised to hear the fear in his voice.

He hadn't intended to scare her, but the tone of Starker's comment brought the "I'm not leaving my children without a mother face," and she nodded.

"Mirch, come get us." He hung the radio handset back on its clip, and said, "Do we drop anchor? How much water are we in?"

"A hundred feet, and no. That would be worse. We'll shut everything down and let it drift until we can get a tow line on her."

Starker nodded. That made much more sense.

Rain pelted the sea as the SAFE boat surged upward without warning, engine yelling.

Two orcas drove the vessel from the Pacific as they breached, and the SAFE boat listed hard to port. Everything in the pilothouse, including Pala, Starker, and Spooky, was hurled in the air as the vessel danced on its portside gunnel for a heartbeat before flipping over. A cacophonous crash boomed through the cabin as everything shifted and the second motor squealed, popped, then fell still.

Spooky screeched, and the pilothouse grew dark, the upside-down SAFE boat bobbing on the tumbling ocean. Starker struggled to his feet and stood on the cabin's roof, staring up at the upside-down command console.

"Dear God," Pala said.

Like a surreal aquarium, orcas could be seen through the pilothouse windows, driving through the dark water, circling the capsized vessel, their black and white forms gliding through the sea like attack submarines.

"We need to get out of here," Starker said.

"What?"

Starker pointed to the steady stream of seawater filling the cabin.

"Yeah." She looked around, eyes frantic.

The radio squawked, but Starker couldn't reach it, so he helped Pala get to her feet. She was shaken, and blood dripped from a gash on her forehead.

"We've got to hurry," Starker said. He knew the SAFE boat couldn't truly sink, but they were extremely vulnerable as the storm battered the sea and orcas prowled the area.

"Meow. Meow."

Starker lifted Spooky and put the cat on his shoulders, and the feline clutched at him like Starker was the last person on Earth with cat food.

Pala waded through the rising water, the boat shaking and vibrating as it was nudged and rammed by the attacking orcas. If the original honor guard of residents was still trying to protect the SAFE boat, they were failing miserably.

Starker went to the cabin door, but didn't try to open it. The vessel rolled in the surf, and he'd have to time the opening of the door to coincide with an upswing, otherwise, the rush of the inflowing sea would prevent them from getting free of the pilothouse.

Pala gasped and Starker looked over his shoulder.

An orca hung in the water just beyond the SAFE boat's windshield, the creature's engorged red, yellow-rimmed eyes staring through the dark water, a large bloody gash running down the center of the beast's head.

Starker reached out and took Pala's hand, Spooky's nails digging into his neck as the cat hung on. "Ready?" he said.

Pala said nothing, but she nodded.

The floodwater in the cabin was three feet deep now, and it pushed Starker and Pala around as the boat shifted and bobbed. He waited a three count, and when the boat's momentum tilted to port, Starker used all the strength he had left to slide open the pilothouse door.

Despite the boat's upswing, water poured through the door, pushing Starker back.

Pala fought through the powerful stream and swam out into the Pacific.

Starker felt Spooky lose his grip, and then the cat was gone. A black hairball flew past him in the maelstrom, and for the second time in two weeks, Spooky found himself in the drink alone.

The upside-down SAFE boat listed back to starboard, and Starker pushed out into the water, the blast of cold freezing him for an instant.

Then he was tumbling through the whitewater as he got flipped and yanked around like he was in a washing machine. He saw white, bubbles, and darkness.

Orcas fought and swam all around Starker, and he sucked in a breath as he oriented himself. Above a faint sheen of light told him which way was up, and he snapped from his daze and stroked hard, driving himself through the water until he broke the surface.

Pala floated several feet from him, her lifejacket holding her above the breaking waves. Mirch and the sheriff's boat were moving in for a rescue, but the orcas were breaching and blocking their path. Starker didn't see Spooky.

Rain lashed the ocean, cold seeping into Starker like radiation, his vision going blurry as his muscles protested and cramped. The day had started well enough, and despite everything that had happened over the last two weeks, Starker never once considered that the orcas might be able to take down the SAFE boat. Bile crept up his throat as a wave of nausea pressed through him and he fought back an urge to throw up. Seawater splashed his face, burning his eyes, pain shooting to the tips of his fingers and toes.

A loud crash echoed over the sea as the SAFE boat came down hard, sending a surge of water in Starker's direction. He used the wave's force to move away from the capsized vessel, and without thought, he started swimming for Seal Rock, which was several hundred yards distant on the eastern horizon.

Starker had only taken three strokes when he saw Spooky struggling to stay above the whitecaps and breaking waves, and he changed course and headed for the cat. No way he was letting the feline drown out here.

"Spooky! Pala!" Starker yelled, water leaking into his mouth as he swam.

The cat's head whipped around, and upon seeing Starker, the feline began doggie paddling through wind-swept sea, rain pounding his little head as he lifted it above the waterline. Starker put out his arm and Spooky climbed onto his shoulders.

"You OK, buddy?"

"Meow. Meow."

"Glad someone is."

The *womp womp* of rotor blades stroking the air echoed over the Pacific.

20

Pala had never been so scared in her life. Irrational anger surged through her as she searched for Starker, thoughts of her children and husband teasing her nerves. The water was cold, her uniform soaked through, and Pala felt icy fingers working their way under her skin, chilling her bones. Heavy rain pounded the sea, pinpricks of cold that stung her face and clouded her vision. Blood leaked into her eyes from the gash on her forehead, the wound pulsating with pain as she gripped her lifejacket, feet out as she floated on the surface of the stormy sea.

The SAFE boat was upside-down, rolling in the waves that pushed east over the Pacific like an advancing army. The thunderous roar of helicopter rotors echoed over the water, and Pala struggled to look up and saw a coastie copter incoming.

"Starker!" she screamed, but there was no response except the angry wind.

Pala rose and fell on the crests of waves, and during her upswings, she managed to see the sheriff's boat moving in, but with the SAFE boat rolling around in the surf and orcas in the area, maneuvering the vessel and getting in close was difficult and dangerous.

She saw Starker eighty feet away as he rose and fell with the roll of the sea, Spooky perched atop her partner's head. A smile broke through her fear and worry. At least she didn't need to worry about the cat. Starker was drifting east toward Seal Rock, but Pala was getting tugged north by the current, the rocky shoreline of Vancouver Island a dark line to the east.

A surge of water pressure pushed Pala upward and to the right as something swam past her, a large red eye rimmed in yellow slipping by in the dark water, the beast's white eye patch standing out like a cockroach on a birthday cake. She sucked on her gums as pressure to scream built in her lungs and surged up her windpipe, but she didn't make a sound.

A tall dorsal fin scythed through the water, the beast's tail flute working up and down. More eyes appeared in the Pacific, white patches easing through the turbulent ocean, the massive missile-like forms graceful, yet menacing. Clicks, bellows, and chuffing rose above the crashing waves, wind, and the roar of the approaching helicopter. Dorsal fins appeared all around her, the orcas rising silently from the depths.

The rain eased, and Pala spun in a whirlpool created by the orcas. She knew what that meant and Pala reached for her Glock, which was still in its holster on her hip. Guns and bullets don't like water, but the law enforcement grade Glock could be fired underwater, so she was confident the weapon would work if she needed it.

Starker was swept away, and Pala could no longer spot her partner and the feline. The faint barking of seals and sea lions fought to be heard above the maelstrom, and her thoughts ranged to Seal Rock. Hopefully Starker and Spooky could make it there.

A wave broke over Pala and she was sucked under, all worries of Starker and Spooky fleeing as she clawed at the water, fighting to get back to the surface.

The Pacific eddied and heaved, and one of the smaller orcas knifed straight at Pala, the beast's white and black nosecone breaking the surface like a submarine coming up for air. The orca's mouth was closed, and as the creature pushed from the sea it flicked its head and tossed Pala like a seal.

Pala pulled in her arms and legs, pressing them to her sides as she sailed through the air, black clouds, rain, and whitewater clouding her vision. She managed to hit the water feet first, but she landed on one of the creature's pectoral fins. The orca jerked and Pala hit the ocean hard, saltwater jetting up her nose and stinging her eyes. Her head wound had stopped bleeding, and blood no longer leaked into her eyes, but the wound throbbed like a drumbeat.

The coastie copter cut through the rain, slowly dropping as it approached. She searched the surface of the sea, looking for Starker, but she couldn't find him.

A massive orca slipped past, its clicking and chuffing like a broken record, its pointy dorsal fin knifing through the sea, the saddle patch behind the creature's dorsal fin solid gray. The orca eased into position alongside Pala but didn't touch her or attack in any way. She knew from the gray markings that the orca was a transient, or Biggs, and until very recently they'd never been seen tangling with residents. A dark black eye watched her, a gray eye patch leaving no doubts that the beast wasn't one of the eleven.

Cold filtered through Pala, and she was getting tired, the freezing sea doing its job, and yet something clawed at her brain.

The Ocean's Eleven, not appreciating the arrival of the Biggs, broke their circle and attacked.

Pala was caught in the center of it all, the water around her a knot of whitewater, black and white flesh and teeth intertwining like a knot of eels. The two opposing pods pushed and rammed each other, the smaller shark-like residents taking strafing runs at the larger Biggs.

The sea flattened, but the rain picked up as the coastie copter settled above Pala like a UFO. The MH-60T Jayhawk hovered two hundred feet above the surface, rotors stroking the air. A coastie wearing a flight helmet with its face shield down waved to her from the copter's open side door as he lowered a safety line, a black harness dangling from its end.

Water sprayed across the surface as an orca breached, its entire body leaving the water, tail flute straight, pectoral fins out like wings. The beast had a long gash along its side, red and white boils bursting from the wound like lobster meat escaping a cracked shell. The orca landed atop the Biggs, and the two massive apex predators struggled as they awkwardly tried to bite each other, neither beast having the speed and range to get the other. Open mouths filled with teeth bit air, and both beasts slipped below the surface, their duel continuing as the orcas slid into the depths.

The Biggs were outnumbered by the Ocean's Eleven, and Pala's rescuers soon found themselves surrounded, along with Pala. The smaller members of the eleven took turns moving in on the Biggs, ramming and pushing them toward their waiting partners. White patches appeared and disappeared in the black water, the rain-pocked surface a chaotic mess of windswept whitecaps and twisting slugs of black and white slithering flesh.

The safety harness splashed down fifteen feet from Pala, and she swam for it, orcas flowing around her, pushing and fighting with each other. Pala could only count four Biggs, and they wouldn't be able to hold off the eleven much longer. A blood slick wound its way through the breaking whitecaps, and one of the Biggs broke off, swimming away from the action.

Memories of her training came rushing back like the tide as Pala swam, the Pacific smacking her in the face, icy tendrils of cold piercing her skin. She drilled on helicopter water rescue twice a year, but they always selected a sunny day when the ocean was flat and accommodating. She'd never had to get herself into the rescue harness with five-foot waves smacking her in the face and a crowd of apex predators nipping at her heels.

The safety harness floated on the surging sea before her, then Pala was falling into a valley between waves, the world disappearing for a heartbeat as she was pulled down into the inky sea. She stopped struggling and relaxed, letting the sea carry her back up. The next wave rolled in, and as Pala was lifted on the swell, she lunged for the rescue line.

She missed it and slid down the face of a wave as it crested, crashing into a knot of whitewater. She felt slick skin, the strong thrust of the sea, then she was being pushed up as if by an unseen hand. A Biggs was below her, driving her up.

The rescue harness floated before her again, and Pala slipped into it, placing the loop over her head and under her arms, making sure the line was padded by her lifejacket. She'd learned the hard way that rope can be as unforgiving as a blade, and as she was jerked from the Pacific, she recalled her first helicopter exercise. Her armpits had been swollen and sore for a week.

Water drained from her lifejacket as rain assailed Pala, wind tearing at her, spinning her around as the dark water receded beneath her. The whine of the hoist motor echoed over the turmoil, and as Pala rose higher, she saw the orcas battling below.

The Ocean's Eleven had gotten the upper hand, and the three remaining Biggs struggled to break the containment circle the eleven had imposed. A roar boomed over the water, the squeal of a massive animal in pain. Two of the Biggs breached at the same time, one launching into the air and crashing down on a resident, the other barely dipping from the water like a dolphin taking a gentle leap. Both beasts managed to break containment, and the remaining Biggs escaped in the ensuing chaos.

Pala laughed as she spun in the air, the loop of rope beneath her arms digging into her armpits despite being cushioned by the lifejacket. With Pala out of the water, the Biggs' mission was complete. She'd never seen anything like it. Starker would—

Thoughts of her partner sent a surge of guilt through Pala as she searched the stormy sea for Starker. The hoist motor whined, and she was almost to the helicopter, its rotor wash pushing Pala around like a fish hanging from the end of a hook. You're never supposed to leave your partner. No matter what, and guilt surged through her, but she brushed it aside. She'd warned him. Made it very clear her children were the most important thing in her world, and they wouldn't be growing up without a mother, even if that meant leaving Starker behind.

Thing was, as hard as she tried not to like the guy, he was like a stray dog, and the more he hung around, the more she cared for him. And if she was being totally honest with herself, she was a little attracted to him. He would understand. What could she do anyway? She was exhausted, chilled to the core, her patrol boat was upside-down, and the storm was showing no signs of abating.

Starker's head popped up through a fist of whitewater, Spooky clinging to his shoulders. He was swimming for Seal Rock.

With Pala out of their grasp, and her pod of rescuers gone, the Ocean's Eleven had homed in on a new target.

The hoist cable shuttered to a halt, the moan of the motor ceased, and the roar of the rotors filled the world. The coastie pulled Pala aboard, undid the carabiner holding the safety loop, and eased her to the deck.

"Are you O.K.?" he asked.

Pala said nothing as she stared out the open door at the dark cloud-filled sky.

"Are you hurt?" the coastie yelled.

"No," she said. "But my partner. He's—"

"Don't worry," the coastie said. "I'll get him." The coastie told the pilot the rescue was complete and asked if he should prepare to do another.

"Negative," came the voice over the comm. "We are to stand down. A police boat is going for him."

The helicopter's engines cycled up, the copter's nose dipped, and the craft shook as the pilot spun the Jayhawk around and rode the thermals east.

Pala rolled onto her side, staring down at the Pacific. She could see Starker, but there was nothing she could do for him now.

21

Spooky hissed at an orca ramming the capsized SAFE boat, waves washing over Starker and burying him in frothing whitewater. The cat's claws dug into his neck, but Starker barely felt the stabbing pinpricks. The Pacific was cold, and his fingers were already numb. The current pulled him east toward Neah Bay Inlet, Seal Rock a dark mound on the eastern horizon.

"Pala! Pala!" Starker thought he heard his partner respond, but with the wind whistling and the rain lashing the storm-torn sea, it was difficult to focus on anything. Cold water slapped him in the face, Spooky shifting and balancing with each wave as the duo got tossed around like trash in a tornado. He went under again, water filling his mouth, Spooky's nails biting his neck, black and white patches of flesh zipping around him in the blackness.

The buoyant life preserver dragged him back to the surface, the gurgle of boat motors echoing over the Pacific, his eyes stinging from the sea water, the air thick with the scent of salt and gasoline. Mirch and the sheriff's boat were driving through the chop, killer whales breaching and diving all around the vessels. Starker searched the sea, and when he didn't see Pala, he swam for Seal Rock.

The coastie copter arrived, and the white and orange bird pulled up short half a mile from his position and hovered. The zap of excitement and the soothing hand of relief fought for control of Starker. If he and Pala were the only ones in the drink, the coasties must be rescuing Pala, and it felt good not to have to worry about her, and by extension her family.

Free of obligation to his partner, Starker doubled his efforts, head down, waves crashing over him as he powered through the surf.

Spooky was a trooper. The cat clung to Starker's neck as though his life depended on it, and perhaps it did. Orcas circled Starker, the big ones staying back and letting the youngsters do the work. The shark-like calves knifed through the sea, bumping Starker as he swam, their engorged eyes manic.

One of the smaller beasts breached—more of a jump, really, and the creature came down like an anvil ten feet behind Starker, and the pressure wave pushed him east on a strong swell. He rode the wave on his stomach, body surfing toward oblivion, Spooky hanging ten atop his head.

The orcas chuffed, spraying water over the surface as they dipped and leaped from the sea, teeth glinting in the gloom. Starker was no marine biologist, but the odd slashes and the swollen eyes of the eleven appeared to have gotten worse. Several of the pustule-filled gashes he'd seen were bloody and pink, the boils broken. When he was a boy, Starker's parents taught him the sea was the ultimate healer, and that saltwater cauterized wounds and promoted healing. He believed that and had evidence to prove it, despite modern cynics claiming seawater can do more harm than good to an open wound. The naysayers said impurities, bacteria, and foreign materials in the water can infect the wound, and to Starker's untrained eye that's what happened to the orcas' lesions. The wounds were festering, and though he'd never done a count, the lacerations appeared to be spreading.

The current was sucking Starker toward the inlet at a steady pace, and he laid back, letting the life preserver keep him on top of the churning water as he rested.

The sheriff's boat backed off, and Mirch pressed forward, but the water was getting shallow as Seal Rock got closer, and the ocean was littered with jagged boulders, many of which hid just below the heaving waves. Seal Rock wasn't far off, and Starker heard Mirch calling to him over the exterior comm, but he couldn't make out what the Lummi cop was saying over the howling wind, screaming rain, and the bark and whine of the hundreds of seals and sea lions on Seal Rock. Mirch's police boat stopped, spinning slowly as it got pushed around, bobbing and listing on the furious sea.

A wave broke over Starker, and Spooky was washed away, but the cat wasn't phased. Starker swam forward hard, nudging the feline before him as Spooky doggy paddled toward Seal Rock which was only a hundred feet away.

The coastie copter thundered overhead as it gained altitude, a person hanging from the end of a rescue line like a pendant at the end of a gold necklace. The rescued person's black hair whipped in the wind, and Starker cackled. Pala was safe.

Starker saw the seafloor coming up to meet him and stood, his feet finding the top of a rock. He stood for a heartbeat, balancing atop the jagged boulder before a wave knocked him off with extreme prejudice. All Starker could think of as he fell was how he'd survived swimming through a swarm of killer whales, only to mash his head on a stone.

He twisted in midair, the dark shape of a jagged rock filling his field of vision. Starker landed in the water, and rolled, water filling his mouth. Waves crashed against Seal Rock, and he let the whitewater carry him forward, the barking of sea lions and the braying of seals blocking out all other sounds.

The rain stopped as if some god had turned off the spigot, and a thick mist swirled above the water. Starker stood and his feet hit bottom and he struggled to right himself, whitewater nudging him forward, pain knotting his lower back.

A roar froze Starker in place. A massive sea lion blocked his way, snout in the air as he screamed. The giant gray slug scuttled toward Starker like an advancing attack dog, walking on its front flippers, snout in the air, dark patches covering the animal's brown skin. Seal Rock was packed with seals and sea lions, a swarm of gulls circling overhead, squawking and arguing.

Starker recoiled, recalling all he knew of the beasts, how they could be aggressive and nasty. The Pacific Northwest supports several types of seals, but harbor seals and sea lions were by far the most common. He knew the marine mammals differed in many ways: the sea lions were brown and walked on land using their large flippers. They bark incessantly and have visible ear flaps, while harbor seals have small flippers and have to wriggle on their bellies when on land like slugs, and they lack visible ear flaps.

Starker inched forward, and the sea lion barked and yelled, bouncing up and down as it pounded its flippers. But the creature wasn't even looking at Starker, and he realized the beast was jawing at the Ocean's Eleven, who were circling Seal Rock. Transient orcas regularly killed and ate both seals and sea lions, tossing them about until they died and then consuming them in much the same way a lion chowed on a gazelle.

The sea lion noticed Starker and dropped to all fours, whiskers gyrating as the massive creature slipped into the sea. Starker pushed forward out of the water, a crowd of seals mewing and shrieking at him.

Spooky sat atop a stone watching Starker as he cleaned himself, his tail wrapped around his legs, the cat's hair flattened to his slender body.

Seal Rock crawled with seals and sea lions, and the black stone looked like a scoop of dark chocolate ice cream covered in ants. Puppy-like faces peered from the dark water, black eyes glistening. The beasts all watched the eleven like a flock of wayward birds, and they paid little attention to Starker as he trudged out of the sea, his muscles aching, his wet clothes clinging to numb skin. He shivered, the cold wind cutting through him.

The steady thrum of the coastie copter echoed over the water.

Starker sat on Spooky's stone and said, "You O.K.?"

"Meow. Meow."

The cacophony of barking and braying filled Starker's head, and he rubbed his temples. Seals and sea lions of every size slithered and walked about the black stone, males fighting as females watched. White bird droppings decorated the stone, and calves hid within the folds of their mother's enormous bodies. Seagulls shrieked and glided over the sea, plucking out small fish and pieces of discarded flesh.

Mirch had anchored his gray police boat fifty yards off Seal Rock and he was working a boom arm and transferring a fifteen-foot Zodiac with a small Yamaha outboard to the water. "Wait there!" yelled Mirch. The Lummi cop eased the Zodiac over the gunnel and dropped it in the water.

Starker waved, relief flooding through him. He hadn't felt in mortal danger bobbing about on the Pacific, but that was because he'd been too busy treading water and concentrating on breathing. Now, as he watched the eleven circle Seal Rock, and he listened to the chorus of sea lions and seals, it was clear how close Starker had come to biting the donut.

Spooky rubbed himself on Starker and meowed.

"You look like a drowned rat, brother," he said. Starker undid the top clasp of his lifejacket to relieve the pressure around his neck. He was shaking, the cold wind assailing him, mist blowing over the water and momentarily hiding Mirch and his police boat from view.

A horn sounded, and to the south the sheriff's boat eased past Seal Rock, cutting through the mist, its RADAR spinning, an array of spotlights slashing through the grayness.

An outboard sparked to life, and Starker lifted Spooky and placed him gently on his shoulder. The cat wasted no time making himself comfortable, the feline wrapping himself around Starker's neck like a scarf.

The Zodiac broke free of the mists and Mirch killed the small outboard and angled it up out of the water to avoid hitting the stones that littered the shallow water like landmines. The seals and sea lions brayed and barked at Mirch. Apparently, only visitors who swam to Seal Rock were accepted by the native population. The Zodiac hit bottom twenty feet from Starker, and he pushed up from the stone and waded into the foam-filled whitewater that rolled and eddied against Seal Rock.

"Holy hell," Mirch said as Starker approached.

Starker waded to the dinghy and transferred Spooky from his shoulder to the Zodiac, then climbed in as Mirch steadied the small boat.

"No claws on the sides," Mirch said. "You hear me, cat?"

Spooky stared up at Mirch as if he didn't understand the question, his wet eyes once again filled with superiority, the fear, and anger of the last fifteen minutes already in the feline's rearview.

"Cats," Mirch said, and chuckled.

Tall dorsal fins still circled Seal Rock, but Starker could only count seven.

Mirch was drenched, his long black hair matted to his head, his wet blue uniform almost black, and somewhere along the line he'd lost his badge. The Lummi cop's light brown skin was dappled with water, and he looked uncomfortable with his long slender legs wedged into the tiny boat.

"Thank you," Starker said. He took a deep breath and let it out slowly as he watched the tall dark dorsal fins scythe through the Pacific.

"No worries," Mirch said as he dropped the outboard. It roared to life, and Mirch spun the boat around and headed back to his police boat.

Spooky sat in the bow, staring at the red light atop the police boat as it spun in the fog. The gray vessel had Lummi Nation Police stenciled on its side in white, and its open pilothouse had no rear wall, and Starker saw the glow of flashing instrumentation within.

The Zodiac made fast work of the rough seas, and two minutes later the inflatable was massaging the police boat, the shriek of rubber scraping against metal like the cries of a dying sea lion.

Mirch scrambled up a Jacob's ladder and tied the Zodiac off on a cleat.

Starker followed, Spooky once again perched atop his shoulders, the wind tearing at them both. As soon as Starker was over the gunnel the feline jumped to the deck. Tail up, poop-shoot on display, the cat sauntered into the pilothouse, jumped into the copilot's seat, spun three times, and sat down.

Mirch laughed as he affixed the hoist cable to the Zodiac. "Cats were certainly bred as management," said the Lummi cop.

When the dinghy lifted from the water, Starker swung the boat into its holding cradles and helped Mirch collapse the boom arm.

The rattle of the anchor chain running over the bow rang over the ocean, the grumble of the anchor hoist like the steady crying of a giant mouse. The rain came again, tapping the pilothouse roof. Waves crashed against the boat, and it listed to port when the anchor pulled free of the water.

"What is this now?" Mirch said.

A line of dorsal fins heading east trailed away from Seal Rock, the orcas moving off.

"Where are they going?" Starker said.

Mirch enlarged the tracking window on his NAV screen. "They're heading inland. And they're moving fast."

22

Pala hooted when Starker reached Seal Rock. Her gut muscles relaxed, the acid creeping up her throat retreated, and relief flooded through her. It was like when her son had been hit by a car when he was five. Pala had seen it happening, like in slow motion, and for half a minute she wanted to kill herself only to see the boy bounce up uninjured like he'd been wrapped in bubble wrap. Now that feeling... She watched Starker crawl from the sea as the coastie who'd pulled her from the drink wrapped Pala in a blanket, helped her up onto a seat, and handed her a water.

The blanket was heavy, and as she sipped her water, warmth returned to her body, the tips of her fingers and toes pulsing with pain. Pala's gaze shifted from Starker to the bottom of her patrol boat as it bobbed and rolled on the tumultuous sea. Black clouds hung overhead, and a steady rain fell, the wind blowing out the three-foot waves that rolled east, lines of foam zigzagging over the inky water.

The coastie that rescued her wore a nametag that read Cureggio, and he was jabbering into a microphone connected to his flight helmet. Wind gusted through the open side door. Pala gripped the coastie's arm and said, "What's happening?"

Cureggio raised a hand, his blue flight suit billowing in the wind. Then he nodded to himself and slid the side door closed. The sound of rotors cutting through the storm filled the cabin, and Seaman Cureggio handed Pala a headset and motioned for her to put it on.

"Can you hear me?" he asked.

Pala adjusted the headset and said, "10-4."

The coastie threw her a thumbs up. "Good. Now you can hear inbound and outbound communications as well as talk with me and the pilot, whose name is Josephine Bender."

Pala returned the thumbs up.

"And my name is Ray." The coastie pointed at his nameplate. "Raymond Cureggio, but please call me Ray." He held out a slender hand.

Pala grasped the hand and said, "Thanks for pulling me out of the drink."

"Don't mention it."

A sharp retort formed in her mind, and she almost said, "But I'm sure you will. Many times." Instead, she smiled. Ray wasn't Joel... or Starker.

Thoughts of her partner caused Pala to inch over on her seat and peer through the window at the mayhem below. Starker was climbing onto the Lummi police boat, tall dorsal fins knifing through the Pacific all around the vessel. Relief filled her for a second time. Starker was safe... for the moment.

The Ocean's Eleven regrouped as they plowed through the sea, a juggernaut intent on crushing anything in their path. The transients were gone, and Pala could no longer see their retreating dorsal fins through the driving rain. Distant booms of thunder argued in the distance, the clouds to the west darker than night. The eleven formed up like a flock of birds heading south, the two massive males leading, their black and white conical heads dipping in and out of the water as the beasts leaped and dove through the sea.

Static crackled over the headset, then, "Coast Guard copter, this is the San Juan Sheriff's Department, do you copy?"

"We copy, over," came the bird's pilot.

"How may we assist?"

"Do you have a visual on the eleven?"

"Affirmative."

"Stay on them. Coast Guard vessels are inbound."

"10-4." Static, then nothing.

Pala watched the Ocean's Eleven peel around Seal Rock, not bothering to stop for a snack. The pod of killer whales was moving fast—Pala judged thirty-five knots, as they rose then dipped into the sea, powering through the Neah Bay Inlet. The beasts left a thick white wake, scattering the whitecaps that broke in sporadic patterns across the Strait of Juan de Fuca. Thick curtains of rain shrouded the horizon, windblown raindrops inching across the copter's windows like ants.

With the eleven racing inland, the sheriff's boat and the Lummi police vessel gave chase. The sheriff's boat hung back, but the Lummi vessel settled into the eleven's wake, the gray boat bouncing and listing.

Radio chatter filled her headset, various agencies calling in for status reports, offers of assistance, and updates about incoming support. The Coast Guard pilot ignored all the babble, but when Captain Raynard's voice boomed over the comm all the other voices fell away.

"What is your current position, USCG-6?"

The coastie pilot said, "Still on scene. Rescue boats are tracking the Ocean's Eleven by sea."

"Stay on the eleven. Support is en route, including drones, over."

"Copy that, Captain."

The Jayhawk's turbine cycled up, the whine of the rotors increasing as the pilot dipped the copter's nose and the craft darted forward into the curtains of rain.

Hills covered in evergreens rolled down to black rock-covered shores on both sides of the channel, boulders dotting the water like an obstacle course. Pleasure craft, fishing vessels, and tourist boats littered the Strait of Juan de Fuca despite the rain, and Pala's thoughts drifted to Joel. He had an afternoon tour, but most likely hadn't left yet and was still processing guests and preparing for departure. If the weather persisted as it had been, he would cancel the trip, so she didn't have to worry about him.

The Strait of Juan de Fuca opened up to the west, the eastern and southern horizon nothing but rain-clouded grayness. To the north, the eleven hugged the shoreline of Vancouver Island, and two people carrying fishing poles walked along one of the small dark sand beaches interspersed between the rocky outcroppings that ran all along the island's southern coast.

Two of the Ocean's Eleven broke off from the rest, cutting due north toward the two people walking on the beach, their rain slickers glistening in the gloom.

The comm burst to life.

"Sheriff and Lummi vessels, what is your estimated ETA to the eleven?" It was the coastie helicopter pilot.

Mirch's voice came over the line bathed in static, the wind and rain wreaking havoc with the communication systems. "Per our SONAR, we're a few minutes back."

"We've got a situation brewing," the pilot said. "Are you going flat out?"

"Nothing left here, over. Why?"

"Two males have broken away from the pod and are heading toward two people walking along the shoreline."

"Copy. Be there as soon as we can."

Captain Raynard broke into the conversation, "This is Captain Raynard. Lieutenant Bender, pursue and attempt to issue a warning."

"10-4," said the coastie pilot as she yanked on the craft's yoke. The copter dipped sharply to port as Lieutenant Bender arced the Jayhawk toward the charging orcas, rotors whining as they bit the air.

"Pala?" came a familiar voice over the comm.

"Starker!" she exclaimed more jubilantly than she'd intended.

"Are you O.K.?" he asked

"Fine. You?"

"A few bumps and bruises, mainly to my ego, but otherwise I'm fine. What's happening?"

"Looks like two of the mid-sized males are looking to pluck some prey from the shoreline like the other night. No way you can get there?"

"We're going full bo—"

"This is an emergency channel," an angry voice boomed over the comm. "Please cease all unnecessary chatter."

Starker went silent, and Pala pictured him standing next to Mirch, stewing, wanting to explain what they'd just been through, but Starker said nothing, and the comm crackled with static.

Below, the nine sea wolves still in formation plowed through the chop, a white line marking their passage like the wake of a cruise ship. The two that had broken away from the group were two hundred yards from shore, and the people strolling over the black beach still didn't appear to be aware of the danger, even though they were peering up at the helicopter as it raced toward them.

Lieutenant Bender brought the chopper in low, the rotor wash churning up the Strait of Juan de Fuca as the Jayhawk tracked the two rogue orcas. Ray got on the exterior comm, screaming warnings, but it wasn't until the helicopter hovered over the threatened people before they realized the danger and headed inland.

The stray orcas were a hundred yards offshore when they sensed their prey was on the move, and the killer whales changed course, swimming east again on a trajectory that would connect them with their pod.

Pala released a breath she hadn't known she was holding.

Boats crisscrossed the Strait of Juan de Fuca, but the orcas didn't appear to notice them. The apex predators surged through the channel, a loose knot of fury, teeth, and muscle. Pala's nerves danced just beneath her skin as she watched. She wanted to warn the boats. Tell them of the threat, but there was nothing she could do but watch, the sound of the copter's engine and the *womp womp* of its rotors cutting the air and filling her head with static.

The pilot arced the copter east, racing back toward the eleven who were clustered together again.

The rabid pod turned north at the Cattle Point Lighthouse, cutting up the San Juan Channel toward Friday Harbor. Pala could make out each killer whale as they looped out of the water, their tall dorsal fins cleaving the wind-torn sea, pectoral fins flexing. Flashes of white appeared in the dark rain-dimpled water, tail flutes driving the beasts through the channel with the force of an outboard, the current giving the orcas extra momentum.

A knot formed in Pala's stomach. It was 4:19 PM and Friday Harbor would be buzzing, despite the rain. The pinkies were running strong, and most fishermen believed the fishing was better in the rain, and she recalled her conversation with Starker about the topic. No. The fishing charters would be going full tilt, even if Joel wasn't.

Rocky beaches strewn with driftwood and flotsam lined both sides of the channel, and tall evergreens and green patches with houses at their centers filled the backdrop. Static leaked over the comm, but nobody spoke.

Pala searched for the sheriff's vessel and Mirch's boat, but she couldn't spot them in the driving rain. Time dragged out as the minutes fell away, the knot in Pala's stomach growing like a tumor.

Her worst fears were realized when the Ocean's Eleven arced west around Turn Island State Park toward Friday Harbor.

The comm exploded with conflicting reports and commands. Captain Raynard took control, but there wasn't much that could be done except attempt to warn the people in the harbor to take shelter away from the water.

Acid climbed up Pala's throat. There wasn't enough time.

The killer whales streaked past Brown Island and plunged into a field of moored boats scattered across the harbor. There were vessels of all sizes, shapes, purposes, and values. The boats were tied off on submerged mooring blocks, and round white buoys floated above each. A miniature tsunami rolled before the fist of whitewater created by the Ocean's Eleven, the boats in the harbor rocking and listing as the sea wolves approached.

The coastie pilot brought the Jayhawk down further until the sleek white craft was flying fifty feet from the surface of the water, the copter's rotor wash stirring the sea around the eleven, but they didn't appear to notice.

Like the explosion of two advancing armies coming together on the battlefield, the Ocean's Eleven jumped into, breached on, and nudged any vessel in their path. Small boats were swamped as orcas drove themselves from the sea, wide mouths open in toothy grins.

The killer whales strafed the moored boats, tall sailboat masts tipping precipitously, mooring lines snapping and pulling free. Loose boats slammed into moored boats like bumper cars, the eleven moving through the chaos, waiting for prey to fall into the water.

Pala gasped when she saw one of the calves toss a young woman in the air like a seal. The blonde came down hard on the water and didn't move as the orca bit into her, blood tinging the whitewater red.

"Shit," said Ray. Pala had been so intent on watching the chaos below she'd forgotten her rescuer was there. The coastie reached behind him, opened a cabinet, and pulled free a rifle.

"What are you going to do with that?" Pala asked.

"Something," he said. "Buckle-up."

Pala complied as Ray slid open the copter's side door, brought the rifle butt to his shoulder, and pressed his eye to the scope. He ranged the gun around and then brought down the rifle. "I can't get a clean shot. The rain, and too much movement." Ray screamed into his helmet mic. "Get me closer!"

The copter shuddered as it banked right, and Pala got a good look at the scene unfolding below

The Ocean's Eleven were tearing up the harbor, boats capsizing, and there were people struggling in the water. Pala shifted her gaze to the docks and the marina, the town of Friday Harbor perched on a hillside in the background. Despite the rain, people walked down Front Street, and workers and tourists packed the docks waiting to get on and off charters.

Pala's stomach knot exploded, acid shrapnel shooting up her throat and settling in her head, her nerves jangling, pain cramping her lower back.

23

The thumping of the Coast Guard helicopter as it streaked away reverberated over the Strait of Juan de Fuca. Waves broke on the bow of the Lummi police boat, throwing sea spray across the windshield. Mirch had the throttle arm pinned, the engine screaming as the thirty-foot V hull trailed after the Ocean's Eleven. Rain tapped on the pilothouse roof, and the wind blew rain through the rear open section of the cabin. The spray felt warm to Starker after being in the chilled Pacific, but the tips of his fingers and toes still throbbed with dull pain.

Mirch worked the ship's wheel, his face a mask of non-emotion.

Spooky was curled up at Starker's feet, the cat cleaning himself, his black hair wet and matted to his slender frame.

The eleven got a good head start, and their dorsal fins appeared and disappeared with the roll of the sea. Tension tightened Starker's neck muscles and lower back, each bounce and jolt of the boat knifing through the water sending a sharp pain up his back.

Starker and Mirch monitored the radio chatter and listened as the two orcas broke away from the rabid pod. Mirch told the coasties his old patrol boat was going as fast as it could, and when Pala came on the line, Starker felt the stress in him release.

The two rogues rejoined the pod and the minutes dripped away, rain pelting the metal roof, the boat rocking and listing, and the engine sang.

The sheriff's boat trailed after the Lummi boat, content to let Starker and the Lummi police take the lead. It was all for the good. He didn't know the deputy sheriff piloting the boat, but based on the young man's actions during the emergency, Starker wasn't impressed, yet he respected the young officer for letting more experienced personnel handle the situation.

A buzz rose over the wind and rain, the sound of a swarm of bees descending on a single drop of honey. The Coast Guard drone pulled up before the boat, surveyed the gray patrol vessel, then continued on its way.

Starker heard the coastie helicopter, but he could no longer see the Jayhawk through the rainy grayness. Brown Island appeared out of the gloom to the north, and Mirch spun the ship's wheel, arcing the vessel around the island into Friday Harbor. The engine sputtered and faltered as the boat knifed through a thick patch of seaweed, but after a few coughs and some white smoke, the engine recovered.

The RADAR and SONAR lit up like a Christmas tree, a field of boats of all sizes and shapes filling the screen. Mirch drew back the throttle arm and the boat slowed, the following sea slapping against the transom, and the vessel was pushed forward by the swell.

A great rending of metal pierced the day, the shriek and tearing of fiberglass booming over the harbor. The constant shriek and thump and pop as boats got pummeled, and the plop and shriek of water being displaced rising in a tumult as the boat lurched.

Spooky got to his feet, his dark wet eyes staring up at Starker as if to say WTF?

The police boat had careened into a moored pleasure craft, but the vessel appeared to be unoccupied. The damage was above the waterline, and the fiberglass bowrider had barely scratched the metal police boat, so Mirch worked the throttle and the wheel and moved around the vessel.

A tall dorsal fin scythed through the water beside the boat, a white eye patch slipping through the black water. The rain lessened to a faint drizzle, the wind pushing away the mist, swirls of fog dancing over the harbor.

The outer harbor was bedlam. Orcas streamed through the field of moored boats, and people struggled in the water as their vessels were swamped and pushed around. Screams of panic and wails of pain echoed over the water, and Starker's mouth fell open. This was his fault. He was supposed to track the orca, ensure they didn't get near people, and disturb the island's premier fishing season. He'd failed, and as he looked out on the destruction his heart sank, the familiar finger of helplessness poking and prodding him to do something, but what?

Mirch escaped his shock first, and worked the ship's wheel, delving deeper into the chaos. He yelled, "There's a store of lifejackets below. Get them." When Starker didn't move, the Lummi officer yelled, "Now!"

Spooky hissed and jumped into the copilot's seat before launching up onto the command console, where he peered through the windshield like he was the captain of the vessel.

The Coast Guard drone was nowhere to be seen, but the helicopter hovered over the outer harbor, and a seaman with a rifle hung out the open side door.

The police boat's engine whined as Starker stepped down into the forward cabin. The storage area was cluttered with lines, small buoys, life rings, and a pile of garbage that was mostly tangled fishing lines and netting. He scooped up as many orange lifejackets as he could carry along with some rope and brought them up on deck.

"There!" Mirch yelled.

Spooky screeched.

Mirch pointed off the port bow where an old woman bobbed in the churned-up water, her red sailboat on its side, her cooler of drinks and sandwiches scattered across the harbor. White patches streaked past her, tall dorsal fins towering over the woman as she called for help.

Starker tied a line to the end of one of the lifejackets and tossed it to the woman. He undershot her, but the woman wasn't deterred. She put her head down and swam hard, reaching the life preserver after five strokes. She grabbed the orange float and gave a thumbs up.

The line went taut in Starker's hands, and he hauled the woman in. Getting her over the side was a bit difficult, but it's amazing what people can do given the appropriate motivation. Starker helped the woman down into the cabin, and by the time he was back on deck, Mirch had a bead on their next rescue. The Lummi cop dropped the boat in neutral and the boat drifted as the two men hauled people from the drink.

The cuddy cabin was almost full when a gunshot rang over the harbor, then another, and half of the Ocean's Eleven started for the marina, leaving the rest of the pod to their business in the outer harbor.

The air was thick with the rusty scent of blood and the tangy-sweet smell of seawater. A blood slick dappled with chunks of fat and gristle streaked the water, and Starker saw an ear floating in the flotsam.

An orca breached beside the boat, and Mirch jerked the wheel and pushed the throttle arm down. The police vessel jumped from the water, and the beast came down next to the boat, the shockwave pushing the ship to port.

Spooky slid across the command console, shrieking, paws splayed out as he tried to steady himself.

A gunshot cut through the chaos.

The orca next to the boat wailed, the sound like a pig getting a rectal exam, and the beast rolled away, disappearing into the muddled water.

Ahead, two orcas tossed around a blonde-haired man dressed in a white suit. Starker's stomach tightened as he watched the tourist get torn apart by the two smaller shark-like orcas, the beasts biting and tearing into the man. It was very un-orca-like, but Starker reminded himself these weren't regular sea wolves. The crunch of breaking bones, and the slap and tear of muscle brought bile up Starker's throat, but there was nothing he could do for the man.

The drizzle ceased, and Starker saw the town of Friday Harbor perched on the hillside overlooking the harbor.

People crammed the marina, and a crowd of onlookers packed the end of the main dock as well as the floating docks that spidered out in a grid pattern from the central concourse. The boats in the marina rocked gently, but none of the eleven had moved in that close… yet.

"We need to get those people off the docks," Starker screamed.

"How the hell do you plan to do that?"

"Get me in there."

Mirch dropped the hammer and the police boat leaped from the water, spitting a rooster tail that drenched the boats behind it. The police boat weaved through the chaos as Starker tossed the last of the lifejackets, orca jumping and breaching from the water. The beasts looked swollen, their white patches tinged with red, gashes of bloody pustules crisscrossing their bodies.

Spooky recovered and jumped into the co-pilot's seat, but this time he didn't continue to the command console, but instead wrapped his tail around himself as he stared forward, though he was too low to see out the windshield.

Mirch jerked back the throttle control and the engine gurgled, water popping and snapping against the hull.

"Stay," said Starker as he pointed at Spooky, but he didn't think it would do any good.

Starker mounted the gunnel and prepared to jump onto the floating dock.

Spooky leaped across the gap between the dock and the boat. The feline didn't look back as he screeched and hissed at the assembled crowd that watched the pandemonium in the harbor with their mouths hanging open, cell phones in the air like cigarette lighters at a rock concert.

Starker jumped onto the steel dock, yelling as loud as he could, forcing the crowd toward land. People tried to slip around him, ignoring what Starker was saying, but when he drew his waterlogged Glock the greased skids of rationality prevailed. Shrieks of panic rose above the arguing crowd, but the throng inched down the dock, Starker and Spooky driving them back like cattle.

"Starker!" Mirch was standing on the police boat's gunnel, holding onto the pilothouse roof. "Pala says there's two coming our way!"

As the crowd merged onto the main path the exodus was backed up and slowed.

The metal dock trembled and shook, and Starker saw a fleeting patch of white through a gap in the metal decking. Every nerve in his body told Starker to run, but there was nowhere to go, and he—

"Help! Help!"

A woman had fallen in the drink, the swelling horde of humanity unaware they'd squeezed the woman off the dock.

Starker inched along the edge of the dock, got to one knee, and gripped the woman's hand. The lady smiled, her brown hair matted to her head, her hazel eyes alight with fear and appreciation. Starker managed to get hold of her other hand, then using his weight as leverage, he hauled her up.

A glint of black and white, a conical head surging from the water, a maw of teeth, then the sound of meat being torn and bones snapping.

Starker was jerked forward and sprayed with blood. He screamed, something in him snapping, his humanity shrinking to a single second. Starker still held the woman's hands, but the rest of her was gone, both arms severed at the elbow, tendons, muscle, fat, and gristle hanging from the limbs.

The water exploded, the dock lifted and bent, and Starker fell on his ass. Water spouted on both sides of the dock, all the boats rocking as if a hurricane was tearing through the San Juan Islands.

He dropped the arms, pushed to his feet, and ran. During his brief rescue attempt, the majority of the crowd had reached the main dock, and he mentally patted himself on the back for accomplishing something on this fateful day. Starker's legs pistoned, tight muscles cramping, his body still half numb with cold. He was running full out, the clang and crack of the dock being driven from the water behind him driving Starker on.

Spooky ran alongside him, but as Starker looked down to check on his partner the dock was nudged up by a killer whale and the cat sailed through the air and landed in the water.

Starker's brain didn't have time to process the halt command because the floating dock beneath his feet was driven up again, and Starker was flicked like a booger. The world spun; gray clouds, the silver metal of the dock, frothing white water, then blackness. He landed on his right side, the steel dock jarring him to the core. Water sprayed Starker as the dock surged up again, and for a second time, he was tossed like a piece of trash.

The last thing Starker saw before darkness took him was the dull metal of the dock, and a swollen red eye rimmed in yellow peering at him from within the whitewater.

24

Island Medical Center, Friday Harbor, San Juan Island, 3:50 AM PT, July 7th. Seventh day of Pink Salmon Season.

Starker came awake in darkness. Pale light leaked around the edges of the drawn window shades, and red and blue daggers of light from the machines belching and farting next to his bed knifed through the blackness. His mouth was dry, and he smacked his lips as he peered around. He wasn't dead, but in a hospital room. Starker took a deep breath and wiggled his fingers and toes. Everything worked, but it hurt when he breathed. He shifted his position and pain lanced his right side. A faint ringing pressed on the inside of his head, but as Starker closed his eyes and let his head sink deeper into its pillow the chiming eased.

He heard a sniffle, and Starker's eyes snapped open. A dark form sat within the folds of the curtains that surrounded his bed. He wanted to call out, but to who? His mother? Cindy? Pala? His stomach felt like it was filled with molten lava, and it hit home that he had no real friends, nobody that would care enough about him to travel to San Juan Island to see him. The thought sent a wave of self-pity rolling through him, and he thought of Spooky. Another sniff, almost a cough, and Starker said, "Hello?"

The figure got up, a light snapped on, and Pala said, "Starker! Welcome back."

"From?"

"I don't know," she said, smiling. "You tell me. You were the one that got knocked to Neverland."

Starker chuckled and his side hurt. "You saw that, did you?"

"I did. Too bad we didn't get a video of it. You'd go viral for sure."

"Did you… where's Spooky?"

Pala smiled. "He's at my house. The kids love having him around."

Starker smiled, and said, "How long was I out?"

Pala glanced down at her watch. "About eight hours. Two tourists fished you out. A little karma there."

He said nothing, his mouth dry as paper.

"Let me go get a doctor. They want to see you as soon as you wake up, and well, you're awake."

"Can I get some water first," Starker said. "Please."

Pala poured some water and Starker gulped it down. She refilled the paper cup and this one he sipped while Pala fetched his doctor.

Dr. Rajim Kapur was a large man, but not overweight. He had broad stocky shoulders, striking blue eyes, and long lanky arms. His glasses sat at the end of a hooked nose as he read Starker's chart.

Pala coughed, and Starker said, "Are you O.K.? Any injuries?"

"Other than my pride and a cold from being in the drink, I'm fine," Pala said.

The doctor shined his penlight in Starker's eyes and made him sit up so he could bang his knee with a little rubber hammer. When Starker almost kicked the doctor in the balls he was allowed to lay back down.

"So, everything has come back clean. No concussion, all the scans came up good and you have no internal injuries. As I'm sure you've felt, the entire right side of your body is lacerated and bruised. I'll give you something for the pain, and some cream for the wound, but other than that, you got lucky, Officer Starker."

"When can you spring me?"

"Your attending physician will be here in the morning, but I'd like to hold you for observation for forty-eight hours, including time served, but if everything goes the way I expect you can go home soon."

Home. Where was that again? Starker nodded and said, "Thank you for everything."

"You bet." The doctor dropped the chart into its holding sleeve on the door and added, "Oh, and a federal agent named Silva has been pestering us to see you if you're feeling up to it."

Starker and Pala exchanged glances.

"If you're not feeling up to it, I can—"

"No, no. It's fine. I'll see him."

Dr. Kapur smiled. "I'll leave him a message."

When the doctor left, Pala sat on the end of his bed and stared at the wall.

"What aren't you telling me?" Starker said. "What the hell happened out there after I... checked out?"

Pala shook her head. "It was a massacre. Nine dead, twenty-eight injured, though some of those are bruised egos and drama queens." She shook her head. "You and Spooky were fished out before the wolves could get you, and the beasts fled when the coastie cutter arrived and the shooting started."

"Shooting?"

Pala rolled her eyes. "It did scare them off."

"Where are they now?"

"The Coast Guard is tracking them and last I heard they're forty miles offshore."

Irrational relief eased the pulsating muscle in his neck, but the peace didn't last long. Forty miles was nothing, and the beasts could be back in the harbor in an hour. "So nothing is being done?"

"Not nothing, but…" Pala put a hand on his leg. "You'll hear all about it soon enough, but two clear factions have formed. One group wants to kill the beasts ASAP using military-grade ordinance, and another group—who I believe has the backing of the government—wants to trap the beasts somehow so they can be studied. Maybe get the Lummi to help."

"Trap them? How? That sounds impossible."

"It might be, but it's not your problem."

Starker lifted his eyebrows.

"The bigwigs called. You're to report to your new post in Seattle as soon as you're able," she said.

Silence filled the room.

Pala stood. "I'm going to head home and get some rest. I'll be back later."

"Thanks," Starker said.

Starker awoke with the rising of the sun to find a man of medium build with dirty-blonde hair and wearing a navy-blue suit and a blue tie waiting on him.

The man came forward, hand extended. "Name's Silva. John Starker?"

Starker nodded as he sat up in bed and the two men shook hands. "How can I help you, Agent Silva?"

Silva said, "Are you feeling O.K.? I heard you took a tumble rescuing people along the docks."

"Rescued? It was more like a warning."

"Semantics."

Starker said nothing.

"So, you're wondering what interest the FBI has in what's happened here?"

"A little," Starker said. "People are dead, but nothing crossed state lines."

"Based on what you know, that is true, but there's much you don't know."

No shit, Sherlock. He said, "What is it you do for the FBI?"

"I investigate anomalies."

"And that's why you're here? Because the Ocean's Eleven are an anomaly?"

"Partly," the agent said. "You know the legal spiel about confidentiality?"

"I do."

"And you're prepared to keep your mouth shut? I mean, I don't see what you could do with the information, but protocol is protocol."

Starker raised his right hand and said, "I swear."

That got a chuckle from Silva and the agent took a seat. "I've been tracking odd mutations in sea creatures for the last year. You may have heard about the incident at the drop off in the Atlantic?"

Starker nodded. "There were rumors that the research station burned to the sea, and nobody knew what caused it."

"First part is true, but the second..." Silva sighed. "The base was overrun by mutant sea spiders."

Starker licked his lips and said nothing. Sea spiders were harmless Arthropods, not predators.

"As it turned out, the creatures were infected with a mutation of chronic wasting disease. You know what that is, right?"

"It originated in deer, though we haven't seen cases out this way," Starker said.

"You have now."

Silence filled the room, the beep and moan of his monitoring equipment the only sounds.

"The bigheads are running tests on a sample mutant," Silva said. "Looking for a weakness."

"Weakness?" Starker said. "From what I can tell, bullets and fire would do the trick."

"Sure does."

Starker asked, "So, what then? Have the researchers found anything?"

"I'm not a scientist, but the bigheads tell me what they've found so far doesn't make any sense."

"Why's that?"

"For starters, the infected sea spiders' DNA doesn't match anything in the known records." Silva paused to let that sink in. Black bags as dark as night hung beneath the agent's eyes, his face marred with worry lines and weariness. "The only connections they've found so far aren't possible."

"Not possible? After everything I've seen in the last two weeks you can still honestly say something's not possible?" said Starker.

"The bigheads found odd macrophages in the sea spiders. Stuff that shouldn't be present four hundred miles offshore," Silva said.

"Macrophages?" Starker said.

Silva sighed. "I hope I get this right…" He looked at the ceiling as if recalling a conversation. "They're a type of white blood cell. Part of the immune system that engulfs and digests cellular debris, foreign substances—anything that doesn't have the type of proteins specific to healthy body cells of the organism it's in. The process is called phagocytosis."

"So there are macrophages in most living tissues?" Starker asked.

"Yes, but the type found in the mutant sea spiders is commonly found in salamanders," Silva said. "The scientists believe this specific macrophage is responsible for limb regeneration."

"Salamanders in the middle of the Atlantic?"

"Like I said, the facts don't add up."

"You said connections. Plural."

"The other is even stranger. The bigheads found prions," Silva said.

Starker's eyes went wide, and he hiked his shoulders.

"Prions are misfolded proteins. They cause chronic wasting disease. This type is specific to deer," Silva said.

"The zombie deer," Starker said. "But if a salamander can't get to the middle of the Atlantic, a deer sure as hell can't."

The chatter of voices filtered into the room and air moved through vents, his monitoring equipment beeping softly.

"Is this disease what was causing the die-offs that were being investigated?" Starker asked.

"Chronic wasting disease is fatal," Silva said.

"Did any of this show up in the dead fish they were studying?"

"The data cross-check showed prions. Different than what's in the sea spiders, but close enough."

"So now what?"

"We need more data, and based on what I saw, the eleven are infected with something. Whether it's the same disease that caused the mutation in the sea spiders, I don't know, but that's what I'm here to find out."

"So, you're in the 'try and trap them camp?'"

"I'm in the federal government's camp. But yes, the powers that be have made it a top priority to get any specimens that may appear to be infected… alive. I'm sure you saw the open wounds all over their bodies… the red eyes."

Starker nodded. "But so what? We can monitor the eleven and act as needed."

The agent shook his head. "I told you the sea spiders overran the base. What I haven't told you is they destroyed it after killing a bunch of people."

"So…"

"This is an issue of national security."

Starker said, "You mean someone wants to weaponize the mutated disease?"

"When in the course of history hasn't man used their greatest technological advancements for war?"

Starker said nothing.

"But that's not what I meant," Silva said. "The disease transforms otherwise harmless creatures into predators, and as more and more marine species are infected, soon the sea will be free of sea life except for the largest and most fearsome apex predators. Not to mention what the losses would do to the food supply, and the worldwide fishing industry that supports millions of workers."

Starker hadn't thought about that last part. He'd been so caught up in what was happening in his little corner of the world that he hadn't had the time, or the vision, to see the bigger picture. "So what are you doing here? Why me? I'm sure the WSCD could have hooked you up with a more experienced investigator."

"Yup," Silva said. "They could have."

Starker waited.

"But whoever they sent wouldn't have been kicked in the ass by the eleven. Wouldn't have your intimate knowledge of the situation."

"What is it you want? Exactly," Starker said. He was getting the loose feeling in his anus that was usually a prelude to him getting shit on.

"Not much," Silva said. "When are they springing you?"

"Sometime tomorrow... I mean later today."

"You'll miss the big briefing meeting today, but no matter. I know what the result will be."

"How?"

Silva licked his lips and smiled.

"Of course," Starker said.

"I'm going to push for the Lummi to assist us, and I need your and Pala's help with that."

"Ah, so this is really about Pala's connection with the Lummi Nation." Starker shook his head. "She hasn't been—"

Silva put up a hand. "Stop reading so much into everything and start thinking about a good spot to lure the Ocean's Eleven. Rest up today and I'll see you tomorrow at 8:00 AM. I'll get us a boat since Pala's boat is... under repair, and my support team is en route."

Before Starker could protest, the agent spun on a heel and left the room.

25

Island Medical Center, Friday Harbor, San Juan Island, U.S., 7:50 AM PT, July 9th. Ninth day of Pink Salmon Season.

A nurse brought Starker the clothes he'd been wearing when he was brought in. The garments were laundered and dried, his boots cleaned, and other than a tear in his jeans everything looked passable. As he dressed, he recalled his small room at the Stags Head Inn. It seemed like a hundred years since he'd last put on the clothes, but it had only been three days.

When he was done dressing, he wolfed down his breakfast before the nurse wheeled him to the exit of the medical center. Pala met him in the lobby, paperwork was signed, and Starker was officially sprung.

"How we doing this morning?" Pala asked.

Starker pushed up from the wheelchair, eager to be free of the hospital, though the two days of rest had helped. His bruised side had gone yellow around the edges, but it no longer hurt when he breathed, and if he limited the speed and abruptness of his movements, he found he could tolerate the pain.

The summer day was bright, warm, and muggy, the moisture from the storm leeching into the air. The sky was free of clouds, and the gasoline-tinged air smelled fragrant after the sterile antiseptic scent of the hospital.

Starker and Pala strolled toward the marina, the thin crowd breaking around them, Starker a little unsteady on his feet.

"How's my boy Spooky?"

Pala laughed. "Loving life. And I have to admit…"

"What?"

"There's something special about that furball. He's like having a babysitter around," Pala said.

Starker waited, eyebrows raised.

"Aurora was sneaking a snack the other night before dinner, and Spooky hissed at her. Even slapped her arm with his paw. I came in and caught her because I heard Spooky's mewing."

"I thought you didn't want a pet?"

"I don't," she said. "All I meant was the cat is… smart."

An awkward silence was filled with birdsong, the thump and clang of humanity preparing for the day, and the faint murmur of the wind.

"So what now?" Starker asked. "Have you met with Silva?"

She nodded. "Yup. Seems O.K.... for a fed."

"What's the deal with Seattle? Did Silva officially pilfer me?"

She nodded again. "Your new boss isn't thrilled, but when the FBI tells you something you don't argue."

"Unless you're a dumbass."

"You argued?"

Starker chuckled. "I didn't have a chance. What's the plan? Did you get..." Starker looked at the ground. He was the worst kind of insensitive ass. He'd been so concerned about his own situation that he failed to consider what his partner had to deal with. She'd lost her vessel, and that was right up there with losing your badge or gun. Worse because of the huge expense, and here he was poking the wound. He left the rest of his sentence unfinished, but the thought made him reach for the butt of his missing Glock, which he figured was on the bottom of the harbor.

"It's O.K.," Pala said as she noticed him reach for his weapon. "The sheriff has your gun, and we'll get it back to you. And transport is covered. Silva has a fancy black Zodiac with a big boy gun in the bow, but that boat will be acting as support."

Starker pursed his lips, but said nothing.

"Mirch has been assigned to us, and the three of us are to meet Captain Raynard at Lummi admin. He's waiting for us."

Starker nodded and said, "Any new restrictions?"

"The basics. Only commercial boats and pleasure craft over thirty feet. And no swimming, which after what happened in Friday Harbor didn't need to be said."

The duo reached the marina, the scent of bacon, gasoline, and coffee thick in the air. Silva fell in alongside them and Starker jumped when he noticed the agent. "Aren't you annoyingly stealthy," Starker said.

Silva hiked his shoulders. "Part of the gig. Mirch is out at the end of main dock."

The marina had been mostly put back together, but some of the floating docks hadn't been replaced and a pile of twisted metal and destroyed boats sat behind the fishery like a zit on a pristine face. The people of Friday Harbor went about their business, but Starker felt the tension just below the surface. Innocence was lost, and the picturesque town of Friday Harbor would never be the same, and its residents wouldn't forget the day their peace was shattered.

"Yo!" Mirch stood on the gunnel of his gray police boat, waving much the same way he'd been last time Starker saw him. "There he is, and in one piece." The Lummi cop jumped off the boat and hugged Starker. "Thought I'd lost you."

"I see you made it out O.K."

"Not before rescuing nineteen people," Pala said.

"Mirch, have you met Agent Silva?"

"I have."

Cops of all colors hated one thing universally; when a higher authority swooped in and took over.

The silence was filled with an incoming seaplane, the cry of gulls, and the rumble of boat engines.

Pala stared across the harbor, and Starker followed her gaze and saw Joel working on his boat.

Silva stepped up onto the gunnel of the police boat, and said, "I'm no seaman, and this boat is no Coast Guard cutter, but I think Mirch is in command when we're on his vessel. Do we all agree?" the agent said.

"You'll be riding with us then?" Starker said.

"As I told you, I want to be where the experience is."

Mirch grunted.

"So are we in agreement?" Silva said.

Nodding heads and Mirch grunted again.

"O.K. Let's get on with it then. I don't want to be late We've got Chairman Spollomen at nine."

"The chief will be there also," Mirch said, and when he saw the blank stares, he added, "The Chief of Lummi Police."

With everyone onboard, Mirch piloted the boat out of the harbor and set a course due east. He cycled up the motors, and soon the police boat was chugging at thirty knots, throwing spray as the vessel arced around the southern tip of Shaw Island, past Canoe Island and Flat Point, and across Eastsound. Orcas Island loomed to the north, and Mirch slowly turned the ship's wheel, arcing the police boat around Obstruction Island.

A knot of big fishing charters clogged Obstruction Pass. Silver scales glistened in the bright sun, and the sound of exultation fluttered over the sea.

"How's the haul been?" Starker asked. The WSCD didn't literally count every pink salmon pulled from the water, but there were limits.

"Nobody's complaining, and the big boats are still heading out despite the… the disturbance," Mirch said.

"People feel safe in boats," Silva said. "At least the ones who haven't studied all the cell phone footage of the Friday Harbor Massacre."

"Friday Harbor Massacre?" Starker said. "A bit grand and showy, don't you think?"

"I do," Silva said. "I'm just parroting our relentless and often misinformed media." Pala opened her mouth to speak, but Silva put up a hand. "I know that's no excuse... but shit. Does pink salmon taste that good? We're up to sixteen dead since the kayaker got killed."

Silva's question hung out there like a fart in church as Mirch piloted the boat north along the Rosario Strait. The wind was a weak puff out of the west, and the strait was flat, save for tiny white wind-blown ripples that laced the sea. The green shores of Orcas Island and Cypress Island fleeted by to the north and south, Lummi Island a distant smudge on the eastern horizon.

"Just so we're on the same page," Silva said, "I spoke with Captain Raynard last night, and regardless of what is decided today, he'll be increasing his patrols and the Navy is on the way. They plan to station patrol vessels at the major harbor entrances, and they will not hesitate to use deadly force if Captain Raynard feels the eleven are putting lives in jeopardy. The Sheriff's Department and the WSCD are to patrol the Salish Sea."

"I've given some thought to possible holding areas for the beasts, and perhaps Reid Harbor on Stuart Island could work. It has a small mouth, it's deep, and there's hardly any residential structures along its edge," Starker said.

"Ding, ding," Silva said. "We have a winner. That's the site that was selected, based on Pala and Captain Raynard's recommendation."

Pala said, "Starker and I talked about this in the hospital. It was his idea, I just passed it on."

"Irrelevant," Silva said. "What's important is that we have a spot I think the Lummi can work with."

Mirch powered down the boat as the vessel roared around the northern tip of Lummi Island into Lummi Bay. The boat's speed dropped to a crawl and Mirch piloted the vessel through a narrow winding channel that led to the Lummi shellfish hatchery. A zodiac with orange inflated gunnels and a silver pilothouse waited at the end of a long dock, and Captain Raynard stood talking to a woman dressed in a blue dress decorated with white flowers.

The police boat bumped the dock and Starker and Pala tied her off.

"Morning," said Captain Raynard.

Introductions were made all around, and Lummi Chief of Police, who had introduced herself as Kendra, led the group down a concrete roadway atop the dam that marked the southern portion of the hatchery. Water roared through the spillway, and pumps hummed and buzzed as they walked through a series of buildings to a waiting police car.

Lummi headquarters wasn't what Starker expected. After a brief drive down a wooded lane, the entourage arrived at a red brick building. The American and Lummi Nation flags flew above a carport, and as the police car came to a stop, Starker marveled at how modern the building looked. Somewhere deep within his white man bias mind, he'd expected a giant teepee or a rounded adobe, but instead what he saw was a building that wouldn't look out of place in any rural town in the United States.

Starker and his companions were ushered into a conference room, where they were met by several of the chairman's aids.

"He's running a few minutes late," said a petite woman with long dark hair and a light brown complexion. "He'll be in shortly. Do you need AV?"

Silva looked around at the assembled, saw no wagging heads, and said, "I don't think so."

The group waited in silence, the sound of air pushing through a vent on the ceiling filling the room.

Like the Lummi administrative building, Chairman Spollomen wasn't what Starker had expected, his mind again conjuring up clichéd and outdated images of what the leader of an American Indian tribe should look like. He'd seen the chairman's face on the TV in the sheriff's conference room and heard his voice, but the limited perspective didn't do the man justice. He wore a dark gray suit, dress shoes, and a Lummi Nation pin on his collar. His hair was gray, short, and slicked back. The only thing that said Lummi Indian to Starker was the bolo tie, its gemstone blue and red. The chairman looked like he belonged trading stocks on Wall Street, not seeing to the affairs of the Lummi Reservation.

The chairman shook hands, everyone was introduced, and the Lummi Nation's top man got right down to business. "Normally I would offer you folks a tour of the hatchery and our new school, but excuse me if I skip the diplomatic pleasantries."

The faint sound of a laser printer pushing sheets leaked into the conference room.

When nobody spoke up, the chairman continued. "Kendra has fed me the basics. You want our help trapping the Ocean's Eleven using our reef netting technique."

Silva said, "That's correct. We need to study these creatures so we can figure out what's infected them. This situation isn't the first of its kind."

"Do you know why orca are called killer whales?" the chairman said.

Starker didn't, but he was sure some of the others did, though nobody spoke.

"Orcas were given the name 'killer whale' by ancient sailors who observed groups of orcas hunting and preying on larger whale species and sharks. The first written description of an orca describes them as enormous masses of savage flesh with teeth. The Lummi, however, see things differently."

"That's exactly why the U.S. government thinks you can help. We don't want to hurt the eleven. We just want to study them."

"Where? The Lummi Nation can take no responsibility for the housing of the creatures."

"Not to worry," Captain Raynard said. "We've picked a good spot. Reid Harbor on Stuart Island."

The chairman nodded. "Narrow mouth, but it's deep. I don't think our nets can handle it and our vessels certainly can't."

"All we need is your best reef fisherman. We'll use the cutter and other heavy boats to deploy the nets, which can be reinforced, right?"

"We have Kevlar strand reinforced nets, but they're not up to the task," Chairman Spollomen said.

"If we provide chain and Kevlar line, can you reinforce enough netting to span the gap? If we provide enough vessels?" Silva asked.

"Perhaps," the chairman said. "How will they be fed?"

"The Lummi Nation does a ceremonial feeding of pink salmon to the orca each season, yes?"

The chairman nodded.

"Any reason you can't supply the expertise for the ritual, the manpower, and we'll supply the fish?"

Chairman Spollomen looked at one of his aides. "There will be a fee for the manpower. Will that be an issue?" said the aide.

"Not in the slightest," Silva said. "I've got my government credit card."

Nobody laughed.

The group went on to discuss the creation of chum, a large baitball, and a supply of mackerel and sardines to lure the beasts in.

"I'd like our police boats on scene at the netting site," the chairman said. "Kendra and Mirch will oversee that part of the operation."

Silva said, "Not a problem."

Speed of supply deliveries and other logistical issues were discussed and hashed out, and when the meeting broke forty-two minutes after beginning, a plan was in place. They would commence trying to trap the eleven when preparations were complete, which was expected three days hence. In the meantime, Pala, Starker, and Mirch, along with sheriff boats and a host of coastie vessels and drones would trail after the creatures when they ventured too close to shore.

"Captain Raynard," said Chairman Spollomen as the meeting broke up. "Please keep in mind that if deadly force is used when not completely necessary, I will recant my offer."

The captain said nothing, but Starker felt the heat in the room rise.

26

Reid Harbor, Stuart Island, U.S., 1:50 PM PT, July 14th. Fourteenth day of Pink Salmon Season.

The clang of metal on metal, the shriek of tightening ropes, and the cries of angry seagulls carried over the water. All pleasure crafts had been removed from the bay, and a knot of boats waited to the south and north, the harbor mouth already partly sealed off. Hills packed with evergreens fell to the water's edge, the underbrush a brown-green blanket of field grass and vegetation. Black stone covered in slick moss ran along the shoreline and fell into the depths to a sea floor covered in black mud.

Starker and crew had spent five uneventful days tracking the Ocean's Eleven as preparations were completed for the mission affectionately dubbed Catch Willy. The rogue orca pod had ventured inland several times to feed on harbor seals, but thanks to the armada of Coast Guard, sheriff, and WSCD vessels the beasts were directed away from civilization. Several times fishing charters had been forced to move because the orcas wanted pink salmon for dinner, but there hadn't been another incident and Captain Raynard had retreated to his cutter, which was the centerpiece of the blockade.

Mirch, Pala, Silva, and Starker were on the Lummi police boat, the vessel floating with the current away from the chaos surrounding the Reid Harbor mouth. Starker took a pull of water as he watched the Lummi fishermen prepare the net for deployment. The Kevlar strands and thin chain sparkled in the sunlight like tiny diamonds were woven into the nets. He glanced down at a white food container bucket and next to it a large rubber storage container. One contained the chum, the other the baitball.

Pala said, "You should have seen Spooky last night." She shook her head and chuckled. "We're watching T.V., and suddenly he vaults to his feet, staring out the front window. I was like, what is this crazy animal doing." She shook her head.

Starker turned to look at her, sipped his water, but said nothing. Gulls screamed and the rank scent of low tide crawled into his nose.

"One of Joel Jr.'s friends was sneaking around the house. Bringing him a toy or some shit. I think the kids were planning to sneak out." She shook her head again. "Spooky."

Regardless of how things went with the eleven, Starker's time in the San Juan Islands was almost at its end, and the looming decision of what to do about Spooky weighed on him. Part of him—a big part—wanted to bring the cat to Seattle with him, but was that fair? To Spooky? And did people give a shit about how cats felt? Did the felines care? He knew dogs got worked up over all kinds of bullshit, only to forget it all five minutes later. Dogs adapted. Did cats? He wasn't sure, but as he sucked in the fresh air and gazed out on the blue water and green trees he wondered if Spooky would like living in a city. Then there was Pala's children. They were—

The radio crackled. "Mirch, do you copy? It's Raynard."

"We're here." Mirch's worried gaze shifted from Silva to Starker to Pala.

"Looks like the eleven are on their way in. An aerial drone has them tracking up the coast to the inlet. Everything a go there?"

"We're a go," said Silver.

The team had been hanging around for days, and Starker was ready to get this done or fail trying. He couldn't take floating around on the Salish Sea any longer or he might lose his mind. Nature was good for the soul, but too much of a good thing dulled it.

Silva got on his SAT phone and ordered his backup team to meet him out on the Strait of Juan de Fuca.

Starker checked in with the coasties on scene and verified the Lummi fishermen were ready.

"Let's go get them," Silva said, and he smiled.

Starker's stomach went sour. Silva reveled in the hunt, Starker didn't. When he'd first arrived, chasing the orcas around was different, fun almost, but the massacre at Friday Harbor changed all that. He wanted this done, whatever that meant, but the dull pain in his side reminded him he had a score to settle.

Mirch cycled up the motor, brought the boat about, and eased down the throttle lever as the engine roared and the police vessel came up on plane. Tension leaked through the boat, everyone except Starker lost in a task. Silva stood in the bow, binoculars pressed to his eyes as he scanned the sea. Mirch and Pala worked the helm, Pala adjusting the SONAR and Mirch arcing the boat around boulders, knots of fishing vessels, and patches of propeller killing seaweed.

Wind gusted out of the east, and the Strait of Juan de Fuca was a blown-out mess, tiny waves breaking in every direction, whitecaps dotting the surface like un-melted drifts of snow on a blue field. As they raced toward the inlet, vessels of all shapes, colors, sizes, and affiliations fell in behind them, including Silva's black Zodiac that looked straight out of a James Bond film.

Silva made his way along the gunnel and slipped into the pilothouse, which had no rear bulkhead. "Do we want to give some directions? Just so there's no confusion?"

"Let's get eyes on them first," Starker said. Then realizing he wasn't in charge, added, "But yes, we should reiterate everyone is to stay back unless called for."

The rocky shoreline of Vancouver Island fleeted by to the north, the green hills of the Makah Indian Reservation to the south. Seal Rock loomed in the distance like a black stain, a dark cloud of gulls circling the small island as if it was a chicken processing plant.

"Trackers and SONAR showing the eleven off Seal Rock," Pala said.

"What angle do you want me to come in on?" Mirch said.

"The tide is coming in, right?" asked Silva.

"Yes," said Starker, Pala, and Mirch in unison.

"High tide is 4:19 PM," Pala finished.

Silva chuckled and said, "Know the tides. Noted."

"I know what he's thinking," Starker said. "Do we want to chum?"

Pala said, "It's a long way and we can't run a chum slick all the way to Stuart Island."

"Let's see if we can get them on the hook before we start reeling them in," Silva said.

Starker stared at the agent and Pala and Mirch looked over their shoulders, smiling.

"That better?" Silva said.

"A little," Mirch said. He arced the ship's wheel, bringing the boat around to the eastern side of Seal Rock. Seals barked, the brown animals covering the dark rock like slugs on a fallen apple. The air was thick with the scent of rot and salt, the constant braying and arguing carrying over the surface of the water.

Tall dorsal fins knifed through the sea, patches of white appearing and disappearing as the Ocean's Eleven circled Seal Rock.

"So who's going to do the dirty?" Mirch asked. He gripped the ship's wheel, his gaze forward as if to say it isn't going to be me.

Silva played with his SAT phone and said nothing.

Pala said, "I'll help."

Starker shrugged. He'd done nothing to earn his pay on this day so he saw no way he could refuse. He bent and searched a bag at his feet, looking for a t-shirt or some such to cover his nose and mouth.

"No need," Pala said, and she fished out medical masks.

"You've done this before," Silva said.

"Sadly, yes," Pala said, but she was smiling.

Starker and Pala masked up and Starker carried the white food bucket to the rear of the boat, balancing it on the gunnel as Pala peeled off the lid.

The smell that assailed Starker was like nothing he'd ever experienced. He'd discovered dead animals, and human corpses, he'd even visited the corpse flower when it was in bloom at the Seattle Arboretum, but the scent that filled his nostrils now made all that seem like a field of roses on a hot summer's day.

The chum was a concoction of the Lummi fishermen. What it contained, Starker didn't know, but as he looked down into the pail of brown sludge, he saw streaks of blood, small bones, and rotting flesh floating within a viscous fluid that could only be described as the devil's soup.

"Jesus," Mirch said.

"Smells dead longer than that," Silva said. The agent stood in the open pilothouse as far from the chum bucket as possible.

Starker adjusted his mask, the reek of the chum burning his eyes. "Ready," he squeaked out.

The eleven had plucked a young harbor seal from atop a rock and were tossing the dead animal around like they were in a circus and the corpse was a beachball.

"Depth is six feet and dropping," Pala called out.

Mirch dropped the police boat into neutral and gunned the engines to get the beast's attention as the tide tugged the boat east away from Seal Rock.

Starker struggled to hold back his lunch, a BLT that was doing its best to make a curtain call. The stench was overwhelming, and his eyes dripped into his mask as he tipped the bucket, pouring a thin stream of the nasty special sauce into the churning water. The surface turned red, pieces of decayed fat and flesh floating in the oily slick as it trailed east with the current, away from Seal Rock into the Strait of Juan de Fuca.

For several minutes nothing happened. The police boat floated lazily inland with the current as Starker fed the channel chum, the slick spreading out and trailing behind the boat.

One of the eleven caught the scent of blood and left its pod mates to investigate. It was one of the shark-like calves, and the beast knifed through the chum slick, its black and white conical head lifting from the water, its massive mouth open as it sucked in the special sauce. But as fast as the young orca had appeared, it was gone, its dorsal fin cycling back to its pod.

Starker stopped pouring chum into the sea, placed the bucket on the deck, and laid the top loosely atop the pail. His legs ached from the constant balancing and shifting, his sea legs worn out, and his bruised side pulsed with pain. He said, "I'm going to conserve this stuff." When nobody protested, he added, "The slick is big enough, right?"

Mirch said, "I think they may need a little more motivation."

"What do you mean?" Silva said.

Mirch sighed like he was talking to morons. "Why would the beasts eat burgers when they can get filet mignon?"

Starker's face screwed up, then he got it. The seals. The orca would never follow a blood slick if seals were easily available. "So we need to get rid of the cows."

"Right," Mirch said.

Silva looked around in confusion, his eyes meeting Starker's.

A confused Fed wasn't Starker's responsibility, so he said nothing.

"Pala, do you care to do the honors?" Mirch said.

A gust of wind tore at Pala's hair, and she shrugged. "Get me in as close as you can."

Mirch nodded as he put the vessel in gear and piloted the police boat within a fish scale of the jagged black rocks that filled the ocean floor around Seal Rock.

Pala went to the bow and Starker trailed after her. "Anything I can do to help?" he asked.

She shook her head no and drew her Glock. Tiny waves broke on the boat's bow, the wind spraying the deck with water. Pala rolled her shoulders and braced herself against the gunnel. She chambered a round and sighted the weapon on a dark patch of stone at the center of Seal Island. Starker heard her exhale, and then two shots rang out over the water.

Both shots hit home, smacking the black stone, the crack reverberating over the sea, shards of rock spraying the nearby seals and sea lions. The beasts closest to where the gunshots struck scattered, pushing their fellow mammals around like a crowd escaping a concert during a fire. Pala squeezed off six more shots, choosing large stones and spots that had already cleared out.

Seals and sea lions slithered and jumped into the water all around Seal Rock, their gray and black forms streaking through the water and disappearing into the depths. A silence fell over the scene as the barking and braying ceased, the hissing of the orcas' dorsal fins scything through the ocean rising above the wind, the scent of cordite thick on the breeze.

The Ocean's Eleven stopped circling Seal Rock as they broke formation, dorsal fins swaying, tail flutes surging from the sea.

"The gunshots don't appear to affect the beasts anymore," Silva said.

"See the gunshot wounds on the big one?" Mirch said.

Silva brought up his binoculars, but said nothing.

Minutes ticked away, the wind, current, and tide pulling the police boat east. Mirch killed the engine, and Starker and his team watched as the chum slick dissipated.

The Ocean's Eleven started out to sea.

"Can we give this another go before we head in?" Silva asked.

"Engage them on the open water?" Mirch said, and the tone of his voice left no doubts that he believed this to be the dumbest idea he'd ever heard.

"Not engage, but entice," Silva said. "Lay the slick right in their path."

"You better decide fast, they're angling southwest toward deep water," Pala said.

Silva said, "Your call, Mirch."

"Fine. Hang on then," said the Lummi cop as he pressed down the throttle arm and the boat jumped from the water. The vessel bounced and hopped as it cut across the sea, passing Seal Rock on the port side on a course that would cut across the Ocean Eleven's path.

Starker took up his position again with the chum bucket, wind tearing at his hair, the mist rising above the transom from the churning propellers coating him with cool moisture.

To the southwest the Ocean's Eleven jumped and dove through the Pacific, their dorsal fins swaying, pectoral fins stroking the sea.

Mirch cut across the pod's path and Starker loosed his stink, the toxic soup covering the surface of the ocean. Pieces of blackened skin, chunks of fat, and bones floated east with the current. Starker had forgotten to pull on his mask, and the scent worked its way down his nostrils and set up camp. He knew it was going to take months to free himself of the smell, but as he poured the chum, he found himself thinking of Spooky, Seattle, and the life he'd chosen.

The police boat arced north as Mirch slowly turned the ship's wheel, the vessel coming around in a wide circle and heading back toward the inlet.

Starker continued to dribble chum into the churning sea, and this time the orcas took notice. Without the seals and sea lions on the menu, one of the younger orcas strayed from the protected boundary of the pod. The shark-like beast surged through the sea, its dorsal fin leaving a wake of whitewater. Above, seagulls argued, and a clock in Starker's head ticked louder and louder.

27

"They're almost on the hook," Silva said into his SAT phone. "Prepare to move in and pick me up."

The plan was for Silva to transfer to his boat and fall in behind the Ocean's Eleven as Starker laid out the chum and baitball from the Lummi police boat. It had sounded so simple back on land, and sitting on a steady boat watching the Lummi deploy their nets. Out on the rocking windswept sea, Starker wasn't so sure they could pull it off. The timing had to be perfect, the entire team's execution without flaws. Even if that happened the eleven might decide to just give up and turn around, and they'd have to start all over tomorrow. Would a delay be so bad? Seattle sat in his stomach like bad clams, but a reckoning was coming.

"Starker, you awake?" Silva called.

Stirred from his reverie, Starker nodded.

"Give the update," the agent said.

Starker nodded again as he picked up the comm handset. "To all vessels. The eleven are almost on the hook. Standby to begin transport. Lock off our route and keep all vessels out of our path and be prepared to make adjustments. Issue local warnings as deemed necessary. Starker out."

Silva rubbed his palms together and said, "Let's go catch us some fish."

"Mammals," Pala said. The wind chose that moment to shower the back of the Lummi police boat, spraying into the back of the open pilothouse.

The Ocean's Eleven had come back together like a herd of gazelles running from a lion. The largest matriarch pushed forward, nudging aside the youngster who was plunging its massive black and white head through the mess of blood and fat, chuffing and squeaking as if asking for more.

"Let's get going," Silva said.

Mirch put the police boat in gear and the vessel inched forward through the chop, the Ocean's Eleven falling in behind them.

Starker continued to dribble chum into the sea, the smell so rancid Silva coughed every few seconds, and Pala had gagged twice.

The buzz of a bee swarm rang over the sea and the coastie drone zipped by. It hovered over the eleven, but stayed high so as not to spook the beasts.

"Bringing up drone view," Pala said. She worked a keyboard and the Coast Guard feed appeared on the NAV screen. She resized the window, and the display was filled with an ariel view of the eleven.

The rogue pod was coming on fast, dipping and surging through the Strait of Juan de Fuca, drawn on by the scent of blood and potential prey. Pus-filled gashes covered all the animals, their once obsidian eyes blown-up red masses tinged with yellow.

"Still hard to believe," Pala said. She'd spun her seat around and was gazing back over the transom at the eleven dorsal fins tracking the chum slick.

"Not based on what I heard, and the pictures I saw," Silva said.

"The incident at the drop off?" Starker said.

Silva nodded. "When the Navy arrived there wasn't much left, and I scoffed when I was told sea spiders had been the cause of the damage. 'You mean those spindly creatures that get sucked away in a gentle current?' I mocked. Yeah, those, and when they showed me the sample..." Silva shook his head. "Let's just say the disease transforms creatures in ways never before seen."

"Any thoughts on what caused it?" Mirch asked. His eyes never left the sea before him.

Silva shrugged. "What causes any anomaly? We still don't know everything about the zombie deer version of wasting disease. This mutation could take years to unravel, which is why we need the eleven. Alive."

That last part sent a tremor of angst climbing up Starker's spine. He had so many questions, but he wasn't sure he wanted to hear the answers.

"Heading north up the Haro Straight," Mirch said as he worked the ship's wheel.

Starker poured the last of the chum into the sea. "Prepare to deploy the baitball," he said.

Silva's boat had fallen in behind the eleven, a shining dark form like a toy Darth Vader might play with in the bathtub. Behind Silva's crew a line of sheriff and coastie vessels formed a blockade a guppy couldn't get through, and police, WSCD, coastie, and sheriff's vessels waited offshore of Vancouver Island to the west and the rocky shoreline of San Juan Island to the east.

Starker stowed the empty chum bucket and grabbed a two-hundred-foot length of polyethylene line.

Silva pried the lid off the large rubber container on the aft deck, and he took a step back as the harsh scent of rotten flesh assailed him.

"Damn," Pala said. "It's worse than the chum."

"The Lummi know their shit," Silva said, and this time he got a laugh from everyone for his double entendre.

The baitball was a teabag of rottenness. Within a tight netting was wrapped all kinds of rancid flesh tied together with fishing line. The bottom of the holding container was filled with viscous fluid and as Starker and Silva lifted the stinky mess it dripped diluted blood and animal entrails. There was a carabiner tied to the rope that bound the baitball together like a ball of fresh mozzarella, and Starker affixed the polyethylene line to it. "Ready!" he yelled.

Mirch grunted and Silva nodded as he positioned himself next to the massive ball of rank flesh.

Without slowing the police boat, Starker and Silva lifted the baitball and tossed it over the side. It hit the water and disappeared under a mound of whitewater before bobbing back to the surface.

Starker grabbed the line and let it play out through his hands as the baitball receded into the distance, the Ocean's Eleven coming on like a pack of giant rats. When the two hundred feet of line was almost played out, Starker tied the end off on an aft cleat and slapped Silva on the shoulder. "Good work, mate," he said.

Silva chuckled. "I think I need to spend a bit more time on physical training." He straightened himself and rubbed his neck.

With a sharp *twang*, the line towing the baitball went taut, and the teabag of nastiness jerked and bounced through the tumultuous sea, the Haro Strait a jumbled mess of whitecaps and ribbons of foam.

"Let's take her up a few knots, shall we?" Silva said.

Mirch looked over his shoulder, eyeballed the baitball, then depressed the throttle arm further. The boat's engine roared, the propeller clawing the water, sea spray drenching the police boat as it knifed up the strait.

Silva brought up his SAT phone. "Come get me." He slipped the phone into a pocket and turned to Pala. "Tell the lead sheriff boat to backfill my crew."

Pala nodded and issued the command as the black Zodiac headed toward San Juan Island and gave the eleven a wide berth. The sleek vessel jetted above the sea, its propellers the only part of the vessel touching the water.

Silva zipped his windbreaker and mounted the starboard gunnel, holding onto the pilothouse roof for support. The Lummi police boat listed and swayed as it cut up the Haro Strait, the wind pushing everything east like a disruptive person in a crowd.

The FBI boat came in hot, jumping over the rolling waves created by the Lummi police boat's wake. The Zodiac's pilot brought his vessel parallel with the police boat, matched its speed, and slowly inched west, closing the gap between the two boats.

"See you on the other side," Silva said.

When the black Zodiac was a foot away from the police boat Silva deftly stepped over the gap onto the black inflated gunnel. He waved as the Zodiac's pilot eased up on the throttle and spun the ship's wheel, the black boat falling away.

With the blood slick in the rearview, the Ocean's Eleven had commenced taking stabs at the baitball as it was dragged north through the Haro Strait. Dorsal fins swayed, tail flutes pounded the surface, and pectoral fins flopped and stroked the sea, a knot of whitewater forming around the baitball, driving it out of the water.

Silva's boat retook its position behind the eleven, and the odd armada sped north at thirty knots.

One of the matriarch's massive tooth-filled maws clamped down on the baitball, and the police boat's engine stuttered, and the tow line stretched and twanged, but didn't break. The baitball flew from the orca's mouth like a cannon shot, and two other orcas strafed the bag of rancid flesh, tossing it in the air with their snouts like they were playing with a seal corpse. Like a horse trough at a popular saloon, access to the baitball was limited to the larger creatures, and as the older killer whales attacked the bait, the two shark-like calves broke off from the pod, circled around in a wide arc, and went after Silva's boat.

"Are you seeing this?" Pala said.

Starker tore his gaze from the sea and looked over Pala's shoulder as she stared at the drone feed via the Coast Guard cutter.

The two smaller orcas took up positions on either side of the black Zodiac, but the FBI vessel held its course, trailing after the baitball as it was dragged through the water like a downed water-skier who won't let go of his tow rope.

Mirch arced the Lummi police vessel around Henry Island and set course for Stuart Island.

Pala opened a channel. "To all vessels, this is the shepherd, and we're bringing in our sheep. Prepare to close the nets."

Without warning one of the orcas running alongside the FBI Zodiac bumped the black vessel, and it listed to port. At thirty knots the small adjustment caused the Zodiac's bow to dip, and the boat caught a wave full on, like a skier catching an edge, and seawater surged over the vessel's sides. The pilot of the FBI boat was skilled, which was easy to see, and the Fed deftly adjusted his course, pushing off the wave and moving away from the attacking orca.

The second calf breached like a subsonic-guided missile, and the beast crashed onto the black Zodiac's gunnel and the boat's twin outboards lifted from the water.

Starker sucked in a breath as he turned away from the drone feed and stared back through the cloud of mist hanging over the police boat's transom.

The Fed boat crashed back into the sea and came to a stop, whitewater covering the vessel. As the water dissipated Starker saw Silva run to the bow where a gun was mounted.

"Oh, shit," Pala said, but Starker barely heard her above the roar of the engine and the howling wind.

"Should I slow?" Mirch yelled.

"No!" Starker said a bit too fast and a little too sternly. "That's not what Silva would want," he finished lamely.

To Silva's credit, the FBI man held his fire as long as he could, but in the end, he had no choice.

The two calves were joined by two of their mates, and the four beasts commenced nudging and prodding the stopped black Zodiac, the two smaller beasts breaching and jawing at the boat. The machine gun rattled, and the water was stitched with bullets, fountains spurting above the churning whitewater.

Starker positioned himself behind Pala again as he watched the drone feed on the NAV screen. "Warning shots," Starker said, and Pala nodded.

A cloud passed over the sun, and everything went dim, the silvery glare on the sea turning black, the sparkle of crashing waves fading into the horizon.

A diseased orca head surged from the water, its black and white conical head landing on the FBI boat, the beast's massive jaws clamping down on the rubber gunnel.

Silva opened up and peppered the sea wolf with bullets.

The killer whale fell back into the sea with a splash and floated on the surface, blood turning the foam red, the beast twisting and squirming in its death throes. It was difficult to see the gunshot wounds amidst the gashes filled with bloody boils, even though the drone was close, but Starker knew the shots hit home because the beast stopped flailing, its corpse rolling in the whitecaps.

The rest of the charging beasts knifed around their dead comrade and abandoned the attack. They disappeared beneath the dark water as they tried to catch up with the rest of their pod, who were still trailing after the baitball.

The FBI boat was moving again, its bow lifting. The radio crackled and Silva's voice boomed over the comm. "I'm sorry I had to do that. Really, but you saw I had no choice."

Starker and Pala exchanged glances. The FBI man sounded genuinely upset. Silva had probably shot—maybe even killed—people. He was a fed, and sometimes that's what they had to do, so the emotions from Silva didn't match what Starker perceived the man to be. Regardless, Silva had been decent enough, so Starker gave the man a little peace. "We saw everything, Silva. Don't worry on it. I would have done the same thing, and so would anybody else at the WSCD."

Static, then, "Thanks, Starker."

"10-4, over."

"Let's get this done," Silva said, and the pop of the comm line snapping closed echoed through the cabin.

The radio filled with chatter as orders were given to secure the orca corpse. A live specimen was best case scenario, but the next best thing was a fresh carcass. As the dead orca rolled in the strait the creature no longer looked as large.

Stuart Island rose from the sea ahead, a black rock covered in greenery. Starker saw no houses, no beach umbrellas, or waterfront restaurants. The island had a population of less than a hundred, and a good chunk of those were summer birds that only flew north from Seattle in the summer months. Most of the year-round residents had been relocated, and Starker had spoken to a couple who had been put up at the Stag Harbor Inn for the duration of the mission.

Starker grabbed the edge of the port bulkhead, eased out the back of the pilothouse, and stuck his head out into the rushing wind. The cool sea air felt good on his face, and it eased his nerves as the knot of boats marking the entrance to Reid Harbor materialized out of the haze. Behind the Lummi police boat, just beyond the motor wash, the baitball dragged over the torn-up sea, the Ocean's Ten coming on hard.

28

The mouth of Reid Harbor was over a quarter of a mile wide, and over twenty boats were positioned across the opening, the Lummi fishermen setting the reinforced netting using Cemetery Island as an anchor because the island sat almost dead center of the harbor mouth. The western side was partially deployed, and the Coast Guard cutter sat in the center of the line, a giant white metal behemoth, an orange stripe cutting across the deep V hull.

Wind gusted, the harbor mouth still a mile distant, and Starker didn't know if the baitball was going to make it.

The ten had broken open the teabag of nastiness, and chunks of rotten flesh leaked into the sea and were quickly consumed by the Ocean's Ten as the beasts took their share and fell back to let others in the pod come forward. Tall dorsal fins cut through the chop, patches of black appearing in the whitewater as the beasts dipped and jumped through the sea, tail flutes stroking the water.

Starker got on the radio. "Silva, do you copy?"

"Right here, amigo."

"I need you to move in closer, really give them a shove. We're getting close, but the baitball looks almost done. Have the coasties and sheriff's office crawl alongside them to make sure they stay on course."

"That's a 10-4."

With that done Starker turned to Mirch. "Bring us down to twenty knots, and Pala, rachet up that SONAR."

The whine of the police boat's engine diminished and the sound of Pala tapping keys carried through the pilothouse. Starker peered aft through the mist that hung over the stern, the ten still churning through the Haro Strait behind them.

Starker counted the seconds in his head as the Lummi police boat cut through the waves rolling east with the wind, the port side of the vessel taking most of the sea spray.

Mirch adjusted course as the police boat roared around a long sandbar that jutted off the southernmost tip of Stuart Island. The line of boats stretching across most of the harbor mouth bobbed and listed in the wind, but everything looked set. Starker sent out a general update, and told the Lummi fishermen they were thirty seconds out.

The sound of engines coming to life rumbled over the water, the ring of station bells and the clang and tinkle of chains dragging over metal rising above the wind.

Starker's heart thumped in his chest, pain racing up and down his spine, his muscles cramping and spasming, his bruised side bitching and complaining. He hadn't been at sea this often since he was in the Navy, and though he had excellent sea legs, there were limits. He heard crashing water when he closed his eyes at night, and everything seemed to sway and shift when he walked on land.

Mirch guided the police boat toward the gap in the string of boats. Despite Chairman Spollomen's insistence that no Lummi assets be used to trap the rogue orcas, the Lummi fishermen had insisted on using their own vessels for the final maneuver. Setting the nets off the Coast Guard cutter and the smaller vessels was simple enough because there was no time constraints and no apex predators driving toward the scene. But the trap needed to be sprung fast, and the Lummi needed the familiarity of their equipment which had been developed and refined for many generations.

The two large metal Lummi fishing vessels were two hundred feet apart, the gap between them a silvery shimmer. A horn sounded, and Starker saw men and women watching their progress from their boats. This was the moment. It would happen now or… it wouldn't. Starker didn't want to think of what came next, because it would likely be more of the same. He was conflicted. On one hand, he was in no rush to get to Seattle, and that was an issue he needed to devote some time to. On the other hand, he wanted to be done with the diseased orcas. Pink salmon season was going strong, and the best thing for all involved would be for the remaining ten to go out to sea and disappear, but as Starker gazed at Silva's black Zodiac pushing the pod of orca forward, he knew that possibility no longer existed.

"Pala, switch me to the emergency channel," Starker said as he lifted the comm handset again. He held it up to his mouth, but paused. The gap in the armada loomed before the police boat. Two hundred yards to go. Starker said, "Standby."

The baitball was nothing but a bloody sack, but it was enough. The diseased orcas still trailed after the Lummi boat, and Starker felt the tension in his chest ease as the police vessel slipped between the Lummi fishing boats.

The rogue orcas slowed as if spooked, but when the two alphas continued to drive through the thinning blood slick the others fell in line. The ten slipped through the gap in the armada, and the heat of pleasure seeped through Starker.

Mirch looked over his shoulder, a question painted on the man's quizzical face.

"Not yet," Starker said.

Dark rock covered in summer grass and evergreens rose on both sides of the police boat as it drove deeper into the narrow bay that made up the harbor. The grumble of the engine and the roar of splashing water echoed over the bay, and when the ten were well within the boundaries of the harbor Starker sprung the trap.

"Releasing baitball," Starker announced over the comm. Then he pulled a utility knife from a pocket and flicked it open. The five-inch stainless steel blade glinted in the sunlight, and as Starker made his way aft his legs ached under the constant shifting and balancing. He cut the baitball loose and yelled, "Mirch. Spin it up and get us to the bridge."

Mirch dropped the hammer and the police boat surged forward, slicing through the placid surface with ease.

The Ocean's Ten drove through what remained of the baitball, but when they reached clear water with no blood slick or morsels of meat or fat, they began peeling off and circling back on the remains of the baitball.

All except the two shark-like calves that continued, falling into the police boat's wake.

The squeal of hoist motors and the clatter of chains rang through the harbor as the Lummi set the final portion of the barricade, the net rising more than ten feet above the waterline in spots.

The orcas appeared unaware they'd just swum into a trap, and other than the two youngsters, the pod was occupied with the blood slick.

The radio came to life. "We did it, Starker," said Silva.

Starker didn't respond. His eyes were locked on the Lummi vessels, and he wouldn't let his guard down until the barrier was fully in place. Silva's black Zodiac and the host of trailing sheriff and coastie vessels disappeared from view as the Lummi fishing vessels came together and the reef net was set, and the Ocean's Ten were trapped.

"You there?" Silva asked, and there was cheering and the sounds of celebration in the background.

"Yeah, I'm here." As Starker watched the two orcas coming at the police boat, and the knot of killer whales strafing the thin blood slick, he didn't feel much like celebrating. He'd had a fish tank as a young boy, but as he got older, he began questioning if wild animals—even mindless goldfish—had a right to live their lives in the wild. His parents, while claiming to understand and empathize, explained that many animals prefer their captivity. Starker didn't think the ten would fall in that category.

The bay narrowed, and no more than five hundred feet separated the eastern shore from the western. The roar of the police boat's engine thundered through the narrows, a metal footbridge spanning the gap ahead, the gleam of its metal like a star on the darkest night.

The two young calves leaped and lunged from the water, their conical snouts rising from the sea like tiny submarines, their tail flutes kicking up whitewater. Behind them, the rest of the pod was done with the remains of the baitball, and the beasts swam around aimlessly like ants who had lost their queen.

Starker cracked his neck and turned his attention back to Mirch and the command console. The seafloor was rising at a precipitous pace, and the depth finder showed the Lummi police boat was cruising in fifteen feet of water. Ahead, the walking bridge spanned the narrow gap. End of the line.

Pala said, "SONAR showing these two little turds still coming on strong."

"Do you want me to circle back? Or should I dock as planned?" Mirch asked.

Starker stared through the pilothouse windshield. The footbridge was low, and there was no way to go under it. Naked floating docks jutted from the steep rock walls along the shoreline, and Starker flashed back to the floating dock in Friday Harbor. "I've had enough. What about you guys?"

Mirch nodded, but Pala pointed at the SONAR screen. The two calves were still coming on, despite the lack of bait.

"Let's tie off on the footbridge," Starker said. "It's attached to the stone and has support columns." He left off, in case these two little monsters try and mess with us.

"Got it." Mirch let the ship's wheel slip through his fingers as he made a final course adjustment, and a proximity warning alarm sounded as the water depth fell below ten feet.

Pala said, "What do you make of these two?"

His partner didn't sound concerned, but as Starker monitored the progress of the calves the knot in his stomach reformed and bile crept up his throat. Starker shrugged, and said, "Curiosity?"

Now it was Pala's turn to shrug.

Mirch jerked the throttle arm into neutral. The roar of the police boat's engine died away as the vessel slowed, the following sea slapping the transom, whitewater bubbling up to the gunnel.

Starker went for the bowline, and Pala went aft. The clang of metal on metal rang like tiny church bells as the Lummi police boat bumped the metal footbridge. It was an incoming tide, and the water level was two feet below the dark high tide line that stained the footbridge.

"Well, I guess that's…" Mirch stood still as a statue, gazing south over the placid water of the harbor. The two orca calves were nowhere to be seen.

"Is the water too shallow for them here?" Starker asked as he finished tying off the bowline.

Mirch and Pala said nothing.

Out on the silvery bay, it was difficult to see the dorsal fins of the orcas. Water popped and snapped against the police boat as it settled, the faint wind carrying the scent of fuel and salt.

Pala said, "Those little ones can swim in less than ten feet of water, though they don't like it from what I've been told."

"How could we know?" Starker asked.

"Bigheads," Mirch said, and shrugged. "Let's go. They're sending a car for—"

The police boat rocked as if jolted and Starker grabbed the gunnel to steady himself.

Patches of white and black slid through the clear water alongside the boat.

"Amazing," Starker said as he watched the beasts.

"Yeah, amazing, let's get the hell out of here," Pala said.

Starker climbed onto the superstructure of the footbridge, a web of metal support poles providing a ladder-like path. The bridge creaked and cried as he climbed, the metal shifting slightly under his weight.

Pala fell in behind him, moving so deftly she was soon waiting on him.

An orca calf exploded from the water, a fountain of whitewater shooting from the harbor and spraying the bridge. The beast landed next to the police boat, and the vessel rocked hard as Mirch clung to the pilothouse roof. He stood with one foot on the boat's gunnel, the other on a metal support beam.

The police boat was forced upward, and Mirch used the momentum to jump from the vessel onto the bridge's support structure. He hit a support beam hard, and for an instant, Starker was sure the Lummi officer was going to plummet into the orca-infested water. But whether it was a pure survival instinct or fear from seeing the patches of black and white circling in the water, Mirch grasped the support with one hand and dangled there like a broken wing.

Pala scrambled down to help him.

The other young orca drove its head into the police boat and the gap between the footbridge and the boat disappeared like the closing of a guillotine.

The three companions climbed, the bridge shaking slightly, the sun glaring down like an accusing eye.

Pala was the first onto the footpath, the clang of her body hitting the metal deck sounding over the bay.

Starker was second up, and he and Pala helped Mirch. When all three companions were on the bridge's path, Starker sat and let his head drop into his hands, pain biting his neck, his muscles cramping.

Below the water frothed and seethed, the two orca calves in a frenzy. Starker didn't know how long he and the others sat there and watched, but when the orcas finally calmed and moved away, Starker pushed to his feet.

The wind brought the scent of earth and moisture as the companions made their way to a Jeep waiting to transport them to the armada for a debrief. It was a steep climb, and worry danced on Starker's last nerve, something eating at him.

The mission was a success, and his job was done here. It was time to leave, yet something gnawed at his insides, and it wasn't just Spooky. It had become clear to Starker that he was at a crossroads. The diseased orca, Pala, Silva—they'd all helped him realize that he'd been floating through life like a leaf on a stream. Hadn't Cindy accused him of that very thing? Had he done right by her? He found the longer he was away from his ex-girlfriend, the more he missed her. That had never been the case before, and his stomach tingled with excitement and angst as he wondered if Cindy was seeing anyone. He made a mental note to call her and mom. He sucked in a deep breath of fresh sea air, and set off down the path toward the waiting Jeep and his future, whether he wanted it or not.

29

Reid Harbor, Stuart Island, U.S., 1:50 PM PT, July 18th. Eighteenth day of Pink Salmon Season.

Starker stood on the rear deck of the Coast Guard endurance cutter, staring west down the length of the barricade net. The Ocean's Ten were at it again, testing the nets, nudging and pushing the anchor vessels. The scientists said that was to be expected, but when Starker had suggested the beasts were looking for weak spots in the blockade, they'd basically laughed at him. Such activities require complex thought, precognition, and killer whales didn't normally display these traits. No one had answered when Starker had asked if those rules applied to the diseased orcas.

Silva's black Zodiac slid through the calm water and Starker waved, though the Fed didn't see him. The FBI man had spoken to the big cheese in Seattle and bought him a few more days, telling Starker's supervisor he was critical to the establishment of the field research center charged with studying the ten. Total whale turd, but there it was. He still hadn't decided what to do about Spooky, and the longer he waited, the less he wanted to go to Seattle.

Pala was issued an old Zodiac that looked like it had been through a war, but the vessel's Johnson outboard ran well, and the boat floated, so there was that. His partner had gone back to her daily duties, and Starker hadn't seen her yet on this day. She was patrolling a knot of charters gunning for pinkies, and she was late picking him up for lunch.

The sheriff and Captain Raynard had taken a step back and let the WSCD take the lead, and Silva had arranged for top scientists and support staff to begin research on the ten, and samples had already been taken. The locals were happy because more people meant more money, and the newcomers would take every empty hotel room, and help fill the restaurants and pubs.

The dead orca was hanging in a fish processing center's main cold room, and a team of scientists was slowly dissecting the creature. So far, all that had been discovered was what Silva had predicted. The disease that infected the Ocean's Eleven had originated with the mutant sea spiders in the Atlantic.

While he waited for Pala, Starker called his mother, had the same conversation for the thousandth time, and then called Cindy. She picked up on the first ring and sounded happy to hear his voice. Their first call the prior day had been awkward and tentative, but they'd slowly shed the chains of their breakup and it was time to crank things up.

"You're still on Orcas Island? I thought you'd wrapped things up there?" Cindy asked, but her voice carried none of the accusatory tone he'd detected in the past.

"Just stalling really," Starker said. "They don't need me here."

"Oh, I thought you said you were concerned the orcas would try and escape?"

"I was... am, but what am I to do?"

She said nothing.

"Listen," he said and licked his lips. Just do it, wimp. Just do it, he mentally scolded. "Would you like to have dinner with me sometime?"

Silence on the line. The gentle breeze brought the stringent scent of salt, and above gulls circled and complained.

"You there?" he asked.

"Yeah, it's just... I thought we'd gotten ourselves into a rut we couldn't get out of? What's changed?"

"Me," Starker said, and his head jerked back in surprise. "I mean, I guess I see things differently now. Long view, and... and I miss you."

Gulls, wind, water plopping and tapping on the cutter.

"I'm not asking you to get married," Starker said. "I'm asking if you want a steak."

Cindy laughed. "I'm not allowed to have fish? Or chicken? You're always trying to control me." The mirth in her voice was obvious.

"You can have whatever you want, as long as it's from the early bird special list."

She laughed again and the sound was like a tonic for a tortured soul. "Oh, and I meant to ask. How do you feel about cats?"

"I don't—"

Yelling and screaming and the rattle of chains carried over the harbor mouth. "Hold on a sec," Starker said.

Several boats down line from the cutter, the net between a Lummi police boat and a sheriff's boat had gone taut. Dorsal fins cut through the sea, and the twang of rope stretching, and the clang of chains being dragged over metal echoed over the harbor. The netting above the waterline swayed and undulated as the beasts cycled into the barrier, pushing, and nudging, and testing.

"Let me give you a call back, O.K.?"

Cindy said, "Sure. Everything alright?"

"Not sure." He tapped end call and dropped his phone in a pocket.

A fist of churning whitewater bubbled above the surface and black patches of slick skin, tail flutes, dorsal fins, and pectoral fins knotted together as the beasts pushed on the barrier net.

"Starker!" He looked down and saw Pala standing behind the command console of her replacement Zodiac.

"Perfect timing," Starker shouted. "Coming down. I want to—"

A shriek carried over the water, the sound of a person in great pain. The line of boats holding the reef nets undulated and shifted, but held. Above, like a giant fly, the Coast Guard drone zipped past, heading west down the net line.

Starker scrambled down a Jacob's ladder to the waiting patrol boat and was met with a surprise.

"Meow."

As Starker boarded the Zodiac, Spooky jumped from his spot atop the command console and ran to him.

"Brought a friend along today. The kids are at camp all day, so I figured…"

"You figured?" Starker lifted the cat and stroked his back, and Spooky purred so hard Starker thought the feline's teeth might vibrate out of his head.

More yelling and screaming and Starker and Pala both jerked their heads toward the sound.

Support boats were moving in behind the section of net the orcas were prodding, and Starker saw Mirch's Lummi police boat inching into the fray.

"Take us over there," Starker said as he put Spooky down and checked his Glock. The gun had been returned to him cleaned, along with fresh ammo, and knowing the weapon was on his hip reassured him, despite it not being of much use when dealing with the orca.

The Johnson coughed and popped as Pala put the boat in gear and spun the ship's wheel, bringing the vessel about as it moved away from the cutter. The knot of boats surrounding the fist of whitewater had grown. Starker counted six dorsal fins swaying and cutting through the surging water that bubbled over the surface like an erupting volcano.

The radio thundered to life. "All available vessels, this is Captain Raynard. Support needed on the eastern end beyond Cemetery Island."

Starker and Pala both looked over their shoulders, and Spooky hissed.

"You got that right, buddy," Starker said.

"A diversion?"

"Which one?"

Beyond Cemetery Island a wake of whitewater trailed up to the barrier netting and then disappeared as the orcas dove, four dorsal fins slipping beneath the surface. The line of boats shifted, and the netting went taut as the orcas bumped the boats and the netting.

"Which way?" Pala said

"East," Starker said. There was plenty of support already on scene at the western attack site.

"I think the second group is the calves," Pala said as she spun the boat around.

"Sure looks like it. I wonder—"

The screech of a struggling winch motor carried over the water as the Lummi fishermen adjusted the drag of their nets, but it didn't appear to be helping. The netting bulged at the original attack site, and the net had been pulled below the waterline. To the west, the smaller group breached and jumped from the sea, and if Starker didn't know better, he would have thought the creatures were playing.

"Starker, you there?" It was Mirch.

"I copy," Starker said. "What's up?"

"The wolves over here are just playing around."

"What do you mean?"

"I mean… it seems like they're just playing around with each other. Like the netting isn't there. One of them got caught a few minutes ago, and the others helped free it, but they don't appear to be—"

The thunderous crash of a massive wave blocked out all other sounds.

The four that had broken away from the pod were making their move, and Starker didn't believe his eyes, and he judged neither could Pala. The two of them stared opened mouthed, the glare of the sun and the push of the wind reminding Starker he wasn't in a movie or dream.

Two of the mid-sized orcas breached in perfect unison like ballerinas after many long hours of practice together, pectoral fins stroking the water, tail flutes driving the creatures from the sea. The massive beasts came down atop the netting, but the barrier held, and the two orcas hung in the netting above the waterline, suspended as they writhed and fought to get back into the sea, pressing the netting down as they thrashed.

The orca calves sprang from the sea like they were performing at SeaWorld. Both beasts came fully out of the water, their black and white forms glistening in the sunlight, the squeal and huff of their exertion rising above the sound of splashing water. Had it not been for the two larger orcas struggling in the nets the two calves would have been caught themselves, but the two calves landed on top of their pod mates and used them as springboards as they wriggled and thrust their way forward.

The larger orcas beneath the calves heaved and struggled, and with their effort, the two calves slithered over the netting into the clear water of the channel, and freedom.

An alarm rang over the harbor, the grumble of motors coming to life, the rattle and pop of gunfire, the buzz of the drone.

Heat spread through Starker. They were losing control.

To the west at the original attack site, six dorsal fins cycled to the net and fell back as the orcas continued to press and prod the barricade. All the lines held, though the netting above the waterline was so tight Starker thought he could play a tune on it.

"Where do you want us?" Pala said.

Starker tapped a keyboard and brought up the tracking signal from the Coast Guard cutter. "Shit," he muttered. All subjects were shown as contained within the harbor. "I forgot we don't have either of the calves tagged."

A cry of pain sounded over the water. One of the orcas that had aided in the escape of the calves was caught in the netting and unable to get back into the water. Its partner had already fallen back and disappeared beneath the surface, leaving only swirling whitewater. A Lummi police vessel raced in and rammed the netting with its bow, pushing the orca backward, but the beast was tangled, and the maneuver did no good.

Starker knew orca could live an hour or two out of the water, but the way the killer whale was thrashing about he feared the netting might not hold, or one of the ropes would break. The beast flipped and jerked, its tail flute smacking the net, the boats holding that section of the reef netting bobbing and listing wildly. Lummi fishermen darted from ship to ship, adjusting the drag of the nets, taking in and letting out line to compensate for the relentless pounding of the orcas.

The Lummi police boat nudged the orca again, but it didn't help. The beast's pectoral fin was twisted in the net and there was no way to free it without getting in close and untwisting the net. The gray police boat looked like Mirch's, but the Lummi cop wasn't behind the ship's wheel. A young man in blue work overalls inched out onto the Lummi boat's deck, a long gaff in his hands. The kid braced himself in the bow and set about trying to unwrap the net from around the orca's pectoral fin.

One of the shark-like calves breached, its black and white conical head missiling from the water, jaws distended. Then the sailor in the blue overalls was gone, and the sea wolf crashed onto the netting, the kid hanging from the beast's clamped-down jaws as it slid back into the water.

Pala screamed and jerked back the throttle control arm. The Zodiac bobbed to a stop twenty feet from the Lummi police boat, but the officer in the blue work coveralls was nowhere to be seen.

Starker felt his bowels loosen, a streak of pain running the length of his body and settling in the tips of his fingers and toes, the memory of holding two severed arms rushing back like the tide.

30

Silva's voice cut through the radio chatter as the black FBI boat bore down on the tangled orca. "Lummi police boat, fall back."

Spooky was on the command console, tail out, head pressed into the wind, tiny droplets of water hanging from his whiskers.

Pala stood rigid, one hand on the ship's wheel, the other hovering over the throttle control.

Starker stared at the Coast Guard drone feed, his stomach a fiery knot.

The orca tangled in the boundary netting struggled and fought, but Starker could see the beast was losing its fight. The pustule-filled gashes that ran all along the killer whale's length were bloody and pink, the wounds having become infected despite the constant massaging of the saltwater.

With nobody at its helm, the Lummi police boat didn't move, and the black FBI boat slid in closer. Two agents dressed in black stood in the bow, one behind the machine gun, the other holding a long rifle that looked similar to the gun Starker used to deliver the tracking darts.

"Looks like they're going to try and knock it out with a tranquilizer dart. Maybe if we—" Pala said.

The Zodiac trembled and Starker gripped the command console as an eruption of seawater bubbled up beside the boat. A calf's head poked from the fist of whitewater, its swollen eyes barely discernable within the puffy red masses before its white eye patches. The beast hung there a moment, appraising, its massive mouth sliding open, blood from its open wounds dripping down slick black skin.

The *pop* of an air rifle spitting a dart carried over the tumult.

The calf slid back beneath the water, disappearing into the depths.

"What the hell just happened?" Pala asked.

"Not sure."

"Meow. Meow. Meow."

"Yeah, me too, buddy."

Starker figured the dart from the FBI agent's rifle had struck home because the orca caught in the net stopped thrashing, and its tangled form lay still, pushing the extended netting below the surface. A squeaking and huffing echoed over the harbor, along with the rumble of boat engines, the whine of tightening rope, and the push of the salty wind.

Scientists have studied whale song for decades, and the generally accepted theory is that sea mammals like orcas communicate with each other via a series of social cues and basic sounds and movements that amount to language. Starker didn't know if he believed the sea wolves could talk to each other, but if they couldn't, they sure were lucky.

As Silva's black boat rammed the unconscious orca in an attempt to get it off the netting, the remaining trapped seven orcas made their move. They came on in a V formation, the two large matriarchs at the head as they streaked toward the gap and the unconscious orca.

One of the escaped calves breached, throwing its gore-streaked body onto Pala's old Zodiac. The beast landed on the transom, the bow rising precipitously as Spooky was tossed from his perch atop the command console. Yelling, screaming and the roar of engines filled Starker's head as he fell to his knees, clutching the Zodiac's gunnel as Pala held onto the ship's wheel as if it were a lifeline and she was tumbling in a storm-swept sea.

Water poured over the sides of the Zodiac as Starker pressed to his feet, the torrent of seawater swamping the boat. As the water drained through the bailing gaps, the calf rolled back into the sea, whitewater bubbling over the sides like an exploding soda.

"Starker!" Mirch's voice burst from the radio. "I'm coming in."

Ahead, the group of seven probed the barrier, the killer whales pushing and ramming the reef netting.

The FBI agent manning the gun in the bow of Silva's boat opened up, the machine gun spitting bullets into the water. The warning shots did nothing to help and may have exacerbated the situation. One of the big beasts breached and landed on the unconscious orca tangled in the netting. The anchor boats all along the line shifted and swayed, the netting and holding lines stretching to their limit, but the barrier held.

The flood waters drained away, and Starker picked up Spooky as the feline was washed down the deck of the Zodiac. The cat looked like a drowned squirrel, but his eyes were aglow with vigor. Starker placed the black furball on the copilot's seat and drew his Glock.

With two killer whales weighing down the netting the remainder of the pod attempted to jump free of their watery prison. Like kids waiting to use the slide at a public pool, the remaining six took turns launching themselves at the nets, landing on their pod mates and falling back into the sea. When one of the mid-sized sea wolves managed to make it over the barricade and joined the escaped calves, Silva's haggard voice came over the comm. "Starker, you and Mirch move in with me and we'll press the things back."

Pala glanced at Starker. It was the "my kids aren't growing up without a mother face." If it was any other time Starker thought maybe he would've backed off, but there was too much at stake, and he'd come to realize that the disease threatened more than just his little corner of paradise. Starker said, "I'll take the wheel if you want."

She pursed her lips. "That's supposed to help?" Pala pressed down the throttle arm and the old Zodiac surged forward through the chop.

The third escaped sea wolf dove, patches of black and white sliding through the water as the beast disappeared into the depths.

Pala brought the Zodiac in next to Silva's black boat, Mirch sliding the silver Lummi police vessel in on the opposite side. Once lined up, the three boats pressed forward, props clawing the water, bows lifting as the vessels drove back the orcas weighing down the nets.

The massive wolf rolled back into the sea, the unconscious orca still tangled in the netting. With the threat of imminent attack gone, Silva's men moved in with knives and gaff poles and cut the unconscious orca free. The killer whale had been out of the water too long and was dead, and as the corpse fell back into the water a tinge of sorrow ran through Starker. The sea wolves were no different than a dog with rabies, or any other diseased beast. The eleven hadn't chosen this path, and its ending wasn't what the animals deserved.

With the weight off the net, the barrier sprang back to its original position, and the netting once again rose above the surface of the water, though there were several holes where the orca had been cut free.

"Anyone have a bead on the escapees? None of them have trackers," came Silva's voice over the radio.

Pala eased the Zodiac away from the barrier, as Mirch moved the police boat in tight against the netting, his propeller spitting water.

Patches of black and white slid through the sea. "I've got eyes on them," Starker said.

Pala spun the ship's wheel, setting a course away from the netting toward open sea.

"Meow. Meow."

Starker agreed with Spooky. Was killing the beasts the best option? They could get trackers on them, and then they'd have wild specimens to study as well as captive ones. But that wasn't his call, and a cop was dead, so he said nothing as Pala eased the throttle lever down and spun up the engine.

But the escapees weren't done. Resident orcas in the eastern North Pacific live in complex and stable social groups. Unlike any other mammals, killer whales live with their mothers for their entire lives. The units are highly stable, and individuals separate for only a few hours at a time, to mate or hunt prey. They will defend their own until their dying breath.

Sensing their matriarch wasn't free and was once again trapped, the calves probed the netting around Mirch's police boat, which still had its bow pressed into the barrier.

The shark-like calves cycled back and forth behind the large wolf as it pressed its conical head into the netting. White and black patches slid through the water on the opposite side of the barrier netting, and the faint squeal and titter of the beasts cut through the whispering wind.

Like a timed detonation, the free orcas surged into the Lummi police boat, pushing and bumping it on both sides. One of the calves breached, driving its tail flute hard, pectoral fins pounding the sea, large clear bubbles popping on the churning surface.

Spooky hissed, and the radio came to life, Silva yelling orders. The FBI man didn't want anyone shooting at the beasts because Mirch was in the line of fire.

One of the escapees was driving at the bottom of the Lummi police vessel, and Starker saw Mirch emerge from the back of the pilothouse, pistol in one hand, his other arm out for balance as his boat surged and bounced from the orca's prodding.

"We've got to help him," Starker said.

"How?" Pala said.

She had a point. They were fifty feet from Mirch's police boat, a mile if it was a foot, and Starker braced himself against the gunnel and brought up his Glock. He wasn't a great shot, and with the boat heaving and listing it was impossible to aim, but he didn't need to be that accurate. Being careful not to hit the Lummi vessel, Starker began squeezing off shots, peppering the water all around Mirch's boat.

The shots were intended to scare off the beasts, but instead, they whipped them into a frenzy. The wolves thrashed on the surface, ramming the Lummi police vessel. Mirch went back to the ship's wheel, and as Starker emptied his clip, Mirch moved his boat away from the netting and the attacking orcas.

With one last thrust of anger and frustration two of the beasts breached, the larger of the two landing on the bow of Mirch's boat. The sound of shrieking metal carried over the water as the Lummi police boat's propeller lifted from the water before crashing back into the sea. The boat rocked and listed as it moved slowly away from the chaos.

The escaped orcas threw themselves at the netting, running along its length, their trapped brethren following along on the opposite side. When the free orcas reached the nearest anchored vessel, they turned hard to the south and dove, their slick forms falling beneath the silvery surface.

Starker let out a breath he didn't realize he was holding, and he put a hand on Pala's shoulder. "You O.K.?"

Pala nodded as she opened a channel. "Mirch, do you copy?" Static. "Mirch?"

Mirch's Lummi police vessel was powering south at five knots, listing slightly as it arced to the west.

"Go!" yelled Starker.

Pala pushed the throttle arm all the way down and the Zodiac jumped from the water, throwing spray, its rooster tail splashing Silva's boat.

"What the hell?" came Silva's voice over the comm, but it was mirthful.

A knot worked its way up Starker's throat as Pala ran down Mirch and the Lummi vessel. He didn't see Mirch behind the command console, and the boat continued to list to the west. Dread crept over Starker as they approached, and when the Zodiac bumped the Lummi vessel Starker's worst fears were realized.

Pala gasped, and Spooky jumped from his spot atop the co-pilot's seat and stood next to Starker.

Mirch's body lay sprawled on the deck, a pool of blood forming around his head and leaking across the boat as the vessel plowed through the sea.

Starker mounted the gunnel and jumped onto the Lummi boat. He went to the helm, pulled back the throttle control, and shut down the motor.

Gulls argued and bitched, water snapped and popped against the hull, and the pounding of Starker's heart filled his head. The police boat floated with the current as Starker dropped to his knees

and took Mirch in his arms. Tears welled in his eyes as he looked around and noticed a smear of blood on the starboard bulkhead behind the helm. The Lummi officer had fallen, smacked his head, and paid the ultimate price.

Suddenly Spooky was there, purring and rubbing against Starker as he cradled Mirch's body. He hadn't known the man well, but he'd always been decent to Starker. Did the man have a family? Kids? He didn't know and the heat of shame washed over him as the sun warmed his face. Starker gazed up at the clear blue sky, a tremor of loss and sorrow consuming him. He thought of Seattle, mom, and Cindy. If he'd died on this day who would've come to his funeral?

"Starker?"

Starker looked down to see Mirch's dull eyes peering up at him.

"I thought Heaven would have better looking women."

"Medic! I need a medic!" Starker screamed.

31

Island Medical Center, Friday Harbor, San Juan Island, U.S., 1:52 PM PT, July 20th. Twentieth day of Pink Salmon Season.

Mirch's room was a few doors down from the one Starker had been in, but it had a nice view of the harbor instead of a treetop. Didn't matter the situation, local be local. The room was packed; Agent Silva, Sheriff Klep, Lummi Police Chief Kendra Sistani, Pala and Joel, and Starker surrounded the bed.

"Why didn't you check my pulse?" Mirch shook his head. "WSCD is all that needs to be said."

"Damn right," Starker said, then his smile ran away from his face. "I thought… The puddle of blood was big. I did my Sherlock Holmes thing in my mind with the blood smear, felt guilty for not getting to know you better, and then you were looking up at me."

"You looked surprised."

Starker laughed and said, "I'll bet."

"So the doc says you'll recover?" Pala said. "Something about you not needing a brain?"

"Clean as bleach," Mirch said. "I cracked my skull and I have a nasty concussion, but thanks to all of you and the coastie medivac team it looks like I'll be OK. What happened after I went to dreamland?"

"Only the three escaped, and they haven't been seen since they fled," Captain Raynard said. "Everyone's keeping an eye out and we'll get trackers on them ASAP."

"But don't worry," Silva said. "More boats have been added to the barricade and a more permanent containment seawall is being put in place. Poles are being sunk as we speak, and a fence made of rope, chain, and Kevlar was added above the waterline. There will be no more escapes."

"Though there might be attempts," Starker said.

"What are you still doing here?" Mirch asked. "Don't you have business waiting in Seattle?"

Somewhere someone cried softly and the buzz of a seaplane coming in for a landing leaked into the room. A sniffle. A cough.

Sheriff Klep broke the silence. "When they springing you?"

"Couple of days," Mirch said.

Sheriff Klep nodded at the Lummi police chief, and she said, "Good. We'll need you to supervise security around the perimeter of the holding area. The Sheriff's Department will patrol the land, and you've got the sea, though based on the upgrades to the barrier netting I figure you'll be spending most of your time shuttling around scientists. You O.K. with that?"

Mirch nodded. "I think I can handle it."

"The state is bringing in a temporary building for the site and there's all kinds of funding coming in," Sheriff Klep said.

"Not to mention the media coverage," Starker said.

"Yup," Captain Raynard said. "That's why I'll be hanging around for a bit. Coastie copters will provide air support. Silva, how you doing with the no fly zone order?"

"Done," Silva said. "With that in place you can run off inquisitive news helicopters."

With business settled, Captain Raynard and Sheriff Klep said their goodbyes and left.

Silva said, "Starker, can I have a minute?"

Starker looked at Pala who raised an eyebrow. "Don't take too long, Joel's got the coals going in the grill."

Joel looked at his watch and said, "Yup, and they should be hot as the sun by now."

Silva and Starker slipped into the hallway.

"I just wanted to say thank you for everything," Silva said. "I know this whole thing hasn't been easy."

There was more coming, and Starker waited.

"Have you decided what you're going to do? Career-wise I mean?"

"I've decided to report to Seattle and give it a chance, but I'm not sure how long that will last."

Silva raised an eyebrow.

Starker sighed. "I'm having dinner with my ex-girlfriend, and I think I want to start things up again, but she hates the city and has no desire to live there."

"Ever hear of the suburbs? I've heard they've got trees and everything."

"Maybe."

"I'm out of here," Silva said. "I'll pop in from time to time and keep an eye on things, but my role here is done."

Starker waited.

"Have you considered joining the FBI? We could use someone like you. You'd have to start at the bottom, of course, but…" Silva looked around. "Or, I can arrange for you to be the WSCD representative for the research project here. Maybe even run it out of the WSCD Seattle office. It's a forty-minute helicopter ride from Seattle to here."

"Just what the new boss wants. The new guy eating up the budget with fuel costs."

"Funding can be arranged," Silva said.

"I'll think on it."

"Don't take too long." He held out a hand and Starker shook it. "See you on down the road." Silva turned on a heel, walked down the hall, and Starker watched him until he disappeared around a corner.

Starker said his goodbyes to Mirch and promised to check in.

"If we don't meet again, it's been a pleasure," Mirch said.

"Bullshit, but O.K. And we'll be meeting again. Count on it."

Mirch laughed, and said, "All the best, my friend."

As Starker, Joel and Pala made their way through Friday Harbor toward the marina, Joel asked, "Have you decided what you're going to do with Spooky?"

Starker felt a pressure building behind his eyeballs and spreading through his head like fog. He said nothing.

"What time is Jesse coming to get you?" Pala asked.

"The weather looks iffy later," Joel said. A line of clouds filled the western horizon, but the day was pleasant and sunny.

"Around six."

"We'll hear him coming in," Pala said.

Fishing charters cycled in and out of the harbor. With the heart of pink salmon season approaching, everyone in the San Juan Islands was happy to be moving on and putting the Ocean's Eleven in the rearview. There had been some local opposition to the killer whales being detained in Reid Harbor, but like with all things, time brought more pressing concerns. The orcas weren't attacking ships and killing people any longer, so they'd been put on a shelf to be forgotten for another day, and that was just fine with Starker.

The trio didn't speak as Joel drove back to the Rankin house for a goodbye barbeque, and so Starker could pick up Spooky. Starker had decided to let the feline decide where he lived. The cat had earned that right, at least.

Starker said, "Re. Spooky. If... and I'm saying if, Spooky would prefer to stay with you and your kids would you be amenable?"

"Will he end up in the shelter if we don't take him?" Pala asked.

"No."

"That's it?" Pala said.

"I don't want you to feel pressured and I don't want to influence your decision."

Pala turned to Joel, who shrugged, but Starker would be lying to himself if he said the man looked happy.

Starker nodded.

When they arrived, Spooky broke away from the game he was playing with Aurora and Joel Jr., some weird kind of tag that always made the cat the pursuer. Starker lifted the feline, and the cat closed his eyes and purred.

Joel's burgers were the best Starker had ever had and the tour boat captain refused to give up his secret.

Pala leaned in and whispered in Starker's ear, "A1 steak sauce."

The afternoon wore away as pleasurable experiences do, Spooky hanging out with the kids as the adults ate and drank their fill. Starker couldn't help but feel lost and alone as he watched the Rankin family, and for the first time in his life he gave serious thought to whether he wanted children of his own. He chuckled to himself. He couldn't decide if he could handle a cat, but he was ready for kids?

When the faint gurgle of the seaplane rose above the merrymaking, Pala caught Starker's eye.

"I'll take him," Joel said. "Starker, your bag is already in the car."

Starker nodded and pushed up from his seat.

"Kids, come say goodbye to Mr. Starker," Joel said.

"And bring Spooky," Pala added.

Out front in the driveway the Rankin family stood together, as if bracing for bad news. Spooky strolled forward like he didn't have a care in the world and planted himself at Starker's side, tail wrapped around himself. The feline looked like a carving on an ancient Egyptian temple, his regal body rigid and attentive.

Starker dropped to a knee and inched his finger back and forth under the cat's chin. The feline purred and closed his eyes, and when the cat opened them, Starker took Spooky's small furry head in his hand. "Listen, I've got to leave now."

Spooky looked up at him with wet eyes. "Meow."

Starker nodded and stood. He took two steps back until Spooky sat between himself and the Rankin family. Starker knew what he wanted; it had become very clear. He wanted Spooky to join him in Seattle. Wanted to pet the beast every day after he came home from a hard day and watch T.V. with Spooky sitting beside him.

But this wasn't about what Starker wanted. It was about what was best for Spooky.

"It's O.K., buddy, if you want to stay here with them."

Spooky looked back at the Rankin family. Joel had his arms around his children, restraining his kids who shifted uneasily on their feet. Tears ran down Aurora's cheeks and Joel Jr. stared at the driveway.

Starker took another step back.

Spooky stood and moseyed over to Starker, but rather than sit beside him, the cat sat in front of him, still in between Starker and the family. Starker's heart superheated and his stomach went cold.

He dropped to a knee again and said, "You want to stay here?"

"Meow."

Starker reached out and patted the cat. "I'll miss you." He bent over and kissed Spooky on the head, and the cat licked his face—a first.

Holding back tears as his chest burned like it was on fire, Starker stood.

Spooky turned and joined his new family.

"You promise to take good care of him?" Starker asked.

An exuberant yes and thank you from the entire family, even Joel.

"You'll come and visit, won't you Mr. Starker?" Aurora asked.

"Meow."

"Count on it," Starker said.

CODA

Atlantic Rift Valley, Atlantic Ocean, Time and Date Unknown.

The Atlantic was a blown-out mess of chop, whitewater, and huge rolling waves. The shearwater coasted on the thermals a hundred feet above the churning ocean, the seabird searching for something to eat.

A dark smudge marred the white foam-streaked sea, and the bird pulled in its wings and dove through the driving wind.

A mangled sea spider rolled in the surf, half of its delicate body burned away, the other half a squished gelatinous mess that looked like a jellyfish that's been in a blender. The bird squawked as it swooped down, alighting on the remains of the sea spider as it pecked at the dead flesh, mountainous waves lifting and dipping the bird as it ate.

A gray dorsal fin rose from the depths, a missile of muscle and teeth. As the knot of whitewater surged toward the seabird it flapped its wings and sprang into the air.

The shark consumed the remains of the sea spider and disappeared beneath the windswept ocean.

Over the following days weariness enveloped the shearwater, and an unquenchable thirst drove the bird north as it followed the migrating seabirds through the Northwest Passage where it slipped into darkness. A relentless hunger drove the bird forward all summer, an anger that drove it to attack its own kind.

When the shearwater broke free of the Bering Sea and glided over the Northern Pacific, the bird was no longer itself.

The harbor seal slithered off its perch atop a rock along the Alaskan coastline. A flock of gulls fought and stirred out on the placid sea, a lone shearwater bullying thirty other birds all by itself. The seal swam noiselessly toward the fray, the birds unaware of the approaching menace.

Gulls argued and screamed, and the shearwater darted about, divebombing any bird stupid enough not to get out of its way.

The seal slid silently through the sea, tracking the shearwater as it jumped about on the surface. The beast's flippers gently stroked the Pacific as it slowly rose through the cold water, its dark eyes locked on the bird. With an explosion of speed, the seal knifed from the sea, jaws open, and the shearwater disappeared into the creature's maw as it crashed back into the Pacific.

The pod of eleven was unusually large. The orcas surrounded Seal Rock, a lone seal frolicking and twisting by itself in the sea. The seal didn't smell right, but easy prey was easy prey, and the orcas moved in for the kill.

Wind gusted and sang as the eleven encircled the seal, who was still blissfully unaware of the approaching danger. The sea wolves created a whirlpool that pulled at the seal, but still the beast didn't notice.

One of the eleven broke formation and cut across the whirlpool, using its conical black and white head to toss the seal into the air. The other orcas moved in, and soon the pod was tossing the seal around like a football at a picnic. The seal fought and struggled, but when one of the orca calves took a bite out of the creature, it fell still, blood spraying the water's surface as the pod that would become known as the Ocean's Eleven ate their fill.

The mutated strain of chronic wasting disease had made its way to the Pacific, the balance in the world's oceans forever altered.

The End

Other Severed Press novels by Edward J. McFadden III: Fortune's Cypher, Crimson Falls, Hell Creek, Barracuda Swarm, The Cryptid Club, Dinosaur Red, Drop Off, Jurassic Ark, Keepers of the Flame, Throwback, Sea Tremors, Primeval Valley, Shadow of the Abyss (#1 Amazon Bestseller Tag), Awake, and The Breach (#1 Amazon Bestseller Tag, Amazon #1 Hot New Audio Release Tag). His other novels include: Terror Peak, the Theo Ramage Thriller series: Quick Sands, Sandbagged, and Too Much Grit, and Dogs Get Ten Lives, The Black Death of Babylon, and HOAXERS. Ed lives on Long Island with his wife Dawn, and their daughter Samantha.

Check out other great

Sea Monster Novels!

Rick Chesler

HOTEL MEGALODON

An underwater luxury hotel on a gorgeous tropical island is set for an extravagant opening weekend with the world watching. The only thing standing in the way of a first-rate experience for the jet-setting VIPs is an unscrupulous businessman and sixty feet of prehistoric shark. As the underwater complex is besieged by a marauding behemoth, newly minted marine biologist Coco Keahi must face off against the ancient predator as it rises from the deep with a vengeance. Meanwhile, a human monster has decided he would be better off if Coco were one of the creature's victims.

Michael Cole

SCAR

Scar is a killing machine. Born from DNA spliced between the extinct Megalodon and modern day Great White, he has a viciousness that transcends time. His evil is reflected in his eyes, his savagery in his two-inch serrated teeth, his ruthlessness in his trail of death. After escaping captivity, the killer shark travels to the island community Cross Point, where prey is in abundance. With an insatiable appetite, heightened senses, and skin impervious to bullets, Scar kills everything that crosses his path. His reign of terror puts him at war with the island sheriff, Nick Piatt. With the body count rising, Nick vows to protect his island community from the vicious threat. With the aid of a marine biologist, a rookie deputy, and a bad-tempered fisherman, Nick leads a crusade against Scar, as well as the ruthless scientist who created him.

CHECK OUT OTHER GREAT DEEP SEA THRILLERS

SHARK: INFESTED WATERS
by P.K. Hawkins

For Simon, the trip was supposed to be a once in a lifetime gift: a journey to the Amazon River Basin, the land that he had dreamed about visiting since he was a child. His enthusiasm for the trip may be tempered by the poor conditions of the boat and their captain leading the tour, but most of the tourists think they can look the other way on it. Except things go wrong quickly. After a horrific accident, Simon and the other tourists find themselves trapped on a tiny island in the middle of the river. It's the rainy season, and the river is rising. The island is surrounded by hungry bull sharks that won't let them swim away. And worst of all, the sharks might not be the only blood-thirsty killers among them. It was supposed to be the trip of a lifetime. Instead, they'll be lucky if they make it out with their lives at all.

DARK WATERS
by Lucas Pederson

Jörmungandr is an ancient Norse sea monster. Thought to be purely a myth until a battleship is torn a part by one.

With his brother on that ship, former Navy Seal and deep-sea diver, Miles Raine, sets out on a personal vendetta against the creature and hopefully save his brother. Bringing with him his old Seal team, the Dagger Points, they embark on a mission that might very well be their last.

But what happens when the hunters become the hunted and the dark waters reveal more than a monster?

SEVEREDPRESS

🐦 @severedpress
f /severedpress

Check out other great

Sea Monster Novels!

Alister Hodge

THE CAVERN

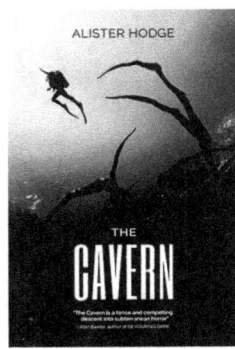

When a sink hole opens up near the Australian outback town of Pintalba, it uncovers a pristine cave system. Sam joins an expedition to explore the subterranean passages as paramedic support, hoping to remain unneeded at base camp. But, when one of the cavers is injured, he must overcome paralysing claustrophobia to dive pitch-black waters and squeeze through the bowels of the earth. Soon he will find there are fates worse than being buried alive, for in the abandoned mines and caves beneath Pintalba, there are ravenous teeth in the dark. As a savage predator targets the group with hideous ferocity, Sam and his friends must fight for their lives if they are ever to see the sun again.

Eric S. Brown

PIRANHA

The rains came, flooding the sleepy, little town of Sylva. Sheriff Hanson never thought that he would be fighting a battle to survive against real life monsters. . . but with the waters came flesh eating, hungry creatures that swept through Sylva's streets like locusts, devouring everyone in their path.

www.ingramcontent.com/pod-product-compliance
Lightning Source LLC
Chambersburg PA
CBHW061231170626
46809CB00007B/2618